AULUS

AND
THE INVASION OF
BRITANNIA

AD 367

BY
ANTONY PELLY

I would like to put in a dedication to the four 'Kenya girls' whose involvement has brought my books into print:-

The instigator, Greta Mattingley.
The empowerers, Sue Duke and Vee Bellers.
The encourager, my wife Sue.

And to
Nathalie McNabb
Our French Canadian saviour who put
this edition into print.

Antony Pelly

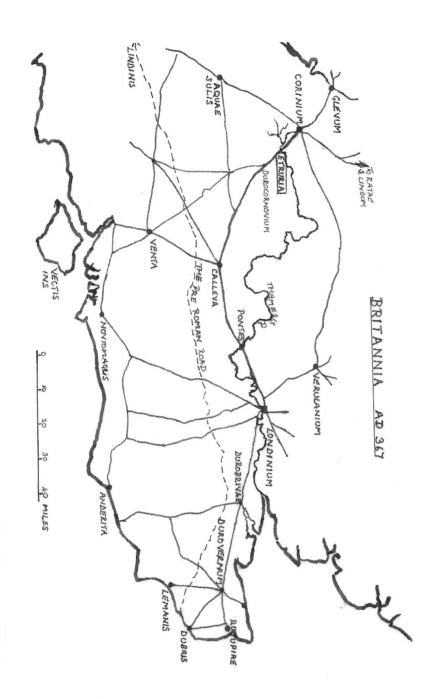

BRITANNIA AD 367

AD RATAE
AD LINDUM

VECTIS INS

GLEVUM
CORINIUM
ETRURIA
DUROCORNOVIUM
AQUAE SULIS
LINDINIS
VENTA
CALLEVA
THAMESIS FL
PONTES
THE PRE ROMAN ROAD
VERULANIUM
LONDINIUM
NOVIOMAGUS
DUROBRIVAE
DUROVERNUM
ANDERITA
LEMANIS
DUBRIS
RUTUPIAE

0 10 20 30 40 MILES

3

AD 367

AULUS

Chapter I.

Spring brought the usual crop of rumours. For years it had been like this, stories of warbands of Scots or Picts or Saxons marauding into Britannia from West, North and East, terrorising everything in their path. But they had never before threatened Corinium and the peaceful country of the South West.

This year was different. Always before, the rumours had been shrugged off. The raids had been sporadic and dealt with by the army. They had been bloody encounters far from the land of Aulus Aurelius and not matters of personal concern; but not this year. As spring slipped into summer the rumours refused to die. They crystallised into uncertainty and then into a gut-gnawing fear. If the stories were to be believed, the raids this year were co-ordinated. Scots, Picts and Saxons had joined forces to attack Britannia from three directions and the army was not strong or plentiful enough to deal with them.

Of course, they were nowhere near Corinium, nor was there any likelihood that they could penetrate this far into the country but fear showed on the faces of Aulus' people. It fanned the flames of their rising panic as they invented ever more horrific stories of the slaughter that was creeping closer, terrifying themselves with tales of rape and torture, of burning farmsteads, of hideous warriors killing everything in their path.

Aulus did his best to calm his people. He laughed at their horror stories, told them not to be so stupid, that the warbands could never come to the farm, that they had nothing to fear. They looked at him with sullen faces: his words had less and less effect. He found himself becoming increasingly irritated while he ordered them sharply to shut up. But the reason he castigated them, he knew full well, was because he was more than worried himself. The rumours were too persistent. Like a plague, they kept spreading and infecting all they touched. Soon, he knew, in ones and twos his farm labourers would begin to disappear, panicked into fleeing like sheep from a wolf. It must be happening elsewhere already – nearly every day now there was a trickle of aimless traffic on the straight military road that ran through the farmlands of Etruria, pitiable flotsam with their possessions loaded onto handcarts or ox wagons, a few cattle or sheep with them, dogs slinking along beside the wheels.

Flavia was as apprehensive as he was. She was trying not to show it but there was a tenseness in her body and their conversation kept coming back all the time to the possibility that the warbands might indeed reach this far South. Aulus tried to reassure her – and himself.

'They'll never get as far as here. The army will be on top of them by now. It could only possibly be the Scots anyway who would have any remote chance of reaching this area. The Picts are much too far North and the Saxons can't get through the defences on the East coast. The forts there are impregnable. I do wonder, though, just in case ... Maybe you ought to go into Corinium to your father's house for a while, until the whole thing dies down. You'd be safe there...'

Of course, she would not hear of it. 'You're my husband and my place is here with you. I'm not going to leave you here on your own. Don't be stupid.'

'Hmm, well, maybe I'll go and see your father and find out just what is happening. If anyone knows what's going on he will. I don't like to leave the farm now, though, with harvest started and the labour as unsettled as they are.'

'I'll stay and look after them. You go. It'll set all our minds at rest to know what really is happening.'

Flavia's father, Tiberius Catullus, had virtually run the town of Corinium for many years, holding in turn all the administrative posts of the town's governing council. Now retired, he still made sure that he was abreast of everything that went on in and around Corinium. Undoubtedly, he would know how serious a threat the warbands really were.

The following day Aulus rode the eight or so miles into Corinium. The morning was bright. Harvest had started in the fields that bordered the straight military road that bisected the farm. Gangs of his men were scything the grain, followed by the women and children gathering the corn, tying it into bundles and propping the bundles into stooks. Perhaps it was his imagination, but the fear in them seemed palpable. They kept stopping their work and looking all about them, like a flock of sparrows ready to take wing and disappear.

His eyes on the harvesting workforce, Aulus did not notice the column of men marching towards him over a low rise in the road half a mile away.

Behind him his groom, Gratian, said: 'Soldiers.' His voice sounded apprehensive.

Aulus looked round. Even at this distance it was obvious that this was a regular unit. They marched as one man, striding in unison in close order, the sun glinting like so many mirrors on their spearheads. There were perhaps forty men in the leading files. Behind them three horse drawn wagons topped the rise. Their grey canvas superstructure swayed slightly as the animals leaned back into the breeching of their harness and the drivers steadied them as the weight changed from drag to thrust. Behind the wagons marched some forty more men. There was no signifier, or standard bearer, but a mounted officer rode beside the wagons on the grass verge.

'So, the rumours must be right.' Regular army units were never in evidence near Corinium. He thought: 'Things must be really bad, but if the army is here we should be all right.' Then: 'I'll ask that officer. He'll know better than Tiberius'. He touched his heels to his horse's flank. The animal changed pace smoothly and cantered forwards towards the oncoming soldiers.

They looked a brave sight, the red of their tunics a bright background to the burnished metal of their chain mail and weapons.

A quarter of a mile away, the officer stopped his horse, looking towards Aulus. He shouted something to his men. The words were indistinguishable at that distance but Aulus saw the soldiers stiffen as they marched. They drew fractionally closer together, and suddenly there was menace in their stride. Involuntarily, Aulus eased his horse back to a trot, then, with a curse at his faintheartedness, quickened his pace again.

The first of the soldiers drew level. Hard, bearded, weather-beaten faces stared up at Aulus with bold, arrogant eyes framed by helmet and cheekpiece. They were strong looking men, thickset and broad shouldered with corded arm muscles. They marched with the swagger and confidence of veterans, in battle order, without back packs, as though in enemy country and expecting trouble. Each man carried a long throwing spear over his right shoulder, with his shield slung down his back over the left. Clipped to their shields they carried two short, lead-weighted javelins. Stubby, broad bladed regulation swords were sheathed on their right hips. They jingled and clinked as the men marched.

The officer was a Centurion. A proud red horsehair crest framed his helmet. He wore moulded body armour. Across his chest he wore a decoration harness that was thickly set with round gold and silver medallions. His legs were protected by tinned greaves that dazzled the eye in the bright sunlight. He looked formidably strong.

Aulus drew rein. 'Good day.' he said.

The Centurion did not reply. He shifted fractionally in his saddle and his horse stopped two yards from Aulus.

He was middle aged. His face was like a weathered rock. Dark, hard eyes gazed at Aulus and then over his shoulder at Gratian.

Aulus said again, 'Good day. Can you tell me what the news is from the North?'

The Centurion's gaze flicked back to Aulus, speculatively. The educated Latin of his speech belied the tunic and breeches that he wore.

'You live around here?'

'Yes.'

'Landowner, eh?'

'Yes, this is my farm you're passing through.' He held the Centurion's gaze. 'If it's anything to you.' He felt a stab of irritation and it flashed briefly in his eyes. The Centurion noticed it and something like amusement passed momentarily over his face.

'It is not.' Abruptly, he neck-reined his horse and squeezed his legs into its flanks so that the animal balanced back on its hocks and sprang forward past Aulus.

'Hey!' Aulus' temper flared.

The Centurion did not look back. He took station beside the lumbering wagons, controlling his horse to a hand canter no faster than a walking pace.

'Rude bastard!'

A young officer marching behind the rear guard grinned in open amusement. He nodded cheerfully at Aulus and winked as he passed.

They left a veil of dust hanging in the summer air as they went.

'Bloody arrogant bastards.' Aulus stared furiously after them. Their shields swung rhythmically across their backs. Not one looked round.

Gratian came up, walking his horse, looking sheepish.

'Did 'e tell thee the news, surr?'

'No, he did not!' The ferocity of Aulus' reply stopped further comment. 'Come on, get a move on', and he clapped his legs to his horse's sides and bounded ahead.

Aulus' temper had cooled by the time they reached Corinium: he was smiling at his anger as he clattered through the great turreted gateway into the city. Immediately, his amusement and all thought of his encounter with the army were forgotten.

He had always liked Corinium. It was a large city, said to be the second largest in Britannia, but – probably because its massive walls enclosed such a large area – it gave the feel of spaciousness and elegance combined with just enough bustle to quicken the blood of a countryman whose visits were infrequent. Like all Roman towns its streets were laid out straight. They crossed each other like the squares of a gridiron, dominated at the centre by the great three storied mass of the Basilica with its colonnaded square of shops and offices enclosing the market place. Close to the Basilica's protecting bulk clustered the jumble of irregular walls and roofs that were the main shopping area and tenement homes of the humbler townsfolk. Spreading out from it, along the regular straight streets, set further apart and then widely spaced, stood the individual houses with their walled gardens and orchards. Trees broke the lines and softened the angles while here and there paddocks and small fields were grazed by cows and horses.

Always in Corinium there was movement; horsemen, pedestrians, animals, the vehicles of the tradespeople but never so crowded that they blocked the streets.

Not so today. The city was teeming with people. At first sight, Aulus wondered if there was a carnival, or games at the theatre but there was no excitement or holiday mood in this crowd. Men and women, they were drifting as though lost. They stood about aimlessly. Their arms hung limply, their shoulders sagged. They were crowding the streets, blocking the paving: blank faces stared up at Aulus as he rode past them. There were carts and wagons everywhere, piled with furniture, bedding and shapeless bundles. Amazed, Aulus saw that they had overflowed the streets and that tents and makeshift awnings had been pitched in the pleasant little orchards and paddocks. Beside the rough shelters some of the carts had been unloaded. The debris of their contents was scattered round them, watched over by ragged children and weary-eyed ancients. There were cooking fires as well, their smoke drifting intrusively into the sunlight. The unaccustomed stink of human excrement kept gagging Aulus' breath.

They pushed through the crowd, Gratian shouting 'Get out the way there! Get out the way!' Sullenly the crowds parted for them. There was hostility in the men's faces now, and anger. There were knots of men at the street corners. It looked as though violence could easily erupt amongst them.

Aulus and Gratian skirted the city centre and turned towards the wide spaced houses of Corinium's leading citizens. Even here, the streets were littered with carts and aimless humanity. Once or twice Aulus stopped and asked the men what they were doing. Their mumbled replies – if indeed they replied at all – were no help. They simply looked at him as though he were some strange animal. He gave it up.

They passed the paddock where Tiberius kept his horses and rode along the windowless street wall of his house. Midway in its length the classic proportions of the front entrance stood with its heavy panelled doors closed beneath their triangular carved stone pediment. Aulus ignored it. He continued along the wall until it turned at right angles down a side street. Forty yards on they came to double gates. Gratian dismounted and rang the bell that hung on the wall above it. A face appeared at a little barred window beside the gate and was gone. The gate opened and they rode into the sudden quiet of Tiberius' stable yard.

Aulus dismounted. To his right Tiberius' orchard and garden, ringed by the perimeter wall, stood empty and peaceful. His gaze moved over the neat flagged walks and cropped grass. On his left, Tiberius' house was a single storied building with whitewashed walls and red tiled roofs. It was built in two wings, connected by a portico and the central gatehouse that Aulus had passed in the street. The hollow square between the wings was neatly laid out in a formal garden. The wooden pillared colonnade on the inside of each wing connected the three sides and gave them a harmony and intimate cohesion.

Gratian took his horse and Aulus walked quickly across the garden and up shallow steps to the house. As he walked he brushed the dust from his tunic and smoothed his wind-tousled dark hair with his fingers.

He called: 'Tiberius, are you there?'

'In here.' There was surprise and pleasure in the voice that answered from the first room that Aulus came to. The old senator was in his study, writing on a tablet at the big rectangular table that was the room's main furniture. His frowning concentration gave way to a smile of welcome.

'Aulus, how good to see you! Is Flavia with you?'

'I'm afraid not.' Aulus smiled back. 'She's minding the harvest for me. She sends her love.'

'Thank you. But I'd rather have her come in person. How are you both?'

'Fine, thank you. Who are all these people in the city? What are they doing here?'

Tiberius looked surprised. He half laughed, disbelievingly. 'Do you mean you don't know?'

'No.'

'Refugees. They're refugees.'

'Refugees? Where from?'

'Where have you been lately, Aulus?'

'On the farm. I've not been off it for two months. I knew there was unrest. It's what I've come to ask you about, but I had no idea...'

'I should have sent you word. I apologise. They're refugees from the warbands.'

'But, surely, there aren't any warbands anywhere near here?'

'No. There are none within fifty miles or more. It's panic.'

Aulus was silent. Whatever Tiberius might say, this was the worst confirmation of his fears.

Tiberius said: 'The northern wall has been overrun by the Picts. The whole of the north of Britannia is in flames.

'So it's true, then.' Fear clutched at Aulus.

'Yes. For the first time in living history they've united; Scots and Picts, and the Saxons on the east coast. They've attacked our borders simultaneously. Not just random raiding warbands. It has been a coordinated invasion.'

'But they'll never get this far south.' It was half a question. 'Will they?'

'Not this year. But the border garrisons have been cut to pieces. They have ceased to exist.'

'That's impossible!'

'It has happened. When he realised what was afoot General Fullofaudes took command in person. The frontier scouts betrayed him. They led him into an ambush. His command was annihilated.'

'Who is – or was – General Fullofaudes?'

'Duke of Britannia – the commander in chief of all the Northern forces. He's dead. He died in the fighting.'

'It really is serious'

'Yes.'

'But we've had disasters before and have mastered them.' He fell silent again, trying to assess how Etruria, his farm and land, might be affected.

There was the briefest of perfunctory knocks on the door. Aulus looked round. Cloa, Tiberius' housekeeper, was peering into the room disapprovingly.

'Good morning, Cloa.'

'Huh. Good morning, Master Aulus.' Her face was accusing. She countered Aulus' greeting like a swordsman parrying a thrust. She had obviously hurried across from the kitchen as soon as she had heard of Aulus' arrival.

'Where is Miss Flavia?'

'She's at Etruria.'

'Huh, so I see.' She shot Aulus a look of malicious triumph. 'The young master's left Miss Flavia alone and unprotected on his farm.' She had never forgiven Aulus for marrying her beloved Flavia. There was at best an armed neutrality between them, verging on open warfare whenever either of them dropped their guard.

'Don't be ridiculous, Cloa. She's perfectly safe.'

Cloa snorted. She was dressed as always in black from head to foot, her hood outlined by a fringe of grey hair. Her sharp, lined old face was imperious. She said, ignoring Aulus: 'The young master has no business leaving Miss Flavia on his farm when he comes into town.'

'I know, Cloa, I know,' Tiberius answered mildly. 'I've already told him so.'

'Well, she's busy, and she sends you her love.'

'Is she having another baby?'

'Not so far as we know.' Aulus frowned. A year ago they had lost their first born with summer fever. The scar had healed. It was a wound that Cloa must always reopen.

'It's time she had another.'

'That's up to her.'

Cloa glared at him and disdained to reply. 'I came to see if you would like wine, Sir.'

'Yes, please, Cloa, for both of us.'

She bobbed the briefest of curtsies, shot Aulus a look of disdain, and withdrew, her back stiff with disapproval. They looked at each other and smiled.

'She does love Flavia so,' Tiberius said apologetically.

From the direction of the kitchen they heard Cloa's sharp call; 'Come on you lazy man. The master's waiting....'

'Age doesn't soften her much.'

'No, but she still runs the house impeccably, and keeps us all in order.'

'Yes.' Tiberius had married late. Flavia's mother had died giving birth to her. Cloa had brought her up, protecting, adoring and scolding her like a fierce hawk brooding its chick. It always amazed Aulus that Flavia had grown up as a normal human being under Cloa's iron hand, let alone as the laughing, vivacious girl that he had first met four years ago in this very room and had fallen in love with on the spot. He supposed it had been Tiberius' balancing influence and the quiet shade of the mother she had never known that had shaped his beloved Flavia.

He switched his mind away from Flavia back to their former conversation and said again: 'But we've had disasters before, Tiberius. The North was overrun when Allectus took the army to Gaul.'

'That was seventy years ago, Aulus. Rome was stronger then. The Empire has grown weak. Our sun is setting. Like the wolf pack, the barbarians are closing in to tear us down. All our frontiers are under attack. Yes, come in, Philo.'

The manservant who came in with a silver wine jug and goblets was plump and fleshy. The tray rattled as he set it down: the sound made Aulus glance at him. The soft white hands were trembling. He slopped some of the wine onto the tray as he poured. Amused, Aulus thought, 'Cloa's been after him with her stick again.'

He said: Hullo, Philo. You don't look too well.'

Philo looked quickly at Tiberius, as though for reassurance. 'It's the refugees, Sir,' he said anxiously. 'I'm just back from the market, Sir. They're all saying it. The army's beaten. We'll all be killed in our beds.'

Tiberius frowned. 'That's enough of that, Philo. Pull yourself together. You're like an old woman, listening to market gossip.'

Philo winced indignantly and busied himself with the goblets. They waited until he had gone before Aulus said: 'Could he be right?'

'I hope not. But he could.' As a senior city senator Tiberius Catullus saw to it that all information coming into Corinium was routed to him. 'There is no doubt that all the frontier garrisons have ceased to exist as coherent fighting units. What is not so certain is what is happening with the mobile field army. There certainly are simply not enough of them to stem the barbarians. I am not sure where they are or who they are fighting. They've not only got to fight in the north. These godforsaken Scots have been pouring in through the Ordovician mountains from the west. They must be trying to fight on two fronts.' He shook his head. 'These mobile warbands are difficult enough for the field army to tie down at the best of time. If they break...' He left the sentence unfinished and spread his hands with a shrug of his shoulders.

'If the field army can't hold them, the warbands really could get this far South?'

Tiberius ran a hand over his thinning hair. 'Ultimately, yes. Reinforcements have been sent for, of course, but there is little hope of any this autumn. The channel will be impassable to troop ships long before the Emperor can put a force together. We've just got to pray the warbands turn around and go back to their homelands for the winter.'

'It just doesn't sound possible.'

'Fortunately, these barbarians know nothing of siege warfare and lack the patience to try it. If the worst comes to the worst we can hold out here until spring without too much difficulty – so long as the plague doesn't do their work for them with all these refugees crowded in here. Then it will be a matter of how soon reinforcements get here.'

'But how many of these raiders are there?'

Tiberius shook his head. 'Try counting fish in water. Thousands, Aulus. Big warbands, and a lot of them. And that's not counting the Saxons.'

'Are they doing the same on the Saxon coast?'

'The news from the east is very sparse. Londinium will be holding without a doubt. But so far as one can gather the Saxon shore forts may have fallen or been cut off. They say Count Nectaridus is dead.'

'He's the Count of the Saxon shore, isn't he?'

'Yes – commander of all the east coast garrisons. If he's alive.'

'Well, if he's dead, and the Duke of Britannia is dead, who's in overall command?'

'It seems that no one is. I assume whoever the surviving senior officer of the field army is will be trying to coordinate the defence. I don't know.'

'Dear gods. What a mess.'

'Yes. But, as I say, I very much doubt we shall see these raiders here this year. No, the worry is whether reinforcements get here in time next spring, because if they don't Britannia will be like a ripe plum waiting to be picked.'

He fell silent, staring out through the open door into the warm brightness of the garden. At last he said: 'You know, Aulus, all my life I have feared this. All my life I have seen the Empire weakening. Our will to survive has gone. We've grown soft and idle and corrupt. The strength of purpose that built the Empire has changed to greed and selfishness. Our world is tottering. Maybe it is about to disappear. It was inevitable that one day the barbarians would unite - probably not for long, but for long enough to devastate Britannia. This summer, it has happened. If Rome fails us now, the country will be lost.

'Surely you're being too pessimistic?'

Tiberius smiled briefly, a smile that failed to touch his eyes. 'Let us hope so. If I hear that the warbands are getting anywhere near here I'll send a galloper out to you at Etruria. If I do, just drop everything and come.'

'I can't abandon Etruria. I can't give up my home and farm without a fight. I'd rather die.'

'And so you would. Painfully'

'I'll have to take my chance on that.' Even to himself the words sounded hollow.

Tiberius said slowly: 'Then perhaps our spirit is not wholly dead. But Etruria's not built for defence and I doubt whether many – any – of your farm people will stay once they get wind of real danger. They'll panic and run, just like these poor wretches who are crowding our streets. There'll be nothing you can do to stop them. I hardly blame them. But bring Flavia into Corinium, Aulus. Don't expose her to such risk.'

'I'll try. But you know how stubborn she can be. She'll say she won't leave her home – and me.'

'I expect she will.' He smiled to himself. 'Just like her mother. But bring her, all the same.'

'I will, I promise. Even if I have to drag her.'

'Thank you.'

Tiberius looked up at Aulus, standing tall and broad in the confidence of youth and strength. He breathed a prayer of thanks to his gods that his beloved Flavia had found and loved a straightforward honest man. The thought gave him deep comfort.

'Well, come on,' he said. 'Let's talk about something more cheerful. Fill your goblet. Tell me all the news from Etruria.'

The mention of the farm recalled the memory of the soldiers on the military road. 'I passed some soldiers coming in this morning. What on earth would they be doing going south?'

'A century, with three wagons?'

'Yes. And a particularly rude Centurion.'

'They came through last night. The officer is a Chief Centurion, I'm told: a very senior man. Unfortunately, I did not have the chance to talk to him.'

'Why are they going away from the fighting?'

Tiberius' face closed slightly. 'Apparently they are on a secret Imperial duty of the highest importance.'

Chapter II

Aulus and Tiberius ate a midday meal together. They tried to talk of Etruria, but it did not work. They were thinking of the warbands: anything else seemed irrelevant. The only important thing was whether the army would hold, whether and when reinforcements would come, and whether Corinium, and particularly Etruria, would be safe that winter.

Aulus left after the meal.

'I'm going straight back to Etruria,' he said. 'I had wanted to see the grain merchant today, but after what you've told me, I can't see any point in fixing a price for any surplus. I don't think it would be wise to sell anything at present.'

'Maybe not. I'm afraid there will be a heavy levy on grain this winter, but the price will be sky high for any surplus.'

'It's not so much that; if things do get bad I'd rather have the grain than the money.'

Cloa appeared as he was mounting.

She glared at him: 'Remember me to my lady and tell her to come herself. She shouldn't be on that farm of yours by herself anyway. She should be safe here at her father's house.'

'I'll tell her so, Cloa, and I'll make sure she comes herself next time. She prefers to be with me on the farm, you know.'

'Huh. You do that, Master Aulus.' She stood and watched them go, unsmiling, her lined face expressionless.

Aulus' heart rose as he left Corinium's walls. It was always a relief to be out in the open countryside again and particularly today to get away from the crowded streets of frightened humanity. Gratian drew level with him, full of the gossip from the servants' quarters. Philo's rumour of the army's defeat was obviously the highlight of the news. Aulus listened with half an ear. No doubt Tiberius' people had taken great delight in filling Gratian's simple country mind with horror stories and his body with their master's wine.

It was hard to think of violence and death in this peaceful countryside. Of course, there was always trouble in the north, there had always been Saxons marauding on the east coast, and the wretched Scots invading from their island on the west. Everyone knew they had all been getting bolder over the years, but the troubles had never come this far inland. Of course, too, Emperors had come and gone, often in quick succession and lakes of blood. There had been insurrections and battles in far off lands, troops had been recalled from Britannia and later replaced, the old legions had disappeared, the army was nowhere near as strong as it once had been, but these things had passed Etruria by. Etruria, his land, had been in his family for four generations and in all that time they had been at peace.

Because of it, the holding had grown over the years. Bought by his great grandfather on completion of his military service, it had been added to by his grandfather and father by purchase and forest clearance until it now boasted several hundred acres of good grain-bearing land. His great grandfather had chosen well. The land was well watered by the river that ran fresh and clear through the northern block, while the farm was well serviced by the military road that ran straight through the centre. Once it had all been forested, a sure sign that the soil was fertile. About half the total area had been cleared. It was one of Aulus' ambitions to clear a good proportion of the remaining woodland.

As he passed his boundary Aulus broke off his daydreaming to look critically at his farm. The yellow green of the pastures blended with the deep gold of the standing crops and stooked corn fields, set against and intermingled with the dark greens of the woodlands. It had been a good season. The grain had grown thick and full bodied. His cattle were sleek and shiny coated, the calves stocky and contented as they butted their mothers' udders and ran, tails in air, playing their simple games.

Away across the fields to his left, connected to the military road by the white ribbon of its drive, lay the farmhouse. Like the farm, it had begun modestly as a conventional row of south-facing single-storey rooms connected by a red roofed portico. Originally it had been surrounded by scattered mud and thatch huts which had housed the cattle and stored the crops. Over the years the family had first added rooms to the house and then, at right angles running north, Aulus' father had constructed permanent cattle shedding, granaries and stores, forming two long, stone- built wings that sprang from each corner of the house. A northern block of living quarters for the single farm men and workshops for the craftsmen completed the square. In the centre of the block he had built a wide arched gateway, so that the farmhouse and its buildings formed a secure inner cobbled courtyard. The final addition, built by Aulus shortly after he married Flavia, was a tall rectangular bathhouse, tacked onto the south western corner of the square, butting up to the house so that its doors opened directly onto the front portico.

As always, Aulus' heart lifted as he looked across at his home. His gaze lingered on the red tiled roof, the dark timber strutting of the house, the windows above the portico thrown open to the sun and the wide shallow steps leading from the house to the garden that Flavia had blended into lawn and flowerbeds. He was still not sure about the bathhouse. It stuck out from the harmony of the square: it was too stark and its tiles too red, though the smoke from the stokehole that heated it was blackening its whitewash and toning it in more quickly than it's scant age should allow.

His eyes meandered on: the farm drive swept out of sight to the east of the buildings, running their length to turn at the north east corner and arc towards the gateway. Beyond, across the meadow to the north of the buildings, he pictured the slavelines –timber framed thatched cottages with a permanent haze of woodsmoke drifting from the open crowns of their roofs, home to the families that had lived and worked there for generations. He smiled to himself. 'Slavelines.' The name was almost an insult on Etruria. They had been slaves originally, of course. They had married, lived and died there, earning their freedom and leaving sons and grandsons to carry on their skills. They were nearly all free now. He fed them and housed them, gave them little plots to grow their vegetables, wool to weave their clothes and leather to stitch their jerkins and fashion their boots, and, on special occasions he paid them in coin. Their lives were simple, creatures of the land like the cattle and sheep and horses they tended but they were content, or they had been until these rumours had taken hold.

And then, surprised, Aulus realised that there were soldiers on the road in front of him, close to the driveway that turned off to the farm. There were three wagons, unharnessed, in the middle of the carriageway, surrounded by a group of armoured men. He felt a stirring of remembered anger.

Three sentries were posted along the road towards him. They gazed curiously at the approaching horsemen, spears in their hands, their shields held loosely across their bodies.

When Aulus was twenty yards from them one switched his spear into his left hand and held up a big authoritative palm signalling them to stop. Aulus said nothing as he drew rein. The soldiers peered at them, weighing them up. One said. 'You're the blokes we passed this morning, aren't you?'

'Yes.'

Their faces relaxed. The soldier waved them past with his spear.

'What's the trouble?'

'Axle's broke on one of the wagons. Smashed the wheels, it has.'

'D'you need any help?'

'Don't 'spect so.' There was good natured indulgence in the reply. 'Chief'll have it fixed directly.'

Aulus nodded and trotted past. It was the back axle of the lead wagon. Aulus grinned wryly. A pothole in the road had been getting worse all summer, deeper and wider as successive traffic had jolted through it. At last, it had claimed a victim. The jarring must have snapped the axle, and the sudden shift in weight had shattered the wheels. The soldiers had removed them and lashed great oak limbs - stolen from his woods, without a doubt – to the frames as drags. From the look of it the task had just been finished. The men were standing around as the hard-faced Centurion inspected their work.

The wagon must have been carrying a very heavy load. Jolting through a pothole, however big, should not have had such a devastating effect. It had been unloaded, but from the way the soldiers were mopping their brows they must have been dealing with a wagon of most unusual design. He rode past. The Centurion straightened from his inspection and turned to look at him. The frustrated fury in his dark eyes killed stone dead Aulus' intention to offer help. He nodded briefly, trotted on, and turned into the drive.

'Hey, you!'

Aulus ignored the shout.

'Hey! Mister!'

Involuntarily, Aulus looked back.

The Centurion was standing, legs apart and hands on hips, glaring at him. 'Is this your place?'

'If I remember rightly, it meant nothing to you whose place it is.'

With obvious reluctance the Centurion took a step towards him. 'Have you got workshops here?'

Aulus did not reply. The memory of the morning's insult was still raw. He let the Centurion walk right up to him. The man had taken off the red horsehair crest, decoration harness and greaves. He looked formidably businesslike. His eyes were angry as he looked up at Aulus.

'Have you got workshops here?'

'What is it to you?'

The briefest spark of humour lit up the Centurion's face for a moment.

'All right, mister, you win.'

Aulus nodded. It had just occurred to him that it would steady the workforce immensely to have soldiers on the farm for a few days. In any case they would have to wait until the wagon was repaired – unless they abandoned it, which they obviously had no intention of doing. The Centurion most probably had already decided that he would use the farm meadow to camp in and would do so whether Aulus agreed or not. 'Yes,' he said. 'This is my farm and I do have workshops. I have a wainwright.'

The flash of humour had gone from the Centurion's features as quickly as it had appeared. Seen close to, and framed by the steel of his helmet, he had one of the strongest and most determined faces Aulus had ever seen. He said: 'It's going to take some time to replace those wheels. You'd better camp on the farm until they're ready.' He indicated the broad meadow stretching out around the farm buildings.

The Centurion nodded. He turned away and raised his voice. 'Optio! Get the men fell in.'

The young, broad shouldered officer who had winked at Aulus that morning had been standing a few yards behind them, an interested listener to his chief's exchange. He snapped to attention, turned and went at the double, shouting orders as he ran.

'Marcus Livius,' the Centurion unexpectedly said. 'He is my second-in-command.' To Aulus' surprise there was a hint of pride, affection even, in his voice.

Aulus searched his memory. 'Optio'. A rank just under centurion. He watched as the men formed up on Marcus' word of command. As the sentries came doubling in, some of the men picked up and shouldered the bulky packs that lay on the grass verge, others grouped themselves empty handed around the crippled wagon while the remainder, burdened with their comrades' shields and spears, formed up half in front and half behind the column. The wagon drivers brought the horse teams at a run and backed them expertly onto the wagon tongues. Within minutes the harness was coupled and the whole column stood ready.

Aulus was immensely impressed. They looked a first-class unit. Their helmets and mail were powdered with dust, but beneath it the metal was burnished white. Like their tunics, their shields were red, freshly painted in gold designs flowing like lightening from the embossed centres.

An orderly hurried from the meadow with the Centurion's horse. He mounted and settled himself into the saddle. Marcus marched across to him and saluted.

'Special Century ready to move, Sir.'

The Centurion nodded. 'Watch that wagon.'

Marcus shouted the order. The lead wagoner cracked his whip over his team. The horses plunged into their harness. The crippled wagon shuddered and tipped as one of the boughs shifted slightly in its lashings.
The horses strained and danced under the dead weight. The wagon inched forward. The surrounding soldiers sprang to steady it and threw themselves onto the front wheels, muscles straining to turn the spokes.

'Hold it.' The Centurion cursed. 'Optio, take two horses from both the other teams.'

Astonished, Aulus said: 'What on earth have you got in that wagon?'

The Centurion turned on him viciously. 'Mind your own business, farmer, and leave me to mine.'

Despite the snub Aulus watched as the crippled wagon was changed from a four horse to an eight-horse team which slowly dragged its way onto the drive.

The sight of their master riding home with a column of soldiers brought all work in the vicinity of the farm buildings to a halt. Word spread like wildfire. Aulus' progress up the drive was surrounded by farm children then, as they neared the farmstead, the old hands appeared, cackling their delight at the strange spectacle. Finally, the house servants and craftsmen dropped their work and joined the crowd to see the fun.

At the same time Flavia was riding back from the northern harvest fields. She was on her favourite mare and riding at a slow hand canter. She was dressed like Aulus in tunic and breeches with soft leather boots that reached to her knees. Her long hair, like old gold in the sunlight, bobbed on her shoulders in time to her horse's stride. She was pleasantly hot and dusty and looking forward to stripping off in the bathhouse. Before she could see the house, she heard the confusion of shouting from the direction of the buildings. She quickened her pace as she splashed through the river and cleared the last belt of trees.

'What on earth is going on?' she said aloud. Then, catching sight of Aulus she felt a prickle of alarm. 'What on earth is Aulus up to? Soldiers? Here?' She urged the mare forward. Someone must have seen her coming because Aulus extricated himself from the throng and came cantering across to meet her. Her heart went out to him, tall and straight, his face lighting up with pleasure at seeing her.

'What is going on?'

'They are a century from the field army, apparently on some urgent secret duty. One of their wagons broke its axle in that pothole just by our turning. They're going to camp on the big meadow until we can get them fixed up.'

'Oh.' She looked past him at the soldiers. They had fallen out and were standing in groups by the wagons. She frowned. 'Is that a good idea?'

'I hope so. I think it'll steady the workforce to have them here for a day or two. Your father says things are pretty bad. Corinium is full of refugees.' He smiled at her as the two horses came together. The mare flirtingly nipped at the gelding's muzzle and squealed briefly.

'You're looking very beautiful.'

She smiled back, warmly crinkling the corners of her eyes and showing white, even teeth. They sat together for a moment, enjoying each other's closeness.

'Is everything going all right?' Aulus asked.

'Yes.' She looked past him at the soldiers. She said again: 'Yes,' absently, 'everything's fine here. Aulus, must they stay here?'

'Who? The soldiers? They'll have to for a few days until Atimetus mends their wagon.'

'Oh.' She took his hand and held it tightly. He turned his horse and they rode together towards the column. 'They won't upset our lives, will they?'

'I hope not. How d'you mean?'

'I don't know.' It was nothing she could explain, just that the afternoon seemed suddenly darker. Looking at the soldiers she had felt a chill of apprehension.

The Centurion saluted her perfunctorily as they rode up.

Flavia said 'Good afternoon.'

He acknowledged her greeting with a grudging nod. 'Ma'am,' he said.

'My husband says that you will be with us for a few days. Will you stay with us in the house?'

'No. We'll camp in the meadow and be on our way as soon as the wagon's fixed.'

She nodded, slightly mollified by the Centurion's obvious authority.

Aulus said ' I'll get my men onto it straight away.'

There was a sudden bellow: 'Get away from those wagons!'

The Centurion turned sharply. Two of the farm boys were scuttling for cover behind their mothers' skirts.

He turned back fiercely. 'Keep your people away from my wagons, mister.' He shouted: 'Optio, get those men back in line and look sharp about it.'

The soldiers doubled to form a protective line on each side of their transport. Aggressively, they faced outwards. The farm people fell back in bewildered alarm. The Centurion looked at Aulus, his face hostile.

'Keep your people away from my men. Just carry on with your business and forget we're here.' He nodded to Flavia - 'Ma'am'- and wheeled his horse away, shouting orders and pointing across the meadow.

They watched in silence as the soldiers left the drive. The crippled wagon swayed on its improvised drags. It lurched across the grass of the meadow to a slight rise some hundred yards from the buildings.

Flavia said abruptly 'I'm going to the bathhouse.' She vaulted off her horse and strode quickly, without looking back, towards the house.

Aulus watched her go. Her short tunic just covered her buttocks, flaring slightly at the hips. He smiled to himself.

Aulus went straight to the workshops. The double doors of the joiner's shop were flung wide open in the hot afternoon. It smelt pleasantly of resinous wood. The three joiners barely had time to pick up their tools before he arrived. He smiled as they bent to their tasks.

'Did you see the smashed wagon, Atimetus?'

The head joiner smiled back slightly sheepishly. 'I did, Sir.'

'Go and measure it up. I want it repaired as quick as ever you can.' He would have gone with Atimetus, but other pleasures called.

In the bathhouse Flavia had undressed. She had passed from the cold room to the warm tepidarum. She was sitting naked on the bench, her oil bottle and scraper beside her, staring frowning at the opposite wall. She looked round, surprised. Her face lit up. She giggled.

'What are you doing here?'

'You.'

'You're not even undressed.'

'Soon will be.' Aulus leant against the wall, looking at her, pulling off his boots. She sat enigmatically still, looking back at him. He pulled his tunic off and threw it back into the cold room.

'You'll get caught.' Her voice was light with laughter.

'Door's bolted.'

She watched as he undid his breeches and kicked them off then jumped up and dashed laughing into the hot room.

He let her go, delighting in her slim hips and neat bottom. The blood surged in him as her trim body disappeared. She called back: 'You can't get me in here. It's too hot.'

He stood in the doorway, grinning at her. She had picked up a jar of water. Grinning back at him she tipped it and splashed most of its contents on the hot paved floor. Steam clouded around her. She laughed again and threw the rest of the water at Aulus. He lunged forward as it came and caught her by the waist. She threw her head back, mouth open. He bent and kissed her fiercely. The steam rose about them. They pressed their naked bodies together.

Later, much later, fresh in clean tunic and breeches, Aulus reappeared at the joiner's shop. Atimetus was busy ferreting in the stack of seasoned timber that he kept for special jobs. He wiped his forehead.

'Those be some real heavy wagons,' he said, his voice slightly puzzled. 'Can't understand it, by rights. The frames be far too heavy, the beds be far too deep. Solid, too, they must be. Ain't never seen nothing like 'em. It's no wonder the axle broke. I'll have to find some real seasoned wood for this job, Sir. I've got some ash for the rims and axle, and some yew for the hubs. What I'm after now is some real solid heartwood oak for the spokes.' He shook his head. 'Be four or five days, it will, Sir, to make the sort of job this wagon is going to need.'

Aulus nodded. 'All right, Atimetus. Drop everything else and get started on them right away.'

'You'd think the army would know how to build a wagon by now.' The old man looked scornful. 'I told that officer so, too.'

'What did he say?'

'Didn't say naught, Sir, not a word. Just stared at me like some wild animal.'

Aulus laughed. He wandered out into the sunlight, through the big arched gateway and across the meadow towards the soldiers.

The three wagons were drawn up close together on top of the little rise. They had pegged out a rectangle round them and the men, helmets and armour discarded, were hard at work removing the turf and digging a trench round the site. They were throwing the sod back with practised skill, piling it to form a rampart within the perimeter. Two men were unloading sharpened stakes from one of the wagons and laying them out on the grass beside the freshly dug soil.

Aulus's good humour evaporated. He quickened his pace, heading for the Centurion who was standing watching his men.

'I never said you could dig the farm up.'

'Military regulations.' The Centurion looked at him stonily.

Nonplussed, Aulus gazed round the scene. Marcus, with what Aulus took to be a tesserarius or junior officer was just finishing marking out tent pitches. There were five at either end of the wagons and two beside them. His interest aroused, Aulus said: 'How many men do you sleep in a tent?'

'Eight.'

'What are those stakes for?'

'To reinforce the rampart.' Aulus nodded. Of course. When the trench and earthwork were finished they would be set, points facing outwards like a bristling hedgehog, to strengthen the camp's defences.

A group of soldiers had started to erect the tents. They began at the pitch nearest the wagons. Within minutes a high sided red leather rectangle with pitched roof had taken shape. Aulus watched, fascinated. The men moved on, joking amongst themselves. The tents they erected beyond the wagons were much lower, like a triangle of brown leatherwork rising directly from the ground.

'Is that big one your tent?'

The Centurion nodded, watching his men.

The horses were picketed in two lines at one end of the camp. The wagoners were brushing them down. One of the soldiers was checking over a pile of hobbles. As soon as the grooming was over the horses would no doubt be taken out for an evening feed. There was an air of order and discipline over the scene. The men looked cheerful as they sweated at their work in the warm sunlight.

Aulus shook his head and sighed. 'Ah, well. I suppose it can all be put back.'

For the first time the Centurion looked directly at him. 'That's right. We'll throw the rampart down when we go.'

'You'd better help yourselves to firewood from the woods. The river is on the edge of the meadow over there.' Aulus pointed. The Centurion nodded. He had long since sent a detail to collect wood and to fill the men's water skins.

'Anything else we can do for you?'

'No, just keep away.' As an afterthought the Centurion added: 'Sir'. He saluted and walked away.

Chapter III

Aulus had been right. The presence of the soldiers had an immediate effect on the farm people. They seemed to relax and to breathe easily again, as though no harm could come to them now that the army was camped on the farm.

Work on the wagon repair went well, unhampered by harvest emergencies. Atimetus retrieved the steel axle stubs and wheel rims which the smith heated white hot and trued to a perfect circle ready to sweat onto the new wheels. He found the timber he needed, and he and the joiners worked full time to copy the axle and duplicate the design of hub, spoke and rim. They fitted the replacement axle on the second day, surrounded by the soldiers and watched inscrutably by the Centurion. Atimetus grumbled fiercely at them: 'Why don't you get out the way and leave us alone to get on with it? If you think you can do a better job, why don't you come and do it yourselves?' He was totally unafraid of the Centurion. 'Trouble with you lot is you don't know how to make a wagon. Look at this bed' – he tapped the oak frame of the wagon – 'Too deep. Too heavy cross section.'

'Save your comments, carpenter. Just get on with it and shut up.'

'I'd get on with it better if you'd clear out of my way. Just because they wear a uniform'- he observed to the world in general – 'they think they know everything.'

The soldiers laughed and strained to take the weight of the wagon as Atimetus fitted props underneath, delighted with the craftsman's spirited attack on their sombre commander.

The Centurion kept his men entirely aloof from the farm. Whenever Aulus passed on his way to and from the cornfields they were being drilled or at weapon practice with sword, spear or javelin. They were improving the camp fortification as well, deepening the ditch, throwing the earth onto the rampart, building it sheer on the outer face to present the maximum obstacle. The sharpened stakes had been set, points outward, into the earth, and thickened up with freshly cut stems from Aulus' woods so that the compact, rectangular camp presented a formidable defence against attack.

Aulus kept away from the camp and ordered all his people to do likewise. They had watched, fascinated, for a while, but then, growing used to the presence of these unfriendly strangers, interest had waned. It was a great comfort that they were there, but if they wanted to be left alone, so be it.

The harvest was going well. The weather held with hot, sunny days and warm nights. Gauging the long lines of stooks and dismounting to examine the ears of corn, Aulus was delighted that his expectation of a heavy crop was correct. Thoughts of the warbands faded in his pleasure at the fulfilment of the farm year's work.

The soldiers had been at Etruria four days when, riding home from the fields at midday, Aulus stopped off at the workshop to see whether the wheels were finished. He found the Centurion there, arguing with a flustered and angry Atimetus.

The old craftsman's face cleared at the sight of Aulus. 'I'm telling the officer it can't be done before tomorrow, Sir.' He wiped his hands on his leather apron. 'I can sweat the rims on in the morning but we just can't have the woodwork ready till then. The officer don't seem to understand that it's only me and the two men and not the whole of his army as works here.' He shot a vicious look at the Centurion who glared back at him with compressed lips.

Aulus nodded. 'All right, Atimetus.' He turned to the Centurion and was opening his mouth to speak when a child ran excitedly into the courtyard and, cupping its grimy hands to its mouth, shouted:-

'There's more soldiers a'coming up the drive!'

Before the words were out, the Centurion had reacted.

He thrust past Atimetus and leapt for the doorway. He was across the courtyard and through the gate before Aulus had moved.

A company of soldiers was turning off the road and marching purposefully on to the drive. They carried full packs, marching in fours, the sun flashing on armour and spear, a trail of dust floating around and behind them.

'Stand to your arms!' Like an angry bull the Centurion roared the command across the meadow. It brought his men instantly alert. As Aulus watched, the order was taken up and repeated in the camp. The men had been sitting around their cooking fires eating their midday meal, the smoke drifting lazily into the blue sky. For a minute there was frenzied activity as they crammed helmets onto their heads, grabbed spears and shields and ran to their stations around the camp. Within minutes of the command every man was at his post and the camp was motionless except for the drifting smoke from their fires.

In silence Aulus and the Centurion stood together watching the approaching column. It was now only a hundred yards away, marching in good order, encouraged on by an officer striding beside the men.

The Centurion stepped into the driveway in their path. He was frowning, his legs planted apart, his fists balled on his hips. It seemed to Aulus that the column stiffened at the sight of him – bodies jerked upright under the weight of the packs, heads came erect and eyes looked straight ahead. As though on the parade ground, the column marched towards them with faultless precision.

Ten yards from the Centurion the officer halted them. He turned his men left into line and gave the order to dress ranks. The movement was carried out with crisp efficiency. The column stood motionless. Aulus counted them. Sixty-two men. Their officer hesitated a moment, looking them over then, satisfied, he turned smartly, marched up to the Centurion and saluted.

'What in Hades name are you doing here?' The hostility in the Centurion's voice was crushing. He was obviously furious. Equally obviously, the two officers knew each other. Aulus looked curiously at the newcomer. He was also a centurion, with red horsehair crest and moulded body armour. Like his men, he was carrying a pack but he stood upright and moved as though its weight was nothing. He was much younger, a broad shouldered and heavily muscled soldier probably in his early thirties, a man at the height of his physical and mental strength. Aulus looked at the man's face. He was immediately struck by the eyes. They were light blue, as cold as ice: a killer's eyes. His skin was fair: Aulus was sure that the hair under the proud helmet must be yellow. Probably he was a Dacian, or a barbarian from one of the German tribes on the empire frontier. Possibly he could even be a Saxon.

The man said: 'Centurion Servius Cenric, Sir.' The Latin was spoken with a guttural accent. 'I am ordered by the Legate to report to you, Sir, with these men. I am to place myself under your command.' There was no emotion in the gaze with which he met the Centurion's hostile stare, but Aulus wondered whether, for all his brave manner, there was not a nervousness about him, something intangible and sullen, as though he expected the Centurion's anger.

The Centurion took his right hand off his hip. Slowly he unballed his fist and thrust his hand, palm upwards, towards Servius.

'Show me the Legate's order.'

'Oral only, Sir. The Legate said it was too dangerous to put anything in writing. The Scots got round to the south of us the day after you left. There was no way of knowing if you'd got through. The Legate ordered me to take this century and go after you. He said we'd be more use to you than dying up there.'

The Centurion was silent, staring at Servius, the angry dark eyes locked with the killer blue. Servius was the first to look away. Without a word the Centurion strode across to the waiting soldiers.

A hand gripped Aulus' arm. Unnoticed, Flavia had joined them. Aulus looked down at her and smiled. She was wearing a simple ankle length dress with short, wide sleeves. The rich blue of the material set off the gold of her hair. She looked troubled.

'What's happening now? Who are these men?'

'Apparently they've been sent to join the Centurion.'

'Oh, no. Can't you tell them to go away.' The urgency in her voice puzzled him.

'They'll be gone tomorrow.'

She bit her lip, frowning. 'I don't like them here.'

Aulus looked across at the newcomers, wondering what was concerning her. In his turn, he frowned.

The Centurion was walking slowly along the front rank of the column. His body was stiff. The colour had drained from his face. His fists were clenched; the muscles corded on his arms and legs. He was shaking with fury.

Flavia dug her fingers into Aulus' arm.

In complete silence the Centurion finished his inspection. He had his temper under control now. Only his eyes blazed, seething like the cauldron of a volcano. His voice was quiet, almost polite.

'What game is this?'

There was defiance in Servius' face as he faced the Centurion. 'The Legate wouldn't spare anyone else, Sir. The situation up there is desperate. He needs every man. It was his idea. He said they'd be least missed with him and most use under your command.'

'The punishment century? You say the Legate has sent me the punishment century? The scum of the army. The criminals. The Legate has sent these men to escort me? What game is this, Centurion?'

'No game, Sir. They're trained men. You know me. I can handle them. And under your command...' he left the sentence unfinished.

The Centurion stared at Servius a moment longer, then turned to face the silent newcomers. 'Listen to me, you scum,' His voice rose to a terrifying roar. 'One false step from any one of you, one step out of line, and I'll have the flesh flogged from your backs till I see every rib in your body.' His gaze swept the men. 'Ah, you, I know you.' He strode forward. To Aulus' amazement he grabbed the mail coat of one of the soldiers, lifted him clean off his feet, shook him violently and flung him backwards crashing to the ground. Shield and spear went flying. The man lay still. The Centurion swung his boot and kicked him viciously.

'Get up, you scum. Get up.' The Centurion lashed out again with his boot.

The soldier struggled to his knees, eyes glazed, his helmet askew.

The Centurion leant forward. The muscles in his arms bulged as he grasped the man's chain mail again and jerked him to his feet. The man stood mute, swaying, his jaw slack. For a moment the Centurion towered over him, then, slowly, he moved down the ranks. At each soldier he stopped, transfixing him with his gaze. Some he called by name, stubbing a finger at the man's face, holding it an inch from his eyes. To others he barked brief questions. It was a frightening performance. The men stared rigidly at nothing, but the sullen - mutinous, Aulus thought - set of their features showed their fear and resentment at their treatment.

The Centurion came slowly back to Servius. 'Very well', he said. 'I'll use your punishment century, Centurion. You'll regroup into two half centuries and you'll scout for me, half in advance, half in the rear. There will be no contact between the two halves, understand? You'll camp and mess separately. You'll have no contact with my men and any man who so much as has a bootlace undone will be up in front of me for punishment quicker than his feet can touch the ground. Now get them divided - and break up any partners.'

The Centurion stood watching, legs apart, hands on hips, his glare nailing the men so that they moved fast avoiding his eyes to take up their new positions as Servius carried out the order. Twice he overruled Servius and ordered men from one half century to the other. When Servius had finished the Centurion stood on, eyeing them. The man he had attacked hung limply between two comrades. The sight seemed to give him a certain grim pleasure.

'All right Centurion. Right half back down the road a mile towards Corinium. Left half a mile on to the east. Set pickets and put out patrols. Any contact between the two halves and I'll crucify the offenders. Understood? Report back to me here in two hours. I'll be watching you. Dismiss!'

Servius saluted. And then, suddenly, his light blue eyes looked over the Centurion's shoulder, full at Flavia. There was no mistaking the message in them. Flavia stiffened. Aulus stepped forward angrily. Servius' eyes switched to Aulus. There was mockery in them now, and amusement. He turned away and in his guttural Latin he gave the orders to his men.

The Centurion watched them go and then, without a word, strode off towards his own camp shouting to Marcus to stand the men down.

Aulus recovered first. 'Come on, everyone.' A knot of farm people and children had gathered while the drama was unfolding. 'There's nothing more to see now. Get on with your work.'

Reluctantly, the group broke up. They looked puzzled. Within minutes, the story, enhanced, would be relayed all over the farm.

Aulus and Flavia were left standing together. Aulus could feel the tension in her body. She said: 'The punishment century? What can he mean? How soon can they be gone, Aulus?'

'Tomorrow. By all the gods, I hope so. I think those are all the criminals of the field army. I think they send them to a punishment century to serve out their sentences.'

She was suddenly furious. 'Damn them! Damn them! How dare they come here? How dare they send criminals? How dare they! I want them off the farm, Aulus.'

'They'll be gone tomorrow.'

'No! Now! Now!' She clenched her fists and shook them at him.

'You know that the Centurion will do exactly as he pleases.'

She strode away from him towards the house. In strained silence he followed her. In her fury she was almost weeping. The corners of her mouth trembled as she said accusingly: 'It's your farm, isn't it?'

'They wouldn't go.'

'Huh!' She went stiffly up the portico steps, tossing her head scornfully, refusing to look at him.

'You know full well I can't order them off.' He caught her wrist and pulled her towards him.

'Let me go!' Her eyes were dark with fury.

'No.'

Angrily she struggled to prise his fingers from her arm. He held her easily, then, as her frown deepened and her jaw jutted, he put his left arm round her waist and pulled her to him.

'Easy.' he said.

'You're afraid of them. You're no man.'

He released her wrist and held her head onto his chest, stroking her hair. She struggled to free herself. He pressed her to his body. After a while she sighed. 'I know. You're right. They wouldn't go but I hate them being here.' Slowly she relaxed against him.

A farm wagon pulled by slow oxen trundled across the road from the southern cornfields onto the drive. Like the oxen, the carters walked with their heads down, half asleep in the warm sunlight. The world seemed at peace.

Flavia looked at Aulus and smiled through tear misted eyes. He took her hand and they walked down off the portico into her garden, drawing comfort from each other and the sight and feel of the land they loved.

The Centurion met Aulus on his way to the fields early the next morning. The day was cooler and overcast.

'I think we'll have some rain in a day or two,' Aulus avoided the Centurion's eyes. He had woken with a feeling of relief that today would see the soldiers leave the farm. The Centurion's appearance made him vaguely uneasy, accentuated by the memory of his violent fury the day before.

The Centurion was plainly uninterested in Aulus' weather forecast. He said: 'The first half century leaves this afternoon. My men will move tomorrow morning.'

Aulus' face fell. 'I thought you were going today.'

'First light tomorrow. The wagon won't be ready until this afternoon. I'd rather spend the night in a properly fortified camp.'

'Oh.' With the soldiers on the farm Aulus had relegated to the back of his mind his conversation with Tiberius in Corinium. The mention of a properly fortified camp brought the memory icily back. He said: 'Centurion, how much danger are we really in from these warbands?'

The Centurion stared at Aulus pensively. He shrugged his shoulders.

'For the gods' sake, Centurion, you owe us something.'

The Centurion nodded. 'You're in more danger here than you realise. If the field army fails – if they overrun us – the whole north and west are wide open to attack. Most likely the Saxon shore as well.'

'Why should you be overrun?'

The Centurion frowned and was silent.

'Well, if it is overrun, will the warbands get this far south?'

'There are enough pickings for that carrion where they are. The Scots won't trouble you this autumn. As for the Saxons, I don't know. I could have told you better in a week's time.' The Centurion almost smiled fractionally as though at some dark joke of his own.

'I see.' They stared at each other. The Centurion seemed on the point of saying more. His eyes bored into Aulus: he made up his mind.

'Make your preparations. This land's well forested. Break your stock up into small mobs. Allot them and your people forest areas. Practice herding amongst the trees. Build yourselves shelters in the thickest parts. If you are attacked don't even think of fighting. Melt into the forest. Get your women into Corinium. Ever seen their handiwork?'

'No.'

The Centurion nodded. It would profit Aulus nothing to describe the horrors that he had seen.

'Attractive girl, your wife. Make sure she's not around if the warbands come.'

'You mean -?' The inference was shocking.

'Mister, if an attractive woman falls into their hands she's lucky if she's raped to death.'

'They couldn't ...' His face went chalk white, but he knew from the expression in the Centurion's eyes that he spoke the truth.

Abruptly, the Centurion held out his hand. In it was a leather purse. 'D'you want payment for the trouble we've put you to?'

Aulus shook his head. He went on staring into the Centurion's eyes, horrified by what he saw in them. The Centurion nodded. He transferred the purse to his left hand. 'I'll thank you for your help, then.' He held out his right hand. There was an unexpected warmth in their handclasp. He saluted, almost smiled, and walked away. He left Aulus sitting motionless on his horse. The gelding tossed its head and snorted. It put its head down and pulled quick mouthfuls of grass. Aulus ignored it. He had never experienced real fear before. It was an emotion that needed all his concentration.

Chapter IV

Aulus and Flavia were woken simultaneously. The greyness of early dawn was at the windows. Neither of them recognised the sound and they lay tense, listening. There was a confusion of shouting and a frenzied clashing like hammers raining on an anvil. A scream cut above the noise, galvanising Aulus into action.

'By the gods!' He sprang out of bed, grabbing for tunic and boots. 'They're attacking us. Quick, quick, get dressed.'

Flavia erupted from the bed as he hurtled from the room onto the back portico, yelling for the servants. The courtyard was empty and peaceful in the misty dawn. Across from Aulus, hazy in the greyness, the big gates were still shut, and the noise of fighting was barely audible. He shouted again, hopping on the wooden floor as he struggled with his boots. In the corner of the yard the door of the house servants' quarters opened and a sleep-sodden face appeared.

'Get everyone out!' He yelled the order three times before understanding dawned on the face and it bobbed back out of sight.

Aulus shot back into the house and through the hall. The heavy wooden bar was across the front door. He tested it, making sure it was seated firmly in its brackets.

Then he paused, listening. Puzzled, he stood uncertain. He bit his lip. Then, sure that he was right, he lifted the bar and inched the door open. He peered round it onto the front portico.

The noise was immediately identifiable. The grey mist lay round the house, restricting vision to forty yards so that he could not see that far, but the full force of the uproar localised the attack onto the soldiers' camp.

Flavia was beside him. She had thrown on a robe. Her eyes, framed by tousled hair, tried to bore through the mist. She whispered 'I knew it would happen.'

Before he could answer there were running footsteps on the back portico. They swung round. The house servants came jostling into the hall, their faces grey with sleep and terror.

'Not this way – get out through the back!' Every second was vital. At any moment the attackers might appear. They would be struck down where they stood, before they could raise an arm to defend themselves.

'Get out! Get to the big wood! It's our only chance while the mist lasts. Quick! Hurry!' He started to push the servants back through the hall and into the courtyard. Men from the northern block were running across the yard towards them. There was a frantic melée as they met. Aulus swore at them. Their panic horrified him. He grabbed two of the younger men and pulled them out of the throng.

'Run to the labour lines. Tell Gair to get everyone into the woods!' He shook them in his urgency, shouting at their uncomprehending faces 'Tell Gair to get them out. Tell Gair! Tell the headman, tell him! Tell him!'

There was a tug at his elbow. 'I'll go, Sir.'

Aulus looked round. The stable lad, Lucian, was tugging at his tunic. His face was alight with excitement.

'Lucian?' Aulus thrust the two men from him. 'Good lad. Tell Gair to get everyone out of the labour lines and into the woods. Everyone, d'you understand?' Lucian nodded and grinned as though this was a game. He darted back across the yard, running for his life and the lives of the farm people. Someone had opened the gates. He vanished through them and, like a sink hole sucking water, the people followed. Suddenly the yard was empty. The tunics of the servants blended into the whitening mist as they went.

Aulus turned back to the house. Flavia was standing on the portico holding his unsheathed hunting sword, its empty scabbard in her left hand. 'Here. Take this.' She held the sword out to him.

'Thanks.' He took the sword in his right hand and grabbed her hand in his left, pulling her down off the portico and across the yard. She resisted his grip.

'Wait! Listen!'

The noise of fighting had changed. The clash of steel on steel still beat its frantic discord, but the shouting was no longer a confusion of individual voices. There were cries, and screams, but underlying them a kind of silence punctuated by shouts of command.

'I think the soldiers are winning.'

'Maybe, but I'm not taking any chances. Give me the scabbard.'

She handed it to him. He slipped the leather baldric over his head and sheathed the sword. The mist was whitening. Soon it would evaporate and their cover would be lost.

'Come on. I'll get you your horse. You'll be safer mounted.'

They ran together into the yard and across to the stables. Aulus flung open the door, snatching saddle and bridle from their pegs. He moved quietly now, careful not to frighten Flavia's mare who looked round, eyes startled, ears pricked. He spoke gently to her and she nickered in greeting. With deft fingers he eased the bit into her mouth and thrust the bridle over her head. He made the throat-lash fast, picked up the saddle and tossed it across the mare's back. He reached under her belly, caught the girth and fastened the buckle.

He led the mare into the yard. 'Up you get. Here, give me your leg.' She grasped the saddle: he caught her left leg and shot her onto the mare's back.

'Go on. Wait for me in the oak clearing in the big wood.'

She nodded, knowing the exact spot he had in mind.

'What about you?'

'I'm going to get some food and clothes. I'll ride by the labour lines and make sure everyone's gone. I'll be with you in ten minutes.'

'Be careful.'

'I will.'

'I'd like to wait for you.'

'No.' He smacked the mare's quarters. She whinnied in outrage and leapt forward.

Aulus ran back to the house. He grabbed clothes for Flavia and bread and cold meat from the kitchen. He threw everything into a bundle in his cloak and knotted it into an untidy parcel.

At the stable he threw the cloak down as he saddled his gelding. He jerked the head collar loose and led the animal out, stooping to gather up the cloak as he went. He stopped. Someone was running into the yard. His heart missed a beat. He looked towards the gateway. The white mist still hung silently beyond the opening. Suddenly there was a figure in the arched frame. One moment more and he saw that it was a Roman soldier. He let out his breath in a whistle of relief.

The soldier saw him and ran straight across the yard to stop, panting, by the horse's head.

'By the gods!' Aulus recoiled in horror.

It was Servius Cenric, the big, fair Centurion who faced him. Servius was in full armour, blood splattered on his face and breastplate, and darkly red on his right hand and forearm: Servius, with blue eyes blazing murder and sweat washing rivulets through the blood and grime on his cheeks and neck.

'I'll have that horse, ploughboy!' Servius' hand shot out to grab the reins from Aulus.

Startled by the sudden movement and sharp blood smell the gelding snorted and shied away, jerking Aulus' left arm taut. Anger surged through him. Unused to weapons, he forgot the sword at his hip and swung his right shoulder back to put the whole weight of his body into a blow to Servius' face.

Servius saw it coming. He ducked and turned his helmeted head. Pain exploded through Aulus' hand and arm and flashed white hot in his brain as his knuckles hit full force onto the metal. He jerked backwards, dropping the reins, his face contorting in agony. His left arm flew to grip his right, fingers digging into the flesh, fighting to hold the pain.

Servius shook his head, dazed from the force of the blow. Automatically he grabbed the reins before the gelding could shy away. He stood for a moment, forcing his brain to clear, then he transferred the reins to his left hand and slammed his fist into Aulus' face.

Aulus' head snapped back, then he doubled in agony as Servius' boot took him full in the groin and crumpled to the ground as the final piston of Servius' fist cracked onto his jaw. Servius aimed a kick at his head, but the gelding reared throwing him off balance and his foot swung harmlessly through the air. He pulled the horse down savagely, vaulted on, dug his boots violently into its flanks and was gone.

Aulus was retching. He could not think where he was nor why the world was floating painfully round his head. His genitals hurt abominably. He vomited and shouted out and retched again.

Slowly the world stopped spinning. Eventually, he lay quiet, light headed, never wanting to move again. His body throbbed with pain. His stomach ached with the exhaustion of retching. His mouth was bitter with acid bile. One eye was swelling and closing and he could not move the fingers of his right hand.

The sun had come out. It shone brightly over the stable roof onto the upper half of the granary. The world was quiet, the only sound was the occasional stamping of the workhorses in the building beside him.

At last, Aulus raised his head. He pulled himself to his knees and sat, legs drawn up, against the wall. He groaned. It hurt to open his good eye and focus it. He peered around. The yard was empty. He remembered that the soldiers' camp had been attacked. He ought to do something about it, but the effort seemed too great.

And then, beyond the buildings someone screamed, high pitched and desperate. Shocking and horrible, it brought Aulus to his senses. Using the wall for support he stood up on trembling legs and with painful, clumsy urgency he edged round the courtyard, up the steps and into the house.

As his strength returned, he started to swear, dredging all the field hands' foulest language from his memory in a long repetitive tirade aimed partly at Servius and partly at himself. He hobbled into the dining room and picked up the water jug. The sweet cold water tasted like nectar. The screaming had stopped. The house was silent.

Left handed he drew the hunting sword and unsteadily, far more concussed than he realised, he went down the portico steps and headed towards the camp.

Only armour-clad Roman soldiers moved around the trampled ground. Whatever else might have happened, the soldiers had prevailed. There was no sign of the attackers. The camp was in chaotic confusion.. By the gateway a wide swathe of the pointed stakes had been flattened. Fighting had obviously raged inside the camp. Most of the tents were knocked down or leaned drunkenly so that the three neatly parked wagons stood up starkly in their midst. There were bodies, some in armour, some in tunics, lying scattered both inside and outside the perimeter. Dark, sticky blood had tamped the dust beside them.

The wounded had been laid in an orderly line beside the wagons. Soldiers were tending them. A detail was gathering the dead. Others were moving to restore the camp defences.

But the worst sight was beyond the camp. An untidy pile of bodies, some headless, some with partially severed necks that lolled like rag dolls lay blood drenched in a mess of blood blackened grass. Soldiers were stripping the carcasses, throwing the armour into a pile, their arms red to the shoulder.

Aulus stopped. Something was missing. His head was too muzzy. What was it?

A soldier stood up from where he had been kneeling beside the wounded and came towards him. It was the second in command, the Optio Marcus, his face filthy with blood and sweat and grime. Blood streaked his body armour and both hands and arms were red. Suddenly Aulus realised what was wrong.

'Where are the Scots?'

'What Scots?'

'The ones that attacked you.'

Marcus looked down at the nearest body. It lay face up, fully armoured. He spat at it and kicked the lifeless head.

'These are Servius Cenric's men.'

'But where are the Scots who attacked you? Or was it Saxons? Or who?'

'We were attacked by Servius Cenric.'

Aulus digested this in silence for a while. His first slow reaction was relief. 'So there aren't any Scots?'

'No.' Marcus frowned at Aulus' slow wittedness. 'Come over here.'

Aulus followed Marcus to the wagons, stepping over an armoured body whose face was a mask of congealing blood.

It made no sense. 'Perhaps I'll understand when my head clears. Thank the gods it's not the Scots.'

'The chief's over here.' Marcus beckoned him on. 'He's badly hurt.'

He knelt down beside one of the wounded. Aulus had never seen the Centurion without his helmet. He noticed that his hair was iron grey and cropped close to the skull. His face was ashen, his eyes were screwed up, his lips drawn back from clenched teeth. Below his armour the skirt of his tunic and his legs were black with blood that had soaked the ground around him.

'Left leg.' Marcus pointed. 'Went for the artery. They didn't get it, the bastards, not quite, otherwise he'd be dead. Look at the blood he's lost and the length of the wound.' It began just above the knee, on the inside of the leg, and raked upwards, ploughing deeper as it ran almost to the groin. Someone had screwed a tourniquet deep into the flesh above it. Aulus' eyes flicked from the wound to the Centurion's face and back. His bemused mind was still grappling with the mystery of Marcus' explanation. Suddenly it clicked into place.

'It was the other Centurion, the fair haired one, who attacked you?'

Marcus glanced at him as though he was half-witted. 'The gods rot them.' He gazed around the shattered camp. 'I must get these tents put right and get the wounded under cover. I want a bed in your house for

Caius.' He shook his head. 'We're going to be with you for some time now.'

'Why? Why would they do that? I don't understand.'

Marcus ignored him. The Centurion's eyes had opened. They were misted with pain and sunk deep into his head. 'How many of them accounted for, Optio?'

Marcus bent forward. 'Thirty-one, Sir.'

'And ours?'

'Fifteen dead, Sir. Including you, Sir, nineteen wounded, some bad. Ten walking wounded. Forty-four fit for duty, including me.'

'Prisoners?'

'Chopped.' Involuntarily Aulus looked beyond the stake palisade towards the pile of decapitated bodies. His stomach tightened at the swift brutality of military justice.

The effect of talking had covered the Centurion's face with a sheen of sweat. A droplet furrowed from his forehead onto his temple. 'Get after them, Optio. No prisoners. Get the farmer to help.' He seemed unaware that Aulus was beside him. He sucked his breath in painfully and gritted his teeth. 'Servius?'

'No, Sir. He escaped.'

'Mithras damn him. The wagons, Optio—' Slowly his face relaxed as he lost consciousness.

Marcus stood up. 'Well?'

Aulus nodded. His own beating was nothing to all this. 'Yes. Bring him into the house. I'll send men to help here.'

'Thank you.' Marcus looked round. 'Tesserarius! Take a detail and get the horses rounded up.' He turned away.

There was nothing more Aulus could do at the camp. He started at an unsteady run towards the big wood.

Chapter V

Racked with anxiety Flavia waited at their meeting place. When Aulus did not come every instinct commanded her to go back. It seemed endless. Terror prevented her: the terror of being caught alive. She was alone. The silent trees had swallowed up her people. At last, in the silence, the waiting became unbearable. She dismounted. Heart pounding, she led the mare back to the edge of the wood where the uncaring river ran past her feet. Across the meadow the labour lines and farm buildings seemed peacefully deserted in the early morning sunlight. Beyond, too far to distinguish detail, lay the soldiers' camp. She could see the red of soldiers' tunics and the occasional glint of sun on their armour.

She stood irresolute. Where were the attackers? The fighting was over, surely? The soldiers must have won.

'I've got to risk it,' she said aloud. 'I've got to find Aulus.'

She threw the reins over her mare's head. As she did so a figure near the camp caught her eye. It was unarmoured, tunic clad. It bobbed up and down, running. She could see the legs and arms working in a clumsy but familiar fashion. It was coming straight towards the wood.

Her heart leapt.

'Aulus!' she shouted. 'Thank the gods!' She clutched a handful of the mare's mane and vaulted into the saddle. 'Aulus! Aulus!' She splashed through the river in a spray of silver water, kicking her bare legs into the mare's flanks. She waved her arm frantically above her head as the horse galloped clear of the bank. The distant figure stopped. It waved back and came running on. She slithered to a standstill beside him, throwing her legs straight out behind her and landing lightly beside the skidding hooves.

'My love, thank the gods! She was laughing and crying at the same time. She dropped the reins and flung her arms round him. 'Are you all right? Are you all right? No! Oh no! You're not! What's happened?' She put her fingers up to touch it. 'Your eye. What happened?

'I'm all right. What about you?'

She nodded. 'Yes. Yes. I thought you must be dead. Where were you? It was horrible. What happened?'

'That fair haired Centurion of the criminal century attacked the camp. There are dead and wounded all over the place. The Centurion is badly wounded. They want us to take him in to the house.'

'Yes. Yes.' It made no sense, but it did not matter. He was safe. Her hands were gripping the solid muscle of his arms.

'There's no one else. No Scots.'

'Thank the gods!' It took a moment for this to register properly. 'But why? Why should they attack each other? He looked a horrible man.'

'I don't know.' He sounded puzzled.

It didn't matter. 'Your hand's all swollen too.'

'It's nothing to worry about. I tried to hit him - that other Centurion. He stole the gelding. I think the Centurion himself is dying.'

'It's all his fault anyway.'

'Where is everyone?' Mentioning the house had reminded Aulus of the labour force hiding in the woods.

'I don't know. I didn't see anyone at all. I don't think they are in the big wood.'

He nodded, took her hand. 'Let's get you back to the house and I'll go and find them.'

When he returned the woods seemed empty. Aulus rode in under the trees, fingering his mouth and jawbone. He threaded his way through the trees. His head hurt when he shouted. Nothing. Nobody.

Cursing, he cantered out of the wood across the fields to where the forest still grew untouched towards the boundaries of the farm. The undergrowth was too thick for the mare. He rode along the edge, trying to call out, succeeding only in a poor sort of a croak.

The farm might have been deserted. Exasperated, he turned away.

'Master!'

He stopped. It was Gair, the farm headman, pushing his way out of the undergrowth towards him.

'Gair!' He turned back. 'Why didn't you answer? Where is everyone?'

Gair grinned. He waved towards the trees. His moustache bristled with pride. 'I've hid them safe, master.' He looked up at Aulus and his face fell. 'Master, are you all right? What's happened?'

Aulus' head was swimming. A second explanation was too much to ask for. The one thing he needed, he realised, was water.

'Just get them back, Gair. It's all right. We're safe. Well done!'

Gair nodded. Age and years of dealing first with Aulus' father and now with Aulus himself had taught him the wisdom of discretion.

'Quick as you can. There's a lot to be done.'

'Yes, master.'

Solid, dependable Gair. He had kept his wits and herded his people to the deepest thickets. He said again 'Well done,' and smiled at Gair. He turned the mare's head away. The mental picture of the cool, sparkling river was overpowering.

From the portico Flavia watched as they brought the Centurion into the farmhouse. Four burly soldiers carried him on a litter improvised from blankets. She stared down at him, hating him, thinking that the gods had paid him for what he had done. He had brought ill fortune to her house, evil onto Aulus' farm, and now he had come to die under her roof.

The fierce eyes were closed, sunk deep into his skull: the skin of his face was grey. There was white stubble on his chin. The sweat was wet on his forehead, matting the close-cropped hair at his temple.

She said: 'Bring him in here,' and they laid him on the bed in the room nearest the bathhouse where the hot air from the hypocaust would warm the chill of autumn.

As the soldiers straddled the bed with their burden she asked: 'Will he die?' And added, 'I don't even know his name.'

The soldiers looked down at their commanding officer. Their faces were tough and impersonal in the steel framework of helmet and cheekpiece. And yet, as they looked, she saw respect in their eyes and something more. Astonished, she thought: 'They like this brutal man.'

One of the men said: 'He is Caius Martius. That's his name. Take more than a traitor's sword to kill this old bugger.' He turned his head, as though to spit on the floor, remembered where he was and thought better of it.

Caius opened his eyes. He looked round painfully, seeking the speaker. He smiled the ghost of a smile.

'There you are.' The soldier grinned, his face coming alive and his eyes triumphant as he looked at Flavia. 'I told you the old bugger was a tough one. He'll be all right.'

Flavia stood looking down at Caius after the soldiers had clattered out on their hobnailed boots. She listened to the gasping breathing in the silent room. She watched his face contort. His lips drew back from clenched teeth, his eyes screwed shut. His body arched and he lay rigid, gripping the sides of the bed with white knuckles and straining biceps. He made no sound. Sweat stood out on his face and gathered into drops that ran into his hair. Involuntarily she moved and rung out the cloth from the bowl of water on the table beside the bed.

Masking her savage resentment, she stooped over him and gently sponged his face. 'You've got us into this mess,' silently she accused him. 'I'll make sure you live. I'll nurse you myself. I'll get you on your feet again and then you can go and take your fighting with you.' – 'There now,' the words came out softly – 'Try and lie still. I'm going to clean your wound properly and then we'll make you comfortable. You're going to be all right, Caius Martius.'

Aulus chose ten of his shocked farm men to help the soldiers. They would not be of much use – not only were they half paralysed by the terror of the morning attack, but the remaining soldiers would no doubt scorn their clumsy efforts. At least they could reset the stakes or bury the dead. There would anyway be no work from them in the fields that day.

The tents had been re-erected. Soldiers were carrying the wounded into them. The wagons still stood untouched. Aulus looked sourly at them, wondering what could be hidden in them to make them so valuable. Something must be. It would explain their curious construction.

One of the soldiers directed him to the big tent nearest the wagons. Marcus, the Optio, was in it, talking to a wiry, dark, bearded soldier with thin features and hollow cheeks. He nodded at Aulus.

'This is Tesserarius Justinian. He'll he in command while I'm gone.'

'Gone? Where to?'

Marcus just looked at him. He said nothing.

'My men can bury those ...' Aulus pointed towards the heap of naked corpses.

'That carrion,' Marcus' voice was brutal, 'needs no burial. It needs to lie for the dogs.'

'We'll bury them.' Aulus felt exhausted. The sprawl of naked bodies had turned his stomach. He gagged to stop himself retching again. Flies were already feasting on the congealing blood of the prisoners that Marcus had executed.

'Please yourself.' Marcus shrugged. 'Burn them. They'll get no burial from us. My men will bury their comrades. Tesserarius, fit in with what this farmer says.' Abruptly, he nodded at Aulus, turned and left the tent. Bemused, Aulus followed him out. Marcus seemed oblivious to the shock of the attack, issuing his orders exactly as he had on that first afternoon when the wagon had broken down. With angry admiration Aulus watched as he formed up some of his men, took post beside them and marched them out of the camp and down the farm drive.

'Where are they going? What are they doing?'

Justinian's eyes were grief stricken, scarcely focused. 'He's after those bastards that got away.'

'Oh I see. What exactly did happen this morning?'

'We was attacked by that bastard Centurion's men. The chief waked us as they came in, otherwise we'd 'ave been killed as we slept. Deserters, they was, so the Optio says. Bastards. Bastards.' Grief was still naked in his eyes.

'Were your friends killed this morning?' Aulus asked the question gently. The Tesserarius' body stiffened. He did not look at Aulus.

'Yes, Sir. Me two best mates.'

'I'm sorry.'

'That's all right, sir. That's how it is.'

'But why should he have attacked you?'

'If you please, sir.' He looked up at Aulus. The bright dark eyes were glistening with unshed tears.

'I'm sorry. I understand.' Aulus fumbled for words. He left the Tesserarius to his grief and walked wearily back to the farmhouse.

Marcus was gone for three days.

The shocked farm community slowly regained its wits. In pouring rain that melted the congealed blood into black jelly and ran red off the broken bodies the farm men buried the dead that Marcus would not touch in a mass grave. They scraped the earth from their spades and fear rumbled in their bellies.

Four of the wounded died. The soldiers buried them along with their fallen comrades in full armour with their weapons laid beside them.

Caius lay and fought for his life. The wound had swollen agonisingly and his body burned with fever. Flavia bathed him with cold water, raised his head to make him drink, watched him, and marvelled at his courage and fortitude.

Marcus and his patrol looked exhausted when they returned, but they smiled in grim satisfaction as their comrades greeted them.

'Caught most of them bastards, they did.' Justinian's dark eyes sparkled maliciously as he told Aulus. 'Tracked 'em down. Got eleven of 'em. They'll not trouble us no more. Crucified 'em.' And he laughed outright at the expression on Aulus' face.

Aulus waited until Marcus had eaten and slept before he tackled him.

'Optio, I have a right to know what is happening on my land.'

Marcus looked fresh and spruce. 'Yes, Sir, you've a right to know. ' His face was open and his eyes direct. 'The chief didn't like it, as you know, when Servius turned up with his century. You couldn't know it of course, but there's no one as dangerous and unpredictable as him. He's a Saxon from one of the tribes beyond Gaul. He's like a mad dog. Chain him or he'll run berserk. No one has a better fighting record than him. He doesn't understand fear. Where the fighting's hottest, that's where you'll find Servius. Like a lion in battle, he is.

'But give him camp life – guards, parades, drill, routine – and he goes to pieces. He runs wild. He's been up and down through the ranks more than once – field promotion and broken back in camp. He's known the lash and punishments that'd break any normal man. But he's won more honours for his age than any soldier in the field army, silver spears, gold crowns- the lot.' He shook his head. 'I never thought of him like this, though. The chief was right after all.

'The chief hated him: called him an animal: wouldn't have him near him. When he turned up with the dregs of the army it wasn't any wonder the chief didn't like it. If you step too badly out of line you end up in the punishment century and that's what he brought with him. The chief couldn't understand how the Legate could have sent them. It didn't ring true. But they were there, and more dangerous if we lost sight of them. So the chief had to make a quick decision and he decided they'd be best controlled if he split them up and kept them under his eye. We've no scouts and no rear guard.

If it was genuine they'd serve a good purpose, and if not, well, at least we could watch them.

'Before dawn the day we were going. the duty Tesserarius was called to the camp gate by the sentry there. He'd heard something outside and, sure enough, no sooner had the guard stood to than a section of Servius' men appeared. They said they'd been sent back by Servius to report there were Saxons not ten miles up ahead. Servius was keeping them under observation and would fall back on the camp himself when he knew what they were up to.

'That's where the Tesserarius should have smelt the treachery. It was out of character for Servius. His style would have been to sit tight or attack, not retreat. But at that hour your brain's not at its clearest. He let the men in before he sent for the chief and me.

'We went to question them. They'd thrown off their packs and were clustered round the guard tent fire. They said they'd spotted this Saxon warband the evening before, several hundred strong, camped across the road.

'Neither of us liked it. The chief said: 'What d'you notice about this section, Optio?' I looked across at them in the firelight. I knew most of them – all troublemakers, not weak like most of the bad soldiers, but wicked. The hard core, the leaders. If Servius had picked them by hand he couldn't have chosen a rougher bunch, and I said so to the chief.

"Right, Optio,' he said. 'And what's more, three of them are supposed to be in the rear guard.' We both knew then what Servius was up to. He said: 'I want some of them alive. There are enough men in the guard tent. Rush them. I'll raise the camp as you close with them.'

'It was just beginning to get light, that greyness you don't notice one minute but the next you begin to see things around you. It was misty, like a dream.

'I strolled across to the tent. I could feel the eyes of those eight men on me. I ducked into the tent and whispered to the men to rush them. But Servius' men were ready. As our men moved so did they, only they were quicker. They had it well planned. A soldier doesn't expect his comrades to turn on him. The guards were slow to realise what was happening and when they did it was too late.

'The chief was yelling like a bull for the men to stand to arms.

'Some of Servius' men ran to the gate and threw it open. Two of them went for the chief. He was ready for them, of course. He'd drawn his sword. He stood braced, yelling for the men to look alive. There's not much he doesn't know about sword drill - but maybe he's slowing up a bit- and the light was non-existent. There's one place you can always get an armoured man – up his tunic. If you can get there you can stab up clean into his belly and disembowel him. One of them threw himself down, rolled past the chief and came up onto his knees behind him. He thrust two handed up into his groin. The chief half turned, seeing it coming, and took it on his leg. As the man struck, so did he. He drove his sword right into the bastard's face. They fell together. Lucky they did because the other man couldn't see enough to distinguish between them and he just chopped down indiscriminately at the tangle of their bodies.

'Our men were coming out by then. I ran to the chief and took the other bastard's head half off his shoulders. I ran to the gateway, taking men to shut it but I was too late. They'd been waiting out there in the mist, though how they got there so quietly I don't know.

'They came storming at us, Servius leading them. If they hadn't had to bottle together to get through the gateway I think they'd have overrun us. But it gave us a spot to focus on. The fight never got much further than there.' Aulus remembered the flattened stakes and trampled ground. He nodded.

'The chief's men are hand-picked: all veterans and good fighting men. Once they realised Servius' treachery their reactions were quick. They closed up fast and went for them. Not all criminals are brave men. There were skulkers and cowards among the invaders who hung back and when they saw it wasn't going to be a massacre they ran. It's not a pretty sight, that, whoever you are, to see your mates running. There's nothing an officer dreads more than his men throwing down their weapons and running. It takes the heart out of the best.

'After those first minutes when I thought maybe we were done for, we checked them and I knew then that we'd beat them. Servius saw how it would end too, because when they threw down their arms he'd vanished.'

Aulus fingered the discoloured bruising on his jaw. Marcus' eyes followed his fingers. He smiled: 'You were lucky.'

Aulus smiled back. Involuntarily he found himself drawn to this man and full of admiration for him. Perhaps he too would have crucified Servius' men. They had deserved that cruel and most painful of deaths.

He said: 'Justinian said you caught up with them and crucified eleven of them.'

Marcus looked mildly surprised, then laughed. 'Justinian said that, did he? Wishful thinking. No. We killed eleven of them right enough, and sure enough they deserved crucifixion, but the quicker we finished the business and got back here the better.'

'How did you find them?'

'I guessed they would not go back towards Corinium and that for a while at least they'd stay on the road. We met some refugees not a mile from here who'd camped the night by the road. They confirmed a party of soldiers had gone past them in a hurry. There were enough people around to keep us on their track. Even so some got away, Servius included, more's the pity. But we've finished them as a fighting unit.'

'I see. But why? Why did Servius attack you?'

Marcus frowned. 'We're on secret Imperial business.' His voice was suddenly impersonal.

'I know, but that doesn't explain everything.'

'I can't say more, Sir. Servius will have known of our mission. Our men are hand-picked from the whole field army. He will have guessed why.'

'Surely to the gods you can tell me. You've completely disrupted my farm and brought death to my house. By the looks of it you're going to be here all winter. I have a right to know what it's all about.'

'Don't ask, Sir. If I was to tell you, you'd not sleep easy again until the day you see the back of us.'

Chapter VI

Autumn would not be long in coming now. The heavy dew of the September mornings and the shortening days warned of the winter ahead.

'I suppose you'll be wanting winter quarters? I'm not giving you my buildings.' Aulus was still irritated by Marcus' refusal to explain their mission. 'At least, not for the bad winter months. If the stock and grain aren't inside we'll all suffer. You can lodge around the farm, I suppose – some in the house, some in the labour lines. We can fit you in somehow.'

Marcus shook his head. 'Spoken like a civilian.'

Aulus frowned. 'You want to stay in the meadow, in tents, through the winter?'

'Give us a free hand in your woods. We'll be snug enough if we can build ourselves a palisade and log cabins in the camp and reinforce the gateway with some of the stone lying about on the farm.'

'Anyway, why don't you leave your wounded here and go on with the men you've got if you're on secret imperial business. You can leave the wagons here over winter if you like. We'll look after them.'

'Give over, Sir. You know I can't tell you anything more. And I have no intention of leaving the chief and the wounded here without us.'

Aulus sighed. 'All right. Go ahead.' And he strolled off, thumbs tucked into his tunic belt.

And thus it was that while the harvest was gathered and the farm made ready for winter, Marcus and his men worked to reinforce their camp. They borrowed farm wagons and collected stone from the field corners where for generations it had been gathered from the land and tossed away. They borrowed axes and saws and spent days in the woods cutting and dressing straight trunks with which to build their cabins and palisade. They built a new gateway in stone, eight-foot high with rounded corners and fighting platforms. The palisade took shape round the camp, the upright timbers butted close together with sharpened tops and inside they built their log cabins and framed the roofs. They asked for straw and, to Aulus' amazement, the soldiers climbed up and expertly thatched the huts themselves.

All the time Marcus had patrols out.

The reports they brought back were disquieting.

Countrymen were drifting away from farm and settlement. The soldiers came to recognise a pattern. A farmer would complain angrily that his labour was running away. On the next patrol the soldiers would find the man nervous and then, as the days passed, they would see the house shuttered and empty, the smell of wood smoke and habitation gone, the buildings locked and deserted.

There was a constant trickle of refugees on the military road. Sometimes they were individuals with lumpy bundles of possessions, sometimes a family group with wagons or handcarts. There was no discernable pattern to their movement. Mostly they moved westwards, towards Corinium, sometimes they drifted eastwards. Always, their faces were blank. Sometimes they camped for the night beside the road. Always, come the morning, they moved on.

Aulus stopped a party of them one day as he was crossing the road. They were as nervous and truculent as frightened dogs. They barely answered his hail, nor checked their pace. They pointed back over their shoulders and shouted 'Saxons' and quickened their stride, frightened by the word itself. Aulus sat his horse and stared after them and wondered how soon it might be before his own people began to follow suit.

But Etruria's community stood firm. The men spat scornfully as the refugees passed through the farm, though Aulus was under no illusions about them. It was not their love or respect for him that kept them. It was simply the presence of the army. His people watched the patrols go out and waited for their return. They felt protected.

At night Marcus' men stood guard. They circled the camp and farmstead and ranged on wide picket beyond the labour lines. Aulus and Flavia, as much as anyone else, came to rely on the slow tread of the sentries. It had become a part of their lives, a warm reassurance of security.

Three more of the wounded died. The crippled limbs of another three would never see them fight or march again. But the rest were recovering. The century should have some sixty men if and when it took to the road again.

Caius too was over the worst. Flavia nursed him with an angry dedication that refused to contemplate his death and her anger turned increasingly to respect as the Chief Centurion fought for his life and slowly began to win. Almost, she came to love him, as far as his withdrawn soul would allow. She watched compassionately as his frame lay wasting and his muscle shrank away, and she strove to cultivate a bond of human warmth to comfort and help him in his lonely battle.

The strain told on her. Her own face became gaunt and dark eyed and her temper was short with Aulus and servants alike.

'Why don't you leave the nursing of him to one of the women?'

She snapped back: 'Why should I? I've saved his life so far and I'll get him right if it's the last thing I do.'

'Why? What's it to you anyway if he lives or not?'

'What d'you mean?' Colour rushed to her face and her eyes blazed.

'You spend all your time with him. I hardly see you. And when I do you're too tired to do anything.'

'I just want him well so he can get his soldiers off the farm.'

Aulus swore. 'Don't we all. I just don't know what's happened to us since they came.'

'Anyway, how dare you imply he means anything to me.'

'Well, does he?'

'Huh.' She glared at him, eyes enormous and black ringed in her white face. She wanted to go to Aulus and tell him she loved him and be comforted by him, but her feet refused to move and her pride forbade her. She had given so much of herself to heal Caius: there was nothing left. Her heart pleaded to Aulus to come and give her reassurance. She glared at him and snapped again 'How dare you? How dare you?'

He sensed the entreaty in her heart. 'Come here,' he said. He caught her wrist and pulled her towards him.

'What d'you want? Where are taking me?' He dragged her struggling behind him to their room and slammed the door shut with his boot. He bent and caught her up behind the knees with his free arm and lifted her and threw her onto the bed.

'I don't want to – I'm not going to...'

'Shut up and lie still.' He lay down beside her and pulled her close to him, hugging her, stroking her hair, and she wept suddenly and clung to him and went to sleep in his arms.

Flavia said: 'Caius is asking to see you.'

September had dimmed into October. Caius' strength was coming back. He had progressed from his bed to a chair where he sat for long hours with his leg propped on a stool. Aulus noticed that his hair had been cut and he was freshly shaved. Despite the pallor of his face and the hollowness of his eyes he looked again, for the first time since his wound, something of the Chief Centurion who had led his men onto Etruria at the end of the summer. Marcus was with him, standing beside him with arms folded.

Caius nodded at Aulus and pointed to a chair. Almost, Aulus felt rising anger and a temptation to ask whose house Caius thought he was in. He checked himself and remained standing in the doorway.

Caius said 'Optio.'

Without preamble Marcus said: 'You know the field army was under strength when the wall was overrun this summer and the Scots landed on the west coast.'

Was it a statement or a question? Aulus said nothing. He sat down.

'Earlier on we had heard that the northern frontier garrisons had been betrayed and overrun. This left only our field army to hold the whole of the north and west. The barbarians had never come in a coordinated attack like this before. There was no hope of reinforcement from the garrison troops holding the Saxon shore on the east. Their hands were full as well'.

'Why are you telling me this?'

'Just listen. Our Legate is – or was – a practical officer. He had little chance of stemming the flood. The warbands don't operate like an army. They're comparatively small, very mobile and impossible to bring to a proper battle. What was he to do? Break up the army into small units and chase them individually? Stay as a united command and have them run rings around us? Sit tight and let them ravage the land? Anyway, he decided to take the fight to them wherever he could find them.' Marcus paused, and looked down at Caius. The Chief Centurion inclined his head. Marcus nodded. 'He called us into his headquarters and tapped his foot on the floor. The safe vault was underneath. He said: "You know what's in there, Chief?" He knew we did, of course. The Chief Centurion knows everything. There was gold there – sent from Rome to pay the men – silver, in coin and bar from the mines. There were the soldiers' savings, plate, ornaments, jewellery and every sort of valuable metal sent for safe keeping, pearls, amethysts, - a fortune! "Your orders, Chief Centurion", he said, "are to empty the vault and take the entire contents to Londinium. You will hand them over to the commanding officer of the reinforcements that Rome will send." '

Caius spoke for the first time, almost to himself, reliving the shock of this unlikely order. He growled: 'I refused.'

Marcus grinned and raised his eyebrows at Aulus. 'Yes. He refused. "Sir," he said. "I'll not leave the army. Court martial me if you will. I'll serve in the ranks rather than desert my post."'

Aulus looked away, embarrassed. He wondered again why they were telling him this. His wound must have affected the Centurion's mind. These confidences seemed totally out of character.

Marcus went on: 'The Legate told us: "Caius Martius, the chances are we will cease to exist. Whatever the outcome I am marching out and I am taking every single man with me. What do you think will happen to all this?" He tapped the floor again. "It will be looted. It will vanish. And what use will that be? Vast sums of money will be needed to re-establish order. I'm ordering you to do this because there is no man I trust better than you." He said more; enough to convince the Chief that what he had ordered us to do was right. He ordered us to pick eighty men from the whole army – eighty-six with the wagoners - the best men we had – to form a special escort century. The Chief swore by Mithras that he would guard the treasure with his life and honour, and hand it over to whoever he judged competent to deal honestly and properly with it.

'Then the Chief picked his men – soldiers we've known for years, steady men who stand out for their common sense and courage, their endurance and loyalty. He had the three wagons prepared with false floors. He packed the treasure into flat iron bound boxes and built them into the space that had been created.'

So! He had been right. Aulus pictured again the soldiers struggling to move the crippled wagon that first afternoon. Of course. He had guessed as much. It explained why Caius had stood his men to arms when strangers appeared and his incredulous fury when the Legate appeared to have sent him criminals as reinforcements.

But why tell him this now?

And Servius? Aulus saw again the bloody figure with the blazing blue eyes and he caught his breath at the determination and treachery with which the man had plotted and almost succeeded.

'Servius knew this?'

'Yes. The whole army knew. It was the chance of his lifetime. But he needed men like himself. He did the obvious thing. He turned to the punishment century. We'll never know how he engineered it or got them away. But he did. Well, there are not many of them left now and the rest have scattered, though I'd rest a lot easier if we had caught Servius himself. I questioned some of them before they died. They'd not seen him since the attack here. My guess is he's still somewhere around hoping for another chance. I wouldn't put anything past him.'

'Why are you telling me all this?'

Caius held up his hand. He said. 'The cargo we're carrying could make the difference between clearing

Britannia of these vermin and seeing the country permanently overrun.'

'Yes, I suppose so.'

'We have to get those wagons safe into the right hands.'

'Yes, so you have.'

'We have, not you have.'

'How d'you mean *we*?'

'My Century is understrength now. The country may be infested with warbands before we can move again. My orders are a lot more difficult and dangerous now. You are a horseman. You have horsemen on your farm. I need you, Aulus Aurelius, to scout for me. I need you and your horsemen to come with us to Londinium.'

It was an absurd idea. Utterly absurd.

Or was it?

There was no reason to doubt Marcus' story. It was probably right that the treasure they were escorting could pay for an army – feed it, arm it, clothe it. The treasure in the right hands might indeed make the whole difference between restored order and chaos. And it would be invaluable to Caius to have eyes and ears scouting for him. The idea was exciting. All the same....

He explained Caius' proposal to Flavia.

'I couldn't possibly go with them. I can't leave you at a time like this. The labour would disappear like they're doing all over the country. The farm would fall to pieces if I'm not here. The seeding and the spring work would never get done.'

Flavia said: 'I could cope, with Gair, while you were away. It wouldn't be for long.' She wondered why she was encouraging him. The thought of his leaving her and the farm was like a dead weight on her heart. Yet it had been half expected. Her closeness to Caius over the weeks had given her an inkling of his thinking and once Aulus had explained the position it was obvious that the situation demanded scouts. Caius would be in no fit state to ride for weeks. By then the cold, the dark and the mud of winter would be upon them; the roads that much more dangerous and the roaming warbands that much more likely to have drifted south to cut them off from Londinium. Aulus and the farm horsemen would be invaluable to Caius.

She voiced her thoughts, 'I think you ought to help them. It would only be for a week or two – a month at the most.'

'Well, I can see that getting his wagons into the right hands is vital. And if the warbands aren't defeated they'll get here sooner or later anyway and then we'll be in trouble. But I can't leave you.'

'If Caius hadn't come our people might have started disappearing by now anyway. What if new troops don't come? What if Rome can't pay for them? We'll lose everything if the warbands aren't stopped.' She listened to her own voice in wonder, and thought "Why am I saying this? Why don't I try to stop him?"

'You wouldn't be safe without me. If anything happened to you...' He remembered Caius' warning "Beautiful girl, your wife..."

'If the warbands come anywhere near here I'll go to father's house and take everyone I can with me. You'll only be gone a few weeks.'

'Yes, I suppose so. And it really would be doing something positive to help. Do you think you and Gair could cope if I did go with them?'

She said 'Yes', and thought "Why are we talking like this? If he goes I may never see him again." The thought was like a great wound in her heart. She tried to smile. 'Anyway, my love, you've got to do it.'

'I know.' He put his arms round her. Neither voiced their certainty that the coming of Caius and his wagons had changed their lives for ever and would lead them now to separation and heartbreak and perhaps to death.

Caius was on the mend at last. Daily his strength returned. Under Flavia's care the flesh began to cover his bones and fill his frame again. Soon he was able to walk, hobbling slowly, favouring his wounded leg, leaning heavily on a thick ash stick that Marcus had cut for him.

Flavia watched his progress with mingled pleasure and sorrow. She had saved his life, but once he was fit he would take Aulus from her.

'You'll take care of him?' She asked him lightly.

Caius did not smile. 'Countrymen make the best scouts. They have the feel of the land. They know instinctively what you'll find over the next hill. Your husband is an intelligent man. He'll be valuable to me. I'll take good care of him.' His dark eyes did smile momentarily. 'I'll send him back safely to you.'

She nodded. Her family had been soldiers for generations. Duty was bred in her, and a pride in her heritage that had found focus in the part Aulus would play in escorting Caius.

Caius explained to Aulus: 'Officers like you don't normally serve as fighting men. They do the staff work. With you, it's different. You've got to command a field troop from the saddle. You've got to train, ride and eat with your men, live with them, fight with them. You've got to be my Century's eyes. Marcus will equip you. I'll instruct you in the basic cavalry drills. Marcus will instruct you in weapons. As soon as you're fit you'll start patrolling. That's where you'll get your real training. You'll find out what you and your men are made of when you're cold and wet and hungry. That's where you'll learn comradeship and reliance on each other.'

Aulus had decided that he could rely on three of his farm horsemen – Gratian, who had been with him the day Caius had come to the farm, Baldur, and Lucian, the stable boy who had kept his wits in the crisis of Servius' attack. All three were competent horsemen. Baldur and Gratian were both steady and reliable men.

'It's not enough,' Caius grumbled. 'You won't be strong enough for a fighting unit. Still,' he growled at Aulus under lowered eyebrows, 'I suppose you'll be of some use.'

Aulus smiled. The frown only partially hid the satisfaction that showed undisciplined in the Chief Centurion's fierce eyes.

Marcus took Aulus and the farm men to the camp armoury. His reaction had been positive. 'Just what we need, Sir, a cavalry screen. And begging your pardon, if we're to fight together I'll drop the Sir. You'll do a fine job, Sir – Aulus.' He grinned and punched Aulus' shoulder in friendly encouragement. 'I'll teach you how to fight.'

Neatly stacked piles of chain mail, helmets, shields and weapons filled one of the tents, a grim reminder of Servius' September attack.

'Not quite right for you, Aulus,' Marcus said. 'As an officer you should have a moulded breastplate. On the other hand, chain mail gives a horseman more mobility anyway. Try this.' He selected a mail coat and watched, amused, as Aulus struggled into it. 'Good. Fits you like a glove. Now, helmet...' Deftly, he selected mail and helmets to fit the four men and laughed at their clumsy first attempts to put them on.

'Now, arms.' he said. 'You should have cavalry swords, of course – slashing, not thrusting. It can't be helped. Balance is the thing,' and he hefted and swung the stacked and oiled swords until he was satisfied. 'Now, daggers – useful weapons, these.' He drew several from their sheaths feeling the cutting edges and squinting along the blades. 'You can slip a dagger into a man's ribs when he's watching your sword arm. There. You take this one Aulus. It's a good one.'

Self-consciously, in the privacy of his bedroom, Aulus tried on his uniform. His boots and breeches were his own, but he pulled on the red leather tunic that Marcus had given him and tied a regulation scarf round his neck. He picked up the mail coat and clumsily shrugged into it. It felt excitingly heavy on his shoulders. He swung his arms several times to settle it easily onto his body.

Flavia laughed as he put on the metal helmet and tied the leather thronged cheek pieces under his chin. There was pride in her eyes as she looked at him.

'You look every inch a soldier' she said.

He grinned back at her and picked up the dagger belt. He clasped it round his waist and slipped the sword sling over his left shoulder so that the short broad bladed weapon hung on his right hip. The cloak that he threw over his shoulders was his own, woven for him by Flavia, dark green, thick and warm.

He examined himself in the mirror, excited and a little bashful.

'Hardly recognise myself.' He drew himself up and puffed out his chest.

'Fool,' Flavia said. They both laughed. She saw the excitement in his eyes and knew it mirrored her own. She smiled archly: 'I always thought it would be fun to marry a soldier.'

He turned and stood in front of her. She fingered the metal coat, then ran her hands up and down it. When she looked up her eyes were sparkling. He grinned and kissed her.

Shouts of glee from the labour lines greeted the three farm men as they returned, shyly, in their chain mail coats from the soldiers' camp. The older men had accepted Aulus' order to train as cavalrymen with the good-humoured tolerance they would have shown had he told them to do some inane trick with the horses. Lucian's eyes had lit up like stars. All three now swelled with importance. They blushed furiously, laughed back at the lewd comments and strutted grandly and uncomfortably round the farmstead.

Marcus groaned theatrically when the four of them presented themselves in the camp to begin their initiation into army training.

'Like a lot of bloody tarts.' The time-honoured epithet raised the time-honoured nervous laugh from his recruits. He shook his head in exaggerated sorrow as they lined up in front of him. 'We've got a long, long way to go. Left turn – other way. Hades! Don't you even know left from right? – At the double' and they trotted, obedient and uncoordinated to begin their new life as soldiers of Caius' century.

The shortening days that followed were so full that Aulus was exhausted by the time he joined Flavia in the evenings. He was strong and fit, but the weight of the armour was at first unexpectedly tiring and his back and shoulders ached from the unaccustomed load. The double weight training sword was no heavier than many of the farm tools that he could swing effortlessly, but the stab and parry of its basic movements brought new muscle achingly into play. With a spear, though, and on horseback, Aulus felt completely at ease. At full gallop he could hit any target.

Unavoidably now he left the running of the farm to Flavia, discussing the day's happenings and the next day's programme as they sat by the brazier or ate their evening meal together in the candlelight. Flavia's fear of taking responsibility for the farm vanished quickly. It was fun to discuss and plan, exciting to manage its stock and its people. With Aulus behind her to sort out any major problems and Gair beside her, solid and sensible, to see that her orders were carried out, it was easy. Over the years she had absorbed the farm routines. Now, naturally and simply, she applied her knowledge. Were it not for dread of the day when Aulus would leave with the soldiers, her life would have been completely full and happy.

Marcus worked tirelessly to teach his recruits. Baldur and Gratian responded willingly and ploddingly, so that Marcus knew that he would make them into competent fighting soldiers able to take their place in the line and hold it by the power of routine and discipline. Lucian, little more than a boy, treated the whole business of soldiering as an enormous adventure, but behind his grinning face and yokel speech Marcus saw the seeds of a quick and resourceful mind that, given time, might raise the boy from the ranks to officer status.

He enjoyed teaching Aulus immensely. Confident in his own ability he recognised in Aulus a far superior brain and a strength of physique that almost matched his own. He smiled to himself as he taunted Aulus to greater efforts, urging him to strike, parrying his blows and countering fast until Aulus stood exhausted, gasping for breath, smiling back at him in growing companionship, the sweat running down his face.

Caius was a different proposition. As his strength returned so he reverted to the grim unsmiling Centurion that Aulus had first seen. There was no laughter in his training. He worked them, as with all his men, mercilessly. He shouted at them, repeating a movement over and over again, buffeting them, hammering them, breaking them but, all the time, while they sweated and united to curse him, he built them into a coherent mounted team.

And they enjoyed it. Through the pain of overworked muscles and the misery of the cold winter rain somehow there was a deep satisfaction and pleasure.

Caius' men treated the farm men with amused good nature. Their own recruit days, when they too had been green farm boys or sharp gutter urchins were long forgotten. They laughed at them, but the recruits were learning the military routines from the best instructors in the army and the veterans also knew that one day their own salvation and safe passage could well lie in the hands of these countrymen.

Over the weeks the weight of the chain mail became as natural as that of a cloak. They forgot the tremble of tortured muscles. In carriage and confidence they became indistinguishable from Caius' soldiers.

Chapter VII

Aulus's horses were beginning to show signs of overwork. Two had gone lame in the last week.

Aulus said to Flavia: 'I'll have to get some spare mounts. I'll have to go into Corinium and see if I can buy some. I'll get some proper military harness made up as well. While I'm there I'll see the grain merchant. I must tell him there'll be no spare wheat this winter with all these extra mouths we're feeding. I'll go tomorrow. Do you want to come?'

Flavia shook her head. 'I can't. We're threshing.'

'I promised I'd take you. Cloa will skin me alive.'

'No she won't. Not when she hears that I'm running the farm.'

'Well, I'll have to risk it. I'll call on your father anyway. He'll know the latest news and he'll want to hear what you're up to.'

Corinium was seething. On every open space there were makeshift shelters crowded with piteous women huddled into shawls and ragged blanket-wrapped children staring blank-eyed at nothing. Their menfolk hunched shoulders against the rain and bunched sullenly in the streets. They were overcrowded, cold, and starving, the flotsam of war, driven aimlessly ahead of its destruction, washed up and held by the massive encircling walls of Corinium.

Tiberius Catullus reflected their misery. His hair was whiter, the lines on his face more deeply etched. 'We can't refuse to take them in, Aulus. Glevum is bursting its walls with refugees. A lot of these people have come south simply because there is no room left for them there.'

'Is there fighting at Glevum, then?'

'No, there are no warbands near Glevum so far as we know, nor any this side of it. They have probably gone into winter quarters wherever they happen to be. Probably nothing much will happen till spring. It's panic. The people believe the army has been wiped out.'

'Has it? Do you know what has happened to the field army?'

'By all accounts they have ceased to exist as a fighting force. There are some soldiers among the refugees. The city council had them up for questioning. They don't seem to be deserters. They say their officers are dead. There may be some units fighting still, but they say they were cut off and had just joined the general stream of refugees heading for the protection of city walls. We've drafted them in to help with the city militia and put them on police work and wall and gate duty. It's been a blessing to have some regular troops. Never the day dawns now without trouble somewhere in the city. The lawlessness is terrifying. You daren't walk the streets. We've had to impose martial law and curfew the city from dusk to dawn. First offence, a flogging – a stiff one – second time, death. It doesn't stop them, but it's the only way to keep some sort of order.'

'Any cavalry among the soldiers?'

Tiberius looked surprised. 'Why d'you ask?'

'You remember that special Century that passed through Corinium at harvest time?'

'Yes.

'Well, they're still on the farm.' And he told Tiberius the story, while from the streets beyond the walls the muted noise of the overcrowded city verified the truth of his unlikely tale.

When he had finished Tiberius sat silent, then said at last: 'I can't say I'm happy, but I am proud of you both.'

'Thank you. You see why I ask about cavalrymen?'

'Yes. I'll find out. If there are any, do you want to take them with you?'

'I doubt they'd go on my orders. I'll have to see Caius.'

Tiberius nodded. 'Ring the bell, will you?' and he reached for a stylus and wax tablet and began to write carefully on the smooth pliant surface. 'We'll send this to the Basilica. You'll have an answer within the hour.'

To Aulus' relief Cloa had not appeared. Having no wish to be berated by her, he decided to visit the saddler while they waited for an answer. He had to sidestep and push through the unhappy streets with their press of damp bodies that stank of sweat and misery. He pulled his cloak tight around him, hand on the purse tied at his belt, wary of cutpurse and footpad.

Normally the saddler displayed his leatherwork – saddles and harness, buckets and tunics, boots and panniers – in a fragrant jumble tipping into the street at the entrance of the long, narrow shop. Today the doorway stood empty, guarded by two useful looking men with legs planted wide.

'It's the times, Sir,' the saddler explained. 'They'd steal everything, this rabble.' He spat derisively. 'Even come into the shop, they do. You've got to look after yourself these days. No one else will.'

Leather was scarce and prices high but the saddler nodded professionally at Aulus' request for military pattern harness.

'Leave it to me, Sir. Did five years apprenticeship working for the military, I did. We've got to look after ourselves now. You'll be forming your men into a militia, no doubt?" His eyes questioned Aulus, openly admiring. 'Look to ourselves, it's all we can do now.'

Aulus did not trouble to enlighten him. His business settled he launched again past the doorkeepers into the drizzling streets.

The doorway of the grain merchant's shop was shut, barred with solid timber doors that filled the square shop front. Aulus studied it in mild irritation. He wondered whether to fight his way through the city to the merchant's warehouse near the western wall. He shrugged his shoulders. Why bother? It was only to tell the man that he had nothing to sell him.

A hail from above made him look up. There was a small rectangular window in the whitewashed wall over the doors. Behind its metal bars someone was beckoning violently.

'Wait, my lord. Wait.' A minute later the bolts rattled behind the heavy doors. One opened a foot. The face of the merchant peered out. He looked quickly up and down the street and beckoned to Aulus. 'Come in, my lord. Quick', and Aulus slipped through into the dark cave of the shop as the merchant peered again up and down the street and slammed the door shut behind him.

Aulus stood still in the gloom, smelling with pleasure the warm harvest smell of grain, imagining the open mouths of the sacks around him.

'Why the barricade?'

'Why, my lord? They'd clean me out in minutes. There's not an honest man among them.'

'The refugees?'

'They're vermin, my lord. Rats. Why we let them in I don't know. If you'll go up the stairs, my lord, with my apologies for the inconvenience.'

His eyes were getting used to the gloom. The outline of a doorway with steps leading up from it pointed Aulus to the merchant's living quarters over the shop.

'I only came to tell you I've got no grain to sell this winter.'

The merchant's face fell. 'My lord?'

'I'm sorry. I need it all myself.'

The man tried to laugh, as though Aulus was teasing him. 'On Etruria, my lord? There's always a good surplus on Etruria.'

'Not this year.'

'I'll offer you a good price, Sir.' The voice was whining now. 'Never better. Don't try selling direct to these vermin, Sir, I beg of you. They'll steal the tunic off your very back. I warn you, my lord.' – His eyes pleaded with Aulus, horrified at this suspected profiteering – 'Let me deal with them, Sir, on your behalf. I know these vermin. I can handle them. You can't trust them – I'll give you a better profit, I promise you.'

Aulus looked at him distastefully. It had not occurred to him that men like this would be making themselves rich from the suffering about them. He snapped 'Not one ear. I need it all myself.'

There was nothing false in the way the merchant rang his hands.

'I need some horses, though.'

Greed flashed in the man's eyes, and malice.

'My lord, the pity of it. There's not a horse to be had in the country.' He shook his head wretchedly, his eyes betraying him. 'You can name your price for a horse these days – if you're selling, that is, of course. Scarce as gold they are.'

Aulus shook his head, half amused, half exasperated. The merchant was careful not to look at him. He smiled deprecatingly and spread his hands wide. 'How many do you want, my lord? I might just possibly find you one or two. It won't be easy though. It'll be costly, and dangerous. Why, my lord, just the other day....'

'Don't bother. If I can't get them at the normal price I'll not bother.'

'I'll try, sir.' The malice in his eyes was angry now.

'Well, if you do they must be good animals, up to weight, with plenty of stamina, and sound.'

'Of course, my lord, of course.' His voice was openly sarcastic. 'For a customer like you, I'll move mountains.'

'Hmm.' There probably was a certain amount of truth in what the merchant said. 'Well, you do that.'

The merchant smiled thinly. Inwardly he called on his gods to curse this farmer. At least, if he could not get Aulus Aurelius' grain he would empty his purse of every coin that he could on the sale of the horses.

Aulus pushed his way back through the crowded streets to Tiberius' house. The messenger was back from the Basilica.

'I do believe that you're in luck.' Tiberius consulted the tablet that the man had brought with him. 'Incredible. There's a Tesserarius from the field army in the city with the remains of one of the regular cavalry units. Fourteen men. They came in last night - what a coincidence – they're in fairly poor shape – three walking wounded, horses in bad condition – hmm – no question though that the Tesserarius – his name's Valerius Lucillus – has his men under military discipline – reported straight to the Basilica – says he's on his way to Londinium to join the reinforcements. What a stroke of luck. They've sent him to camp near the South gate, outside the city – he wants to stay a few days to give his horses the chance to rest up a while.'

'That's marvellous.'

'They could be just the men you're looking for.' Tiberius spoke absently. He was reading a second tablet that the messenger had handed him. He frowned and clicked his tongue. 'I don't know how we're going to keep all these people fed this winter. We'll have to close the gates to any more of them. We're not going to be able to cope. The gods help us if plague breaks out – though I suppose it will solve the problem for us. I don't know which I dread more, this winter or the start of the warmer weather.'

'Our patrols keep reporting on deserted farms. There must be grain on them, and stock running wild. Why don't you send your militia out? Better you than the warbands next spring.'

The old man nodded. 'We're doing that already – bringing in anything we can lay hands on. The tax gatherers will be out to Etruria too, I'm afraid.'

'Yes.' Aulus had been expecting them. Normally the mention of tax gatherers threw him into a rage. The problems facing them all now were so deep, though, that he could view the prospect of losing sheep, cattle and grain with equanimity. 'If we don't all stand together in a few months we may all be dead.'

'Yes.' The bleakness in Tiberius' voice left Aulus in no doubt that he had voiced his father-in-law's own fears. He tried a brighter topic.

'If Caius agrees I'll come back tomorrow and make contact with these cavalrymen. I'll bring Flavia.'

Tiberius' face cleared. He smiled. 'I don't see nearly enough of my daughter these days. I think you keep her locked up on that farm of yours like some sort of vestal virgin.'

Aulus laughed. 'Some virgin!'

Caius and Marcus listened to Aulus in silence. Both had been sure that the field army had been annihilated, but confirmation brought no relief.

Suddenly, Caius looked older. He turned away from them. Aulus and Marcus stared awkwardly into the brazier. There seemed to be nothing to say.

With his back to them, Caius said: 'I've served with the army all my life – twenty-eight years.'

There was a long silence. Charcoal tinkled in the brazier. Caius said again 'Twenty-eight years.' And again, almost surprised, 'Twenty-eight years!' He turned back to face them. His hard eyes were blank. 'What else did you hear?'

'There are fourteen of your cavalrymen in Corinium. They came in yesterday.'

Marcus brightened immediately. 'Now that is good news.' He could understand, but not quite share, Caius' grief. The field army had been home and family to him, but there were other armies in other lands. His trade was war, death was accepted philosophically in friend or foe. He looked at Caius speculatively. It hurt to see him like this. His wound must have affected him. It shook his confidence in Caius' invincibility.

'Valerius Lucillus.' Caius repeated the name. He nodded to himself. Marcus said: 'I'm not surprised he's turned up. He's a lad with a lot of intelligence and enterprise.' He looked at Aulus. 'He was drafted to the cavalry for just those qualities. The army has – did have – regular cavalry units. They're used as gallopers and scouts. They're the bright boys who'll think for themselves. The sooner we get him out here, the better.'

Caius nodded. 'Fetch him.'

'And those other soldiers that Aulus says are in Corinium?'

'No.'

Marcus opened his mouth, raised his eyebrows, and thought better of it.

'They'll do as much good where they are.' Caius volunteered a rare explanation. 'They may be deserters. With Valerius and his men we'll have two useful mounted troops and over seventy men – all men I can trust.'

'Valerius will be under your command. He'll see nothing odd in it. He'll accept you as an officer and take orders from you quite naturally.'

Aulus' heart leapt. 'Valerius will accept you as an officer...' Caius and Marcus must have done so themselves.

They rode back to Corinium in the gloomy dawn, Aulus and Marcus with Flavia between them. The three farm men jogged abreast behind them. Caius watched them go and grunted with satisfaction. They looked like soldiers. He smiled to himself. So they should. The individual attention of two of the army's best officers could hardly have failed to turn them into soldiers. He had been right to enlist Aulus. His brain and leadership would be useful in the coming dash to Londinium.

They took Flavia to Tiberius' house. They clattered bravely into the stableyard, a lady with her proud escort of warriors. The household came running to greet and admire them. Flavia's eyes sparkled with laughter. Tiberius hugged her. Cloa fretted behind him for her turn to fling her arms round Flavia's neck.

'My child, my child.' Cloa's face shone with love. She cradled Flavia's head, her fingers buried in the golden hair.

Goblets of wine were brought running from the house and drunk in the saddle with a flourish and a swagger. Everyone laughed and crowded round marvelling at the transformation of the farm men into soldiers. Aulus caught Tiberius' eye. The pride and admiration in them warmed his heart.

They left Flavia, waving and laughing as the gates closed behind them, her arm linked with Tiberius', Cloa hovering beside her. Tiberius looked younger and happier than Aulus had seen him for months. And Cloa – Aulus smiled to himself – Cloa was like a fierce black old cow mooing round its golden calf.

Valerius had camped his men in a spinney half a mile outside the city gates. A sentry posted on the edge of the wood shouted a warning, and half a dozen men appeared as Aulus and Marcus rode up. One stepped forward, Valerius, without a doubt, a strong looking young man probably in his mid-twenties, alert and confident despite the bedraggled look of the group.

Marcus hailed them. There was a visible start of recognition, a guarded pleasure mixed with apprehension. Valerius called his men to attention and saluted, his features carefully blank.

Marcus returned the salute. 'Surprised to see me, Tesserarius?'

'That I am, Sir.' His voice was as deliberately neutral as his face. Marcus smiled. Instantly Valerius' manner relaxed. Relief showed clearly on his face.

'We're not deserters, Sir. Everything's gone to hell up there. Our last orders were to fall back south till we made contact with the reinforcements. That'll be you, Sir, I guess? I've thirteen men with me, three of them walking wounded. We're just about fit for duty, Sir.'

Marcus dismounted. 'Let's have a look at them.'

Lined up on the edge of the wood, the little company were a sorry sight. They were gaunt-faced and hollow-cheeked. Their eyes were sunk and black rimmed.

Uniform cloaks were wrapped tightly round thin bodies, much stained and muddied, torn and patched. They huddled into their cloaks with teeth clenched against the hunger and cold. Beneath the ragged hems their boots were worn and wet with fresh mud.

But, Aulus saw, they were all properly dressed as far as their condition allowed and all presented polished and sharpened weapons for Marcus' inspection. Thirty yards into the spinney two army regulation tents were neatly pitched with fires in front and empty picket lines behind.

'The horses are out foraging, Sir. I'd been planning to stay here a few days to rest them. They're in poor shape.'

Marcus accepted this with a nod. He had sized up the situation within seconds. He was more than pleased with what he saw. In times like this, of chaos and defeat, there is a fine dividing line between a military unit and a wolf pack. One order too many, one rash action when men have reached their limit, and the dividing line is there and past. Valerius had done well. He had kept his men in hand when many officers, junior or senior, would have failed.

Valerius was explaining still. 'I'm sorry you don't find us in better order, Sir. We've been in the field for six months or more. Food's been short. It's been a hard time.'

'Call the men to the fires.'

The troopers broke ranks and gathered round. They were burning deadwood, dry oak and beech that flamed hotly and pushed back the dark gloom of the day. The men held out their hands to the blaze and opened their cloaks to let the heat warm their bodies. They were silent, looking guardedly at Marcus and his companions. There was a subdued hope on their faces.

'Never thought we'd see you no more, Sir,' one of the troopers spoke with a ghost of a smile.

'Never thought the day'd come when I'd be glad to see a bloody officer.' The speaker was unidentified. Several of the men smiled briefly, a little ray of sunshine on a winter's landscape.

Marcus said: 'You've done well – all of you. I'll hear the full story from the Tesserarius, but I can see you've fought well and have kept your honour and the honour of the army. You'll be wondering how I've got here and what's happening. Chief Centurion Caius Martius is camped a few miles from here. This is tribune Aulus Aurelius. He'll be commanding you from now on.'

The men said nothing. Their gaze shifted speculatively to Aulus, who nodded, unsure what was expected of him. They seemed to accept his brief acknowledgement, more concerned with the set of his features and his build and bearing, curious that an officer should appear in trooper's armour.

'You may be thinking the Chief has brought reinforcements,' Marcus went on. 'Don't. Because he hasn't.' The eyes swivelled away from Aulus, their attention fully caught. 'He's only got the special Century he left with. As of now, you're part of it. You'll break camp here at first light tomorrow and join us.'

All eyes were on him. No one moved. Watching them, Aulus thought: 'That's got them thinking. I wonder if they know what Caius is carrying.'

As if in answer to his thoughts Valerius said: 'Beg pardon, Sir. It was common knowledge what the Chief's orders were when he left and what he was doing. Have you been to Londinium, Sir?'

'No. Did you know Centurion Servius Cenric had deserted?'

'Yes. He murdered the guard and sprang the punishment Century.' Valerius sounded faintly puzzled.

'They followed us and attacked us. The chief was wounded – amongst others. That's why we never got to Londinium.'

There was a sigh round the fire.

'Don't worry. Most of them are dead.'

Again, the sigh, and a sudden burst of talk. Marcus held up his hand.

'You're part of the special Century now. You'll be scouting for us.' He looked round at the thin, pinched faces. 'Don't worry. We're in winter quarters. We'll get you in good shape again before we move out. Any questions, Tesserarius?'

'Down the military road, sir?'

'Yes. I'll have a man posted to guide you in. You've got food to last till then? Good. All right lads, see you tomorrow. And well done.'

They mounted and turned their horses for Corinium. As they left the spinney the silent troopers found their tongues. The babble of noise that followed them made Marcus laugh aloud. 'That's given them something to think about,' he said.

Around noon the next day the survivors of the field army's cavalry arrived on Etruria. It was raining and blowing a chill wind. The men rode slowly up the farm drive hunched against the weather, heads down, cloaks clenched around their shivering bodies, spears cradled loosely in the crook of their arms. Rain dripped from their helmets and faces, from numbed hands and from their sodden boots. The horses stumbled as they splashed through the potholes. They were in worse shape than their riders. Their heads drooped on emaciated necks. The bones of rib cage, shoulder and hip started through the staring and dripping fur of their winter coats. Several were lame. They hobbled painfully at the back of the column, their dismounted riders leading them in a picture of the purest misery.

'By all the gods!' The words came in a whisper of disbelief from Caius, who had laid aside his stick and walked part way down the drive to meet them. Words failed him. In his mind he saw the army formed up on the parade ground, a thousand men, splendid in ceremonial uniform. He saw the sun flashing on burnished metal and enriching the dancing red helmet crests and cloaks. He saw the Legate, magnificent in a gold-embossed breastplate, riding his prancing white charger in front of his cheering men. He saw the deep yellow and black leopard skins of the standard bearers and the proud standards themselves. The rain dripped down his neck: the image vanished and he saw again the handful of starved, freezing troopers struggling through defeat and the icy mud and rain of the dark mid-winter day.

He turned off the drive. He drew himself stiffly erect, head high, his shoulders thrown back as though the whole army was to pass in review before him.

Valerius turned in his saddle. His order was snatched by the wind, but the men came achingly upright. Numbed fingers uncurled painfully from the tightly clasped cloaks, grasped their spears and held them upright.

Valerius ordered 'Eyes left,' and the last surviving unit of Rome's proud field army of Britania saluted their Chief Centurion as they passed in front of him.

Winter closed in on them, dark and cold, when the sap of the spirit sinks, hemmed in by short days and the routine of camp life. Caius kept them working. They extended the campsite to build quarters for the cavalrymen and stabling for their horses. They strengthened the palisade and fortified the gate. Every morning they drilled and trained with spear and sword. They patrolled ceaselessly and they guarded Etruria at night.

The battle weariness receded from Valerius and his men. Fodder and corn filled their horses' frames. It was not long before Caius passed them fit to begin mounted patrol.

From the first, Valerius had accepted Aulus' authority. Young patrician officers were a normal part of life – some were playboys or fools, some came to serve their time as a rung on the political ladder, and some, like this one, were men you wanted to follow: men who in years to come would command armies on the frontiers of the civilized world. Valerius counted himself lucky and quietly took Aulus in hand, steering him with the companionly interdependence of an experienced junior officer who knows that in military ways he is far older and wiser than the man above him.

Caius split the troopers into two contubernia – the old tent group units of eight men – and gave Aulus the five most experienced troopers to join his three farm men. As the days began slowly to draw out they started their scouting patrols.

The patrols served two purposes, as Caius had told Aulus when he had first asked for his help. They gave the special Century eyes and ears fifteen miles from the camp and they welded officers and men into the two halves of a self-contained and self-reliant fighting unit. They began by leaving before dawn and returning to camp the same night, then, as January gave way to February they planned two and three-day patrols and Aulus learned the hardships of sleeping rough and cold. He learned to pick a campsite sheltered from wind and rain with a good supply of dead wood and running water close by. But chiefly he learnt about himself and about his men. He found that he could take this life in his stride and that when they were soaked through, tired and hungry he could laugh with them and cheer them on and lead them with his own example.

There was little that could usefully be done on the farm apart from the everyday feeding routines. Flavia and Gair had it well under control. So Aulus devoted himself to soldiering, throwing himself heart and soul into the adventure of this new life.

Servius Cenric too was surviving the winter.

His wits had not for one second deserted him on that misty September morning when he had stolen Aulus' gelding and fled from Etruria. He did not go far, sure that there would be other survivors from the fight, guessing that some would instinctively flee back the way they had come, towards country that they knew. He had not been mistaken. Six hardened rogues had vanished from the battle shortly before Servius himself. Seeing that Caius' men were getting the upper hand and knowing that capture was certain death they had slipped into the dawn mist and fled together back towards Glevum.

Servius spotted them running across the fields, continually looking back in fear of pursuit. In silence he walked the gelding towards them.

'Where are you going, boys?'

They bunched together and stood scowling up at him.

'Lost your tongues have you, as well as your guts?'

They muttered then and cursed him under their breath. Servius watched expertly as they tensed themselves to rush him. His blood coursed with the excitement of danger and action.

He taunted them: 'Well, you scum? You gutless gallows birds!'

One of the men stepped forward on stiff legs. 'Out of the way, Centurion.'

Servius smiled. 'Are you threatening an officer?'

'Get out of our way if you know what's good for you.'

'I thought so.' In one movement Servius drew his sword and spurred the gelding so that it leapt and plunged forward towards the man. He dropped forward along the animal's neck, right arm extended straight, and the point of the weapon took the soldier in the throat before he could move. The terrified gelding crashed into the knot of men. It skittled two of them and scattered the rest. Servius drew rein and wheeled to face them.

'Stand fast, you scum! Don't anyone move.'

They stayed motionless, staring at the ground where the blood pumped blackly from the throat of their dead spokesman.

'Who's next?' No one looked at him. 'You?' Servius pointed the dripping sword at the man nearest him. 'Speak up, carrion. I rescued you from the executioner. D'you want me to do his work for him?'

The man looked up at Servius. He swallowed painfully and dropped his eyes. Servius dismissed him contemptuously.

Cautiously the two men on the ground picked themselves up. Servius drove the gelding at them. Frantically they scrambled to avoid him. Servius aimed the flat of his sword at one of the helmeted heads. It knocked the man off balance and tumbled his legs from under him. The gelding reared and shied, terrified, and Servius sat easily in the saddle and quietened him.

'If any one of you scum steps one inch out of line again I'll crucify him. You're coming with me, gallows birds. You're under my orders still, and you'll follow where I lead. Do I make myself clear?' He looked at each man in turn, challenging them with his murderous blue eyes. Satisfied, he let his tone become conversational.

'There's still an emperor's fortune in those wagons. We're still going to have it. We're going to use different methods, that's all. We've got to use a bit of cunning. I'll lead you to it, I promise you. We'll all be rich men, rich as emperors.' His voice changed subtly. 'Where d'you think you would have run to, anyway?' There was no answer. They stared at him, sullen and fascinated. 'There's nowhere to run. I'll tell you where you'd find yourselves. On a cross, that's where. They'd flay the skin off your backs and nail you up as tight as drum heads for the crows to pick your eyes out. Unless the Scots got you first. And you all know what that means.'

He paused, weighing them up. Fear and greed. Two emotions they all understood. He had them where he wanted them. His voice changed to a bark of command. 'Get fell in you sewer rats! We're going back. We're going to wait and see what our friend the Chief Centurion and his honest veterans do now.'

He led them in a wide detour back past Etruria and on down the military road. They passed Durocornovium on the edge of the Downs and hurried on until they found an isolated farm nestling close to the road in the fold of a valley.

Servius galloped up to the house. 'You shouldn't be here.' His face knotted with concern and his eyes shone with compassion at the surprised farmer who answered his shouted warning. 'Haven't you heard? The Saxons are not twenty miles from you and heading this way. You should have been warned long since. Get out now, quick, while you still have time. They'll be here in a day.'

With his own hands he laboured with them to load their cart in desperate haste, urging them on with a continuous stream of encouragement and warning. With gentle compassion he helped them onto the cart and lashed the oxen, shouting 'Don't stop until youreach Corinium. Go! Go fast, and the gods protect you.' The whip hissed and cracked in his hand and the dazed farmer and his family vanished westwards in confusion and heartfelt gratitude to this humane and brave officer.

The braziers were still warm. The larder was full. The granary held enough grain to feed ten times the number of his company. Servius' authority was restored. The five men recovered their spirits and thought again of the treasure that would be theirs.

And so they passed the winter. Servius held them, through the force of his personality, in a strict military routine of drill and weapon practice, guard and duty rota. He joked with them and jollied them on through the dark cold days and long nights. But he used his fists at the first sign of argument. On a freezing January day he stripped and flogged one of the men who had left his post to warm numbed fingers at the fire.

All the time they watched the road, waiting for Caius and his wagons. When they did not come Servius went back to Etruria. He went at night and lay soaking wet on the edge of Aulus' woods, watching. In the moonlight he saw the slowly pacing sentries. Satisfied, he slipped away. One day they would come. He would be there, waiting.

Chapter VIII.

There was a spell of spring-like weather in February. The sun had regained a little warmth and the earth dried out so that the farm was busy with plough and harrow, turning the land and working the soil ready for the sowers to spread out across the fields and fling the grain for the new crop.

Aulus distrusted it, knowing that winter was not yet over. Caius distrusted it, knowing that if they moved now the March rains and gales could catch them unprotected and strand the wagons in a morass of mud.

The calm weather stirred the blood of a warband of red-haired Scots camped away to their north. There were forty-six of them in an explosive brotherhood of young warriors who had been cramped together for far too long over the winter months. They had sailed from Hibernia in three warboats the summer before and had rampaged through the Ordovician mountains on to the flat plain land around Deva. In their trail of destruction they had also lost some of their number in early contact with the Roman army and some at the desperate hands of the Britons whose farms they had looted and burned. Undeterred, they had drifted south-east and had wintered in an Imperial posting house north of Glevum.

Their gods had been good to them. They had wintered well. There had been meat for all. There were women. There were slaves. They had had plunder enough to satisfy the greediest.

But the winter months were long and tedious. Their pleasures palled. The fights between themselves grew more bitter and more lethal. They welcomed the sun with an orgy of drinking and feasting. In boisterous spirits they butchered their prisoners and sharpened their weapons. The winter was dying. They were on the move again.

They followed the sun god and moved south. They burned everything in their path but they moved through a deserted countryside. Black smoke billowing on the horizon alerted any lingering country dwellers to their proximity. Like the bow wave of their boats, they sent a flying surge of panic ahead of them to swell the numbers of refugees in the cities until the harassed officials swore that the dangers of plague and starvation within the walls were greater than the risks of fire and sword without.

Valerius spotted them first.

At the northern limit of their patrol he and Aulus had picked a hilltop with a sweeping view to the north. The fine spell had already dimmed into cloud when Valerius rode up the hill on a cold dead morning and noticed a blur of smoke on the grey horizon. It was so far away that an untrained eye might have missed it but he knew its significance and sat watching with the tingling excitement of imminent action.

'Look, lads,' he grinned as he turned to the troopers behind him and pointed out the smoke. 'See there. We're in business.'

He sent two men galloping back to Etruria and remained on the hilltop whistling quietly through his teeth, eyes narrowed as he concentrated on the smoke.

Caius listened to the gallopers' report without comment. He sent for Marcus and Aulus. 'The warbands are on the move. Valerius has reported smoke to the north.'

'Do we move out?' Marcus' face lit up at the prospect of action.

'No. This may be an isolated band. It may not come anywhere near us. We watch and wait. Leave at first light, Aulus. Take six days' rations. Join Valerius and advance to contact. I want to know who they are and how many of them. When you've found out send Valerius back. Stay in contact and don't lose touch with us. It goes without saying – don't be seen. Don't attack. Watch them. Fall back if they come this way. Mark your route. I'll give Valerius two days to rest up and send him back to relieve you. Clear?'

'Yes. What about the farm?'

'It's up to you. The weather's broken. The warbands may go to ground again. My advice is to keep your people here. Once you send them to Corinium you may not get them back.'

Aulus nodded. This was the moment they'd been waiting for. But nothing had prepared him for the shock of reality. He hoped his voice sounded normal. 'Yes. They'll stay. Caius....' What could he say?

Caius looked at him. The dark eyes understood. 'Don't worry, lad. I'll see no harm comes to her. She'll be all right with us.'

'Thank you.'

He was outwardly calm as he gave his orders. But he could not hide his fear for her and the farm when he told Flavia that the warbands were on the move. She took his news calmly. She had already heard what Valerius had reported. She had analysed her reaction – not fear or panic, just a resolve to stay and fight this out.

'I'm staying here.' Her voice was hard, as though she expected him to argue.

'Yes. But remember my promise to your father.'

'We'll be all right while Caius is here.'

'Yes. Yes. I know. Yes, we must stay.' But he thought: 'My wife. My home. My farm. Everything that I hold dear. I'm going to be leaving them. I've been wrong. I should never have got involved in this. I'm going to desert them just when I should be here with them.' He said aloud: 'But you've got to go to Corinium if they come this way. I'm not risking you staying here while I'm gone.'

'Aulus, what are you saying?'

'I can't leave you alone. I must have your word or I won't go.'

'Oh, darling, don't.' And she thought: 'He mustn't think like this. Neither gods nor man would understand or pity us if we showed weakness now.' Aloud, she said: 'Why do you think Caius is sending you off? He wants to give you the opportunity to prove yourself. And he knows you can do it.'

'Yes. It was just ... We'll be all right, though. Whatever happens, if the war bands get this far... Caius'll look after you. I'll come back. I'll be here if they head this way.' He smiled shakily.

When Aulus reached the hill-top meeting place the next morning he was momentarily surprised by the appearance of the watching troopers. Faces, hands, legs, armour and harness were all smeared and daubed black.

'Charcoal,' Valerius explained, his teeth white as he grinned. 'Stops you being seen. At this sort of work it doesn't pay to ride around like you were on the parade ground. A flash of sun gives you away for bloody miles. Here you are, Sir, we've got paste all ready mixed for you.' He watched, grinning, as Aulus spread the black mess on himself.

'Fun, ain't it, Sir. You spend half your life cleaning your bloody armour. Does you good to muck it up.'

They moved off across country, picking landmarks, constantly using high ground for their bearings and woodlands for cover. They reached and crossed the road running North East from Corinium to Ratae and Lindum that evening and camped on the edge of the broad valley that they found beyond. Before dawn the next morning they stood to arms, but the land was deserted. There was no sign of smoke or warband, foe or friend. Away in the valley they could see farmlands and buildings, but nowhere any sign of life, save some distant pigs that wandered, unherded, across the pastures. They waited, standing beside their saddled horses, cloaks drawn close against the cold, watching.

Towards midday there was a hail from one of the men. All eyes turned to him, and then in the direction he was pointing. Away to the north from beyond the distant treeline a black oily billow of smoke was rising and mushrooming into the sky.

They watched in silence, then Aulus gave the order: 'Mount up.' It was utterly matter of fact. They had found the warband. Sooner or later blood would flow.

Slowly, cautiously, sometimes together, sometimes a single horseman carefully scouting into open country, they moved forward. They made contact that evening. The smoke from a timber framed building guided them. Until today the house had stood beside a lane running from east to west across their front. Hidden among the trees, they watched the raiders at their cooking fires.

'Scots.' Valerius' voice was heavy with scorn and hatred.

They could hear their shouts. There was a loud cheer when a last corner of the roof fell in with a whoosh and a cloud of sparks, and prolonged yelling when some cattle were driven bellowing at full gallop along the road towards them. To Aulus' horror he saw that they had captured a man with the cattle. He was sickened with disgust by the screams which rose suddenly above the hubbub.

Beside him Valerius growled 'Bastards. He clenched his teeth and repeated 'Bastards. Bastards. May they rot in hell for ever. I count about forty to fifty.'

'Yes. So do I,' Aulus tried be matter-of-fact. The reality of the warband was terrifying.

'Time to report back to the chief, don't you think, Sir?'

'Yes.' With an effort Aulus quelled his fear both of the warband and of being left by Valerius. But he was also aware that anger was rising in him. 'What d'you think? Send someone off now or wait till morning?'

'It'll be dark directly. Better to get our bearings in the light.'

'Right. Do we reckon this is the only warband?'

'I'd say so, but you'll find out in the next few days.'

Valerius and his troopers left at dawn the next morning. They left Aulus feeling alone and inexperience; eaten with such nerves that he shook as he watched the Scots' departure from the ruined building.

With his troopers beside him he waited until they had disappeared. Against reason he half believed that the prisoner of the night before might still be alive. One glance was enough. He had to grit his teeth and clamp his lips shut against the nausea. The man had been flayed.

In that second Aulus faced reality. He realised now that deep down he had never truly believed that Etruria would be attacked. It had almost been a game, this playing at soldiers. But this was no game. It was deadly serious, totally lethal. Either they destroyed the warbands or he and everything he knew would die. The civilization of Britannia could cease to exist.

The warband followed the lane for a while, then, for no apparent reason, they left it and headed south. Aulus followed. For three days he watched. Heading always South the warband crossed the Corinium to Lindum road, but they did not move far. They were in a fertile country of deserted farms. They made for any buildings they saw and looted and burnt them. They rounded up any stray cattle and sheep they found and added them to their herd. Incredibly, they found people as well, and Aulus grew accustomed to the distant shrieks as they amused themselves with their victims. Each day they killed some of the cows or sheep and gorged themselves on the roasted flesh.

With the help of the regular cavalrymen Aulus found it relatively easy to track them, to keep out of sight, and to leave markers to guide Valerius back to him. In their arrogance the Scots had no reason to think they were being watched. It only needed prudent common sense to keep it that way.

Valerius reappeared on the third afternoon. He looked hard at Aulus with his quick alert gaze. He said nothing, but he smiled to himself. The invisible balance between them had tipped. From now on, Aulus would lead. Valerius would follow. They would make a good team.

As Aulus and his contubernium rode back it started to rain, hard rain that slapped onto the ground and threw up little droplets from the puddles.

It rained for three days. The soldiers cursed it and drew their cloaks tight. The mounted patrol sat sodden and miserable with teeth chattering as the rain washed their helmets clean and ran the gritty charcoal paste in rivulets down the inside of their tunics. Frozen with inactivity they damned the weather as they watched the farm into which the Scots had crowded when the rain began.

For two days the warband stayed inside, only emerging to check the cattle or, sometimes, to answer the calls of nature. They were in explosive mood. They enjoyed fighting. They wanted new women. They wanted young, strong prisoners and fat cattle. The few Britons they had found were wretched creatures and the cattle hardly worth rounding up. This deserted land was cheating them. Cooped up, frustration boiled into furious argument and vicious fights. Above the din the strongest voices rose insistently, shouting for a strike into fresh country, and by the second night they had carried any waverers with them. Amidst cheers and laughter, they agreed to leave this spoiled land and head fast to the South where the women would be ripe, the men unprepared and the cattle fat.

They moved before daylight. Abandoning their cattle, they erupted from the farm and vanished into the darkness. Their speed and purpose caught Valerius unprepared. His sentries, paralysed with cold, were slow to realise what was happening. By the time they had roused Valerius the steady swish of the rain had drowned any sound of the Scots' progress.

There was no point in trying to follow them blind. Cursing, Valerius waited for enough light to see the tracks that they had left in the mud, then at a cautious trot he went after them.

The Scots' euphoria did not last long. After two days under cover the rain was cold and the ground so sodden that they sank into the mud. They were in unknown country. In the dark they could not even see where they were heading. It was with relief that they came onto the military road running north east from Corinium, swinging in a wide loop towards Verulanium. They paused to argue about which way to go now. They had had enough of the sodden ground. They turned right onto the road.

Valerius was not far behind. Soaked and numb with cold his brain had refused to wake up. He felt leaden and stupid as he slithered through the mud. He recognized the paving with relief.

'Naso.' He singled out a young trooper on a big, powerful chestnut. 'Get back to camp and report to the chief. We must be a mile or so from our turning. It's just up there.' He pointed to the left along the road. 'Tell him they seem to be heading for Corinium, but the gods only know what they're up to. Faber, go with him and link up with Tribune Aulus and bring him back here.'

The two men wheeled their horses and set off at a fast canter along the road verge, vanishing quickly into the grey of the morning. Valerius waited. To ride on the open road would be to court disaster. He was not sure what to do. His brain felt dead. True, visibility was poor, but without cover the six of them would be too easy to spot.

The Scots solved his dilemma. They had not gone half a mile down the road before they changed their minds, turned around and started back towards him.

One of the troopers said: 'I think we got company, Tesserarius. Listen.'

Faintly through the rain came the sound of shouting.

'What the hell's that?'

'Sounds like them Scots is coming back this way.'

'Shut up and listen.'

They sat straining to hear above the rain. There was a frightening familiarity in the noise.

'He's bloody right, Tesserarius. Them bastards is coming this way.'

Valerius sat uncertain, his numb brain searching for an answer to this sudden crisis.

'Was you thinking of taking them on, Tesserarius? I don't feel none too strong on an empty stomach.' The man beside Valerius grinned as he spoke but his face was strained as he peered through the rain.

'No, I bloody wasn't. Move it lads, back along the road. And keep to the carriageway.' His voice rose. Galloping horses would leave deep hoof prints in the soft wet grass of the verge.

They crowded onto the road, spurring their horses in sudden panic.

'Keep together, keep together.' Valerius waited for the last man to go and started off behind them, cursing the mud that flew from the galloping hooves spattering its telltale trail. He glanced at the verge and swore. The hoof prints of the gallopers he had sent on ahead were deeply etched into the grass.

The troopers spurred heads down against the rain and wind. They were wet, cold and hungry and the frustration of their long, sodden inactivity watching the Scots suddenly coalesced into fear. For a brief moment of panic all they could think of was to put the maximum space between themselves and the warband. They galloped undisciplined and unchecked.

They had gone well over a mile when the leading trooper recognised the track they had been using over the winter on their northerly patrols. The double line of Naso and Faber's hoofmarks had turned off here. It led invitingly back towards safety. Without hesitation he swung his horse off the paved road. The rest of the contubernium followed without a second thought.

Valerius, riding in the rear, yelled to stop them, but their momentum and the horses' excitement carried them three hundred yards along the track before the last horse had pulled up in a slither of mudlines ploughing through the grass. Strung out along the track they sat shamefaced at their panic. Valerius rode through them, yelling at them to close up, swearing every profanity in his vocabulary. Clouds of steam rose from the horses. Over-excited by their race they tossed their heads and pawed the wet ground to be off again. Without a word, avoiding each others' eyes, the men closed up behind Valerius. He turned on them furiously.

'You've done it now – you've bloody done it now. Mithras and all the gods. We've left a trail a bloody mile wide for those bastards to follow.'

They sat stolidly, eyes averted, waiting for Valerius to calm down.

'Naso and Faber's been down here anyways,' one of the men regained his wits. As always, the best defence lay in attack. Valerius glared at him.

'It's true, Tesserarius, and Faber'll bring the tribune back this way anyway.' A second man joined in.

Valerius bit his lip. 'The gods damn it all.' The realisation of what had happened had woken his brain at last. It chilled his blood with a cold dread far worse than the misery of his soaking clothes and body. Now he must act. Now make the best of it. 'Come on. It's no use us sitting here moaning. The fat's in the fire. We've got to get back and warn them. Come on.' He clapped his legs to his horse's sides. The animal bounded forward. The troopers headed back towards Etruria.

Aulus and his contubernium had left Etruria at dawn. He was in a vile temper. Before he had seen the Scots, it had seemed all-important to stay on the farm and hold it together. Now he realised the futility of the idea. The raiders would sweep over the land come what may. Resistance would be useless. They must find the farm empty – truly empty – no cattle, no sheep, and particularly no humans to die slowly for their amusement. Above all, of paramount importance, Flavia must not be there.

And she had refused to leave. They had argued furiously into the night. Then they had lain tense beside each other, neither wanting nor willing to be the first to heal the wounds. He had got up, bleary-eyed and dull-witted to find the rain still pelting. He was soaked within minutes. He left wordlessly and rode at the head of his men in a rage that the rain seeping through his clothes did nothing to cool.

The day was little more than an hour old when he met the two mud-streaked, sweating messengers of Valerius' contubernium. Aulus saw them some hundred yards away, their horses straining through the mud, moving slowly in a plunging run.

He spurred forward to meet them. 'Naso. Faber. What's up?'

'The Scots – moving fast.'

'Where are they going?'

'Don't know, Sir. They went off towards Corinium on the military road.'

'I'm to guide you back, Sir.'

Aulus looked at their horses, standing heads down on trembling legs, gasping for breath, nostrils flared.

'Where did you leave Valerius?'

'About a mile from where we cross the road, towards Corinium.'

Aulus nodded. 'Right. Get on back to camp, the pair of you. I'll find Valerius' tracks in this mud. Take it easy. Those horses are spent. Alert the camp.'

They went on at a fast trot. 'Thank the gods.' Aulus kept repeating the words over and over. 'If they head for Corinium they shouldn't come near us.' The relief, after the stab of terror at the messengers' news, was like the warm sun of spring. The rain seemed to beat less coldly and his rage was forgotten.

They came upon Valerius unexpectedly as they hurried through the bare trees and muffling leaf carpet of a patch of woodland. For a moment Aulus' brain refused to believe his eyes. He pulled up, automatically raising his arm for his men to halt.

'What in Hades' name are you doing here?' The fear was there again. It came out as anger.

'They turned back towards us. We nearly bumped into them.' Valerius could hardly look at Aulus as he saluted. 'They were coming along the road towards us.'

'Why didn't you get off the road and stay with them?'

Valerius did not reply.

'Why?' Furious, Aulus shouted at him.

'Tracks, Sir. We'd left hoof prints.'

So! The hunter was now the quarry. 'Are they following you?'

Valerius could not meet his eye. 'I had to warn you. It's my fault.' He stared desperately at his horse's ears.

'Did you see them – or they see you?'

'I don't think so. We didn't see them. But they weren't far off from us. It is possible.'

No matter whether they had or not. The Scots would follow fresh hoof prints. Dispassionately he could assess his failure to send Flavia to Corinium. It was too late now. It had happened. The warband must be stopped.

'What's done is done, Valerius. They would have seen the tracks we've used regularly over the winter anyway. Go and warn the chief. Tell him I'm going to try to divert them.' He wondered whether to add a message to Flavia, to tell her to ride straight to Corinium. Somehow the words would not come. 'Ask Caius to look after my people.' He turned in his saddle. 'Come on," he said to his conterbinium, 'Let's see what we can do.'

Shamefaced and silent, Valerius and his dejected companions moved aside to let them pass.

As Aulus cantered on he tried to visualize every yard of their way to the road crossing. How much time had he got? Should they fight, or try to decoy the Scots away? For a moment he visualized a charge and the Scots scattering before them. Six or seven to one, probably. He smiled faintly. Not a chance. It must be a decoy. But how to do it? Just ahead they would reach an area of bush and dense, tussocky old grassland. It should barely show their hoof prints. Perhaps it would be possible to lay a false trail there.

They reached the place and his heart lightened. It was criss-crossed with tracks where successive traffic had threaded around the bushes. He could barely see where Valerius and his men had been. On the far side where the track began again he pulled up. Hoofmarks showed clearly here and divots of fresh mud lay as they had been flung from the horses' flying hooves. He gazed round. A sheep trail led away to his right, heading, meandering, down a gentle slope to a river at the bottom. It ran muddy and angry, swollen with rain, the water lapping its banks.

He looked at his men. Their faces were tense.

'Let's see if we can lead these barbarians onto a false trail.' He pointed to one of the men. 'Throw down your corn sack along this sheep track.' The man grinned as he untied the sack that he carried behind his saddle.

'Mill around. Get the hoof prints muddled up.'

Satisfied that they had churned the area enough they trotted onto the sheep track. Close to the river Aulus had a second sack thrown down. He pushed his horse towards the water. It put its head down and sniffed nervously, its front feet dancing on the muddy bank.

'Get on.' Aulus dug his heels into its flank. Snorting, the horse launched into the water and floundered across. The current pushed them downstream until, with a bound, it reached the far side, heaved itself out and stood, legs apart, shaking vigorously. Aulus watched as the men followed. They broke down the bank in a dozen places as the reluctant horses scrambled and knapped and struggled to get out.

'Let's have another corn sack for good measure.' And a third sack was flung down to encourage the Scots on over the water.

They detoured eastwards, then cautiously north in a long left-handed circle that brought them eventually back onto the Verulanium road. They turned west along it and rode in a nerve stretched silence that Lucian at last broke with a whispered 'There's the track.'

Hoof prints overlaid with running foot prints told a clear story. The Scots had turned here in pursuit of Valerius.

In silence they followed. The Scots were ahead of them now. At any second somewhere – anywhere - they might meet. The troopers peered through the rain, ahead, around, back over their shoulders. Tension mounted with every step. They reached the sheep track where Aulus had planted the corn sack.

'Thank the gods.' For a moment Aulus felt almost euphoric with relief. The first corn sack had gone. They spurred down to the river. Both the other sacks had gone.

The men shouted with glee. They swung their horses round and headed back to Etruria. They reached the farm's labour lines soon after noon, tired men on tired horses, hungry and numb with cold. Aulus roused himself and spread the men out to go through and check that they were empty. A glance at the first huts was enough. The grey ash was cold in the hearths. Treasured possessions had been snatched from their places. Blankets were gone from the beds. Food stores were empty. They left the huts and cantered on across the sodden grassland towards the camp.

Caius was standing in the gateway. The medallion harness covered his chest. The red horsehair crest framed his helmet. The greaves adorned his legs. He said: 'Where are they?'

'I don't know. I tricked them onto a false trail, but they may follow us if they've got their wits about them.'

Caius nodded. He looked past Aulus. 'Optio,' he barked, 'Come here.' Marcus was supervising a group of men above them on the gate's fighting platform. He hailed them and hurried down the ladder.

'Get any farm hands left here across the road into the woods. Send Valerius with them and make sure they're properly hidden with the women and children. We can expect an attack today. Get the men fed. Parade in half an hour.' Caius turned back to Aulus. He nodded again. 'Well done. Your wife is across the road with the farm women. She's all right. She's a plucky girl. Get your men fed and get back here in half an hour. And get some food yourself. Go on, move it' he added as Aulus sat unmoving, wondering why he had placed himself so completely under this man's authority.

Chapter IX

'If the Scots pick up the trail they'll be here this afternoon.' Caius said. 'Assuming that, we will bait the trap. This place is going to look deserted with the gate open as though we'd decamped. I want them to run in here like rats into a grain store before they realise what they're doing. Then the grain store is going to come alive.' He almost smiled. 'And you'll be outside to catch any who get out.' He looked at Aulus as he spoke. 'Position your men on the reverse slope over there.' He pointed out beyond the camp to where, a couple of fields away, the land sloped gently downhill. 'Put the men out of sight. You and Valerius keep far enough up the slope to see what's going on. When the moment's right, get here fast.'

Aulus looked dubious. He had grabbed a quick meal washed down by two goblets of wine. He felt slightly light headed and warmer for the food in his stomach. He had applauded Caius' action in clearing the labour lines, but he was worrying about Flavia and the farm people hidden in the woods across the road. He said: 'How do I know what the right moment is?'

'You'll know.'

Marcus broke in: 'Don't worry, Aulus. This fight's going to be short and sweet and won in here. All you'll have to do is run down any Scots who escape. We don't want any survivors to return to the North and bring back their friends.'

'And what if they don't come into your trap?'

Marcus smiled and spread his hands with a shrug of his shoulders. 'If they come we'll have them. They're no match for us in a straight fight.'

Caius said: 'I'll be on the fighting platform at the gate. If they don't take the bait we'll come out and deal with them. If that happens watch for my signal. Don't move until I give it. Don't worry.' He relaxed slightly. 'If they come, they're dead.'

Valerius reappeared from escorting the farm men into the woods. He reported that all was well. Together he and Aulus trotted off to take up their position with their men.

'Sorry about this morning, Sir.'

'Forget it. I'd have done the same thing. Did you see my wife?

Valerius brightened. 'Yes Sir. She's a rare one, Sir, if you don't mind my saying so.'

Aulus smiled. 'No, I don't at all mind you saying so.' He gripped Valerius briefly by the arm. Valerius smiled back. The black cloud of the morning evaporated and was gone. They reached the dip and sent the men on beyond them down the slope. Together they turned and rode slowly back up until they could see the farmstead and camp.

Aulus whistled in admiration. The camp looked deserted. The gates stood wide. One had been unhinged. It hung forlornly. Nothing stirred.

'The cattle are all with my people over there?'
'Yes Sir.'

They fell silent. Steam rose from the horses and their bodies. The smell of wet wool, wet leather, sweat and wet horse was strong. The rain fell steadily.

The cold crept in on them. Sitting still the chill stiffened their legs and arms and stole over their bodies so that they shivered involuntarily in great spasms that shook their frames. They gritted their teeth: heads down and backs hunched they waited in bovine misery. Rain dripped from helmets and cloaks.

It seemed an eternity.

Aulus saw the first of the Scots before his distant shouts drifted across to them. He had outstripped the others and appeared suddenly from the labour lines, waving his arms to unseen companions behind him.

Aulus' heart and stomach lurched. Beside him Valerius drew in his breath sharply. The numbing cold was forgotten. Suddenly the labour lines were full of Scots. They came on towards the farmstead like stampeding cattle, axes and swords waving above their heads. A high- pitched nerve grating war cry flowed with them. The man leading them shouted something above the cry and pointed to the camp. In a body they swerved towards it. They hardly checked at the gates. They bunched and jostled each other to be the first through. Caius had placed his men well. The Scots were into the camp before they realized that anyone was there. Then it was too late. The soldiers erupted from their hiding places and fell on them.

Across the fields Aulus' voice was choked with excitement. 'Come on.'

Stiff legs kicked stiff horses. They floundered up the slope, the frozen bodies of men and animals responding slowly and grudgingly to the command. Aulus bullied his mount into a protesting canter. In a ragged bunch they headed towards the camp.

Almost at once Aulus realized his mistake.

Some of the Scots had stayed in the labour lines. The sound of fighting flushed them out like bees to a honeypot. In ones and twos they appeared from the huts, racing over the pasture towards the camp. The sight of Roman cavalry materialising out of the ground stopped them in their tracks. Had they been bunched together they might have stood their ground but singly they wavered. One turned and ran back, then a second and suddenly the distant figures had vanished back into the sheltering cover of the huts.

Beside Aulus Valerius was cursing furiously.

Aulus yelled: 'Get after them, Valerius. Stop them.'

Valerius wheeled apart, followed by his contubernium. For a moment there was a wild confusion of swearing men and horses as they disentangled themselves, then they were clear, kicking their horses into a gallop, splattering mud as they went. Valerius' voice rose in urgent command 'Ride, you bastards. Don't let 'em get away.'

Aulus galloped on towards the camp, but not one of the Scots who had dashed so eagerly through the gates came out alive. They had been on the move for ten hours. They were outnumbered by fresh, disciplined soldiers. They were caught by surprise and they were cut down in a short and merciless bloodbath. They died in a disorganized and muddling rabble, taking only two soldiers with them as they fell.

Valerius caught up with five of the fleeing men among the huts. They turned bravely to face the thundering horsemen and were skittled into the mud like bloody ninepins. He knew there must have been others, but somehow, they had vanished.

They dragged thirty-three bodies out of the camp and piled them outside the gates. It was the first time Aulus had seen Scots close to. Their bodies stank of rancid fat, sweat, filth and fresh blood. Long, tangled, matted red hair flamed from their skulls and cheeks and beneath the grime there was an almost transparent whiteness to their skin. Blood and rain mixed and trickled from the carcasses. They were as shocking and horrible in death as was their reputation in life. Aulus gagged as the dripping corpses were loaded onto a farm cart to be taken and burned.

Caius showed neither pleasure at his victory nor anger at the escape of the rest of the band. He handed his bloody sword to one of the soldiers to be cleaned and resharpened, and impassively called Aulus and Marcus to his quarters. Marcus had a long cut in his forearm. A rivulet of blood ran from it across the back of his hand as he came to attention in front of Caius.

Caius nodded briefly towards the wound. 'Deep, Optio?'

Marcus smiled. 'Just a scratch, Sir. Nothing to worry about.'

'Let's have a look.' Marcus held up his arm. Caius examined it. He picked up a cloth from a pile on the table. 'Here. Bandage it up. You'll do. What's the wounded count?'

'Thank you, Sir.' Marcus wound the linen carelessly round his arm. 'Five wounded. Three of them serious.'

'Get them seen to. Valerius is to take his contubernium and pursue until dusk. Then get back here. We'll have everyone inside the camp tonight – men, women, children, everyone. Your people are no longer safe here, Aulus. Tomorrow you'll abandon the farm and send the entire work force into Corinium.'

Aulus said nothing. He stared blankly at Caius.

Marcus said: 'They'll be back after dark, Aulus. Then they'll return northwards to find some of their friends. This farm is marked now.' His voice was gentle and his face compassionate. 'It would be suicide for anyone to stay. You've seen what they're like.'

Aulus nodded. He looked from one to the other. Marcus' eyes were sad. Caius returned his gaze without emotion.

'But we're here. We can....'

'No. As soon as this rain stops we move out.'

'You can't....' Again, Aulus faced a moment of truth.

'If they come back and bottle us up here we could be trapped. Spring's not far away. The warbands will all be on the move. We've got to get to Londinium as quick as we can. We have to take the risk and make a dash for it.'

'They'll burn my farm if we go.'

'Yes. That's probably going to happen anyway.'

'My stock – my people – everything.' Aulus shook his head. He spread his hands in a helpless gesture as though his outstretched fingers were letting go of his possessions and the outflung palms were throwing his farm to the marauders. He said, uncertainly: 'I'll only be gone two weeks. I can get some of the men to herd the stock in the woods till I get back. Then I'll stay and keep the farm going.'

'Well, that is up to you but I don't advise it. Take your men now and get your farm people organised. I want everyone in here before dark. Clear?'

Aulus nodded. He turned to leave. Caius' voice behind him was quiet: 'And don't let your wife try any heroics.'

As Aulus left the camp the rain slackened. For the first time in three days he saw ragged patches of washed blue in the sky towards the west. By the time he had found Flavia the rain had stopped.

They greeted each other in unspoken full-hearted relief. In front of their frightened and shaken farm people they could not show their love, nor their joy at seeing each other after the previous night's bitter argument.

Sheep and cattle were turned into the woods close to the homestead, shelters rigged from every wall and roof in the camp and, as dusk came they closed the gates. Valerius had seen no one. The night would tell if others of the warband had indeed escaped and were bent on revenge. They settled down to watch and wait the night away.

They ate together in Caius' tent. It was a silent meal, the shadow of the coming days heavy on the four of them. Marcus tried to cheer them with stories and jokes, but Caius sat grim and unheeding, and Aulus and Flavia were in no mood to listen.

Eventually Flavia put out her hand. Briefly, she took Marcus' hand and squeezed it.

'You're very dear,' she said. 'Thank you.'

He pulled down the corners of his mouth in exaggerated disappointment. 'We do our best', he said lightly, but his eyes were troubled as he looked at her.

He fell silent, and shortly afterwards he excused himself to go and check the guard.

Caius spoke suddenly. 'You've made all your arrangements to leave tomorrow?'

'Yes. Some of the men will stay and herd the stock in the woods away from the buildings. Everyone else will go to my father-in law's house in Corinium until I get back.'

Caius nodded. He turned to Flavia. 'You realise they'll rape you to death – or worse – if they catch you.'

She flushed, guilt written so plainly on her face that Caius knew his shot had gone home. He watched the colour drain from her face and fury blaze suddenly from her eyes.

'What d'you mean – how dare you?....'

'You're to stay in Corinium, Flavia. There's to be no heroics, no coming back out here on your own, no trying to be clever. Is that clear?'

Their eyes locked, ice and fire. At last she said 'Damn you, Chief Centurion.'

His face relaxed. A ghost of a smile lit his features and was gone. 'That's my girl,' he said gently, and after a moment she looked back at him and said: 'I promise.'

The night closed round them, dark with ragged cloud, chill and sodden from the rain. There would be little sleep for the legionaries. With double guards set, turn-and- turn-about in two hour watches, they would be alert all night.

The night seemed endless. Aulus and Flavia lay close together by the brazier in makeshift curtained off quarters, silent, ears cocked for any sound outside the walls. The muted burble of talk from the huddled farm people mingled with the hollow tread of the sentries on the wooden fighting platform and the ring of their boots on the masonry ramparts. Every so often they heard the duty Tesserarius, or Marcus' light footsteps as he went round the men, silently listening with them as they stared into the darkness.

Sometime in the middle of the night a shout from the walls jerked them fully awake. Before it had died Caius's bellowed roar 'Stand to your arms! Don't move, the farm people!' brought the camp to its feet. Jostling the legionaries, Aulus and Flavia climbed frantically onto the rampart.

Out in the darkness there was a pinpoint of light. It floated in the darkness and grew until it was bright enough to shadow the outline of a hut.

'They're firing the labour lines!'

From below in the camp there was a groan, a communal cry of despair from the farm people. A woman began to weep. Flavia winced at the sound.

The fire grew, and spread, jumping to a second hut, and then another.

She thought: 'How could they burn after all that rain?' and she clutched Aulus' arm, her free hand involuntarily across her mouth, smothering the cry that rose in her. She could see the Scots now, prancing like demons among the flames, and she could hear their triumphant shouts. And then, above the clamour they heard the roar of the fire as the heat grew fiercer and helped to dry the thatch and timber of the next huts in line.

When all the huts had gone, and the fires had died to glowing mounds in the darkness, Aulus and Flavia went silently back to their quarters. On the rampart the tears had run silently down her cheeks. Now they came in great heartrending sobs. He took her hands and pulled her to him. They clung together, numb with the shock of the destruction of their farm. And tomorrow he would leave her, perhaps never see her again. In the dying light of the brazier he bent and kissed her. 'Come,' he said, and he laid her gently onto their makeshift bed and wrapped his arms around her.

'It's like talking to a fog,' Aulus swore in exasperation. As soon as it was light he had called his people together in the farm courtyard to load all his wagons with the possessions they had salvaged from their huts and as many sacks of grain as they could carry. They stood apathetic, overwhelmed by the burning of their homes and the enormity of their loss.

'Come on, everybody,' he shouted for the twentieth time. 'Help and get these wagons loaded.' They milled uncertainly. A few of the men moved half-heartedly to the granary. 'For the gods' sake, Lucian,' he turned to the youth standing beside him, 'Go and ask Marcus for some of his men. We're going to be here all day at this rate.'

Eventually, with the legionaries' help, they were ready. Valerius, with Baldur and Gratian, were sent on ahead to warn Tiberius. The farm wagons stood harnessed and laden, flanked by the numb farm men and their women, the loads topped by the very young and very old. No one spoke. They looked utterly wretched. They stared longingly about them at the yard and buildings with misery in their eyes.

Aulus gave the order to move. Escorted by the cavalrymen they shambled hesitatingly forward out of the yard and away from their home.

Flavia rode with Aulus at their head. They spoke little. She was withdrawn into herself, but at peace with him. Once she reached for his hand and gripped it hard. She smiled at him, a full loving smile that turned his heart over. 'I know you'll come safely back.' she said. 'I know no harm will come to you. Then we'll rebuild the farm. I'll look after everyone until you come. So long as we have each other we'll always be strong, won't we? It's going to be all right. We're going to survive this and rebuild our lives stronger than ever before.'

'Yes, my love, I'll be safely back. Don't worry while I am gone and we'll rebuild Etruria between us better than ever it was before.'

'I love you, Aulus.'

Valerius was waiting at the city gates. They bunched the wagons nose to tail and stationed the troopers ahead and on either side. The city was even more crowded and it stank. The farm people huddled close to their possessions, terrified by the noise and throng.

The doors of Tiberius' stable yard were flung open at their approach. They hurried through, from noise to quiet and the tranquillity of Tiberius' walled garden and lawns. The gates were slammed shut behind them. The troopers dismounted. The wagons were unharnessed and manhandled onto the grass. Valerius began immediately to rig awnings from their sides.

Tiberius was overjoyed to see Flavia. He had been sick with worry since news of the warband had reached the city. His face was thinner. Its network of lines seemed deeper, his hair sparser and whiter.

'Thank the gods, child', he hugged her to him. 'Thank the gods you've come. Why didn't you come sooner? But there. You're here. That's all that matters.'

She clung to him. 'Oh, father.' What could she say?

'I know, child. I know.'

She kissed him, love and pity mixed. 'You're too thin, father.' Was it pity for him, or for herself?

'I'm all right. It's been a worrying time for us all.'

'Yes, I know.' She disentangled herself. Cloa was almost jumping up and down beside her. She threw her arms round Flavia. 'My baby, my little girl'. Her arms were fiercely strong as she gripped her. Her eyes were wet with tears.

'Why, Cloa,' Flavia tried to laugh, 'You're crying. Come on. We can't have that.'

'Indeed, I am not, mistress'. She dabbed her stole at her eyes and clamped her jaw shut. 'Indeed, I am not.'

Aulus came across to them. 'I've brought as much grain as we could carry, Tiberius.'

'Good. Excellent.' He welcomed the diversion. 'We need it and all the more with all these people. How many have you brought? It looks like hundreds. We must get the grain under lock and key before the mob smells it and pulls my gates down. The city is lawless, Aulus. It gets worse every day – though it's no wonder it is happening, poor devils.'

Aulus went with Flavia to her childhood bedroom. He shut the door carefully behind him and took off his helmet.

'I'll be back in two weeks.'

'Yes.'

'You'll be all right here?'

'Yes. I can't tell you to be careful, but I'll pray to all the gods every minute you're gone.'

He nodded. 'Look after them. As soon as the shock wears off they'll be bored. The young ones will disappear into the town I expect, and the old will lose heart. It won't be easy for you.'

'I'll manage. There'll be plenty to do for two weeks.' She was fighting back the tears.

'Yes.'

'You could send the wagons back tomorrow for more grain.'

'Yes.'

They looked at each other. Suddenly, there was nothing more to say. He moved quickly to her, wrapped her in his arms, kissed and hugged her. He grabbed up his helmet. 'I love you.' The words were thick with unshed tears.

Then he was gone. Proudly and sadly she watched the troopers disappear into the crowded street. He turned in the saddle to smile and wave as he went.

Chapter X

In the gloomy dawn of the next morning Caius Martius' special Century set out for Londinium. Aulus left first, splashing through the muddy puddles of the driveway with his eight men. He did not look back.

Half an hour behind them, Caius waved his legionaries forward. They set off with the careless swagger of veteran troops. Life was for the day. Change and adventure lay ahead. The dangers of their task were unheeded.

Beside them Caius rode a little more stiffly, but his face, framed by the steel helmet, was as hard and bleak as when he had first ridden onto the farm.

The wagons pulled heavily from their long winter's rest. Above their hidden cargo the wounded legionaries lay stretched uncomfortably among the grain and equipment that were piled high under their canvas superstructure. The wagons seemed to move reluctantly, creaking and protesting, rutting the packed stone of the driveway.

Valerius and his eight troopers watched them go, standing beside their saddled mounts. As the wagons turned off the driveway onto the military road he ordered his men to tighten their girths and mount. They made a last sweep round the ashes of the labour lines, searching again for any sign of the Scots' presence and then trotted slowly in double line down the drive. They were a tiny, forlorn little band against the massive grey clouds of the March morning and the empty stillness of the land they were leaving behind.

Despite the rain of the past few days the Century made good progress along the metalled road.

They almost took Servius and his men by surprise.

Like the Scots, Servius had had enough of winter. Only his leadership and iron will had kept his men together through the endless cold and wet. The fine spell in February had temporarily raised their spirits. With renewed hope they had watched the road for Caius and his wagons, but the recurrent rain had dashed their morale and the men sat together in a tight knot, talking in low voices, faces dark with frustration. They moved sullenly and grudgingly when Servius went to break up the group, hatred in their eyes.

'All right, you bastards,' Servius spoke scornfully. 'We'll move when this rain stops. We'll take ourselves a little trip back up the road and pay a call on the Chief Centurion – maybe I'll hand you lot over to him.' He smiled round the men. 'That makes you cringe, doesn't it? Get up off your arses, you gutter scum. You.' He pointed to the man nearest to him. 'Outside! Get out and watch the road.'

The soldier opened his mouth to argue, shifting in his seat, refusing to rise. Servius moved like lightening. He sprang at him, his dagger rasping from its sheath as he moved. His left hand grabbed a fistful of the man's hair and jerked his head agonisingly back. The point of the dagger broke the skin of the tightly stretched throat and sent a quick trickle of blood zigzagging down to soak into his neckscarf. The man's adam's apple bobbed violently, his eyes terrified.

'No one move. Keep still - That's better. Now, scum, you heard my order.' The man tried to nod. 'This time, you're lucky. Any more insubordination and you'll not find me so easy. Got it?' The dagger pressed harder into his throat. 'Right. Get moving.'

He withdrew the dagger. The man rolled his head painfully. Reluctantly, he stood up. Immediately Servius kneed him viciously in the groin, and as his head jerked forward in sudden agony he knocked him sprawling amongst the others.

'You bastards never learn.' Servius stood over them, poised, commanding the situation. His voice was pained. 'Now get up when you're told or I'll teach the lot of you some real and painful lessons.'

He sent two of the men into the pelting rain to watch the road. Their patience was soon rewarded. A trickle of refugees was scurrying eastwards. Their frantic haste alerted the watchers and brought Servius to question them. An unholy glee was rising in him.

'Just a minute.' He stepped into the roadway in the path of a couple pulling a laden handcart. Their simple faces looked terrified, then confused, and they turned and peered back up the road.

'No need to be worried. We're an army patrol, collecting news of the north. What's up? Why are you running?'

The man shook his head. He mumbled incoherently, looking from Servius to the road behind him. It was the woman who spoke.

'Let us pass, your honour. They're coming after us, Sir, in their hordes. Let us pass, I beg you.'

'Who's coming after you?'

'Them killers it is.' She looked back over her shoulder again.

The man said 'For the love of God, your honour, it's the warbands. Burning and looting. Haven't you heard? Let us go, Sir. Let us go, I beg you.'

'I thought there was a detachment of troops back up there.' Servius jerked his chin towards Corinium.

'So there is, Sir, so there is. A few. Too few. Not enough.'

'What are they doing, then?'

Tears started to the man's eyes. He opened and shut his mouth wordlessly. The woman stepped forward and knelt at Servius' feet, clasping her hands up at him, entreating him. 'We don't know, your honour. We're simple people. Please, your honour, please, we beg you –we don't know nothing but that they'll kill us if they catch us. Let us go.'

Servius smiled down at her. Her sodden clothes clung like rags to her thin frame. Her hair hung lank round her terrified, rain-streaked face. He savoured her misery for a moment, then jerked his thumb over his shoulder.

'On your way and move fast. They're close behind you.' He stepped aside and laughed as they scrambled and slithered to heave the handcart away through the downpour.

On the morning that Aulus was escorting Flavia to Corinium, Servius had left his winter quarters. With the greatest caution he had led his men back along the road towards Etruria. Anxious to meet neither Caius nor warband and ignorant of the movements of either he had taken advantage of every scrap of cover and every hilltop.

He had found Durocornovium deserted and spent the night there, barricaded without fire or light into a stone-built barn away from the empty settlement and Imperial posting house.

In the morning they left the settlement and were moving stealthily through woodland when Aulus passed them. The mounted troopers were ignoring the trees, concentrating on the road ahead and they had had time to hide themselves. The troopers trotted past without noticing the watchers lying motionless in the tangle of last year's bracken and undergrowth.

Servius frowned savagely. 'Cavalry,' he whispered.' Where in Hades' name have they come from?'

They lay still, the sodden ground soaking their tunics. The road was empty now, seemingly drained of the trickle of refugees.

They heard the Century first in the faint rumble of the earth under their bodies. Then, in the distance, the rhythm of one of the army's marching songs with the cries of the drivers lifting occasionally above the singing.

Servius smiled and sighed, a long, full sigh of relief and anticipation. He eased himself up and counted the Century past. Including the cavalrymen probably sixty men or more, and the unmistakable figure of the mounted Caius. He was pretty sure Marcus was amongst them and he spat with venomous profanity towards them.

Again, they lay still. Half an hour later he nodded his grudging approval as Valerius and his rear guard trotted past.

They stood up then, laughing, stamping their feet to ease the cramp, their mutiny forgotten. Two of them playfully started to wrestle and they crashed down and rolled in the bracken, encouraged with shouts from the others.

The euphoria lasted several minutes before the laughter faded and they fell silent as they watched Servius. He stood apart, frowning, his fierce blue eyes glaring into the distance. Caius' force was stronger than he had expected and the addition of mounted patrols meant they would have to keep their distance, at least by day. He tried to gauge the pace they had been going. Barring accidents they might reach Calleva Atrebatum, the nearest walled city across the Downs, by the following evening. He was wondering if their best opportunity might be to wait and create some diversion in the crowds that were bound to be in the city, and run off one of the wagons, when there was a sudden startled exclamation and a sharp word of warning from one of the men.

'What in Hades' name's bothering you?'

'Over there, Sir, on the road.'

There were three of them. Their hair bobbed on their shoulders as they loped along the grass verge of the military road.

'Scots!' Servius sucked in his breath. 'Scots. Following that bastard Caius.' A grin of pure evil lit up his face. 'Well, now, if that doesn't beat bear fighting...'

The Scots jogged silently on and vanished from view. Servius sat down and leaned back against a tree.

'Shut up, you bastards and let me think. Those animals must be keeping tabs on Caius. They must be a warband scouting party. What a stroke of luck.' The humour of the situation appealed to him. He grinned round at the men. 'There's justice for you. A good reward for all our waiting. We let those red-haired bastards deal with Caius. We let Caius deal with them. We move in, clean up, and pick up the pieces.'

He fell silent again. How much further would Caius go that day? How far behind would the warband be? Caius should have passed through Durocornovium by now. He would be bound to press on until he reached the open country of the Downs. Probably he would try to get well across them before picking some lonely hilltop for the night's halt. Please the gods, the warband would be close on his heels by then and would attack him there.

He scowled again. What would the warband do with the wagons? They wouldn't realise that their real cargo was hidden under the floorboards. Would they take them, or burn them? Either way it raised fresh problems. Would fire reveal the treasure? 'Possibly not', he thought dubiously. 'It's all seasoned oak and the loot is in oak boxes. It's like steel. With luck, and if the wood's wet, it'll scorch but not catch on properly.'

And if the Scots did not appear? 'We'll have to think of some way of slowing them up,' Servius deliberated, half aloud. 'The best bet would be to leapfrog ahead of the column during the night and wait for Caius somewhere where the wooded country begins again on the far side of the Downs.' They would soon find a culvert or bridge that could be smashed in to stop the wagons long enough for the Scots to catch them up. Besides, he had no desire to cross those empty hills in daylight. There was far too little cover.

He stood up. 'Come on, lads. We don't want to hang around here too long. We'll move on down the road nice and gentle and see if we can't find ourselves a good ringside view to watch the fun.'

Besides the Scots who had fled from Valerius in the labour lines there were half a dozen stragglers who had not yet reached the farm. Warned of the massacre by the fleeing survivors they had scattered and lain hidden in wood and ditch until they were sure the pursuit had been called off. Towards evening they had started to move, locating each other with bird calls whistled or hooted through their fingers.

As night fell they had crept back, the urgent need for revenge obliterating fatigue and hunger. Unseen and unheard in the darkness they had crawled close to the camp and lain motionless, listening, straining their ears to catch the rhythm of its life. Finally, they had melted back away from its walls, their numbers too few to attack. They had moved naturally towards the labour lines and the leaping flames slaked the rage in their hearts. As the fires died down their eyes had turned again to the hated Roman camp. Leaving three of their number to watch the Romans the rest stripped themselves to the waist. They set off northwards through the night to search for companions to return with them and avenge their kinsmen.

With the dawn their stride became a loping run that ate up the miles, and in the afternoon, guided by the smoke of a burning building, they met up with a strong band who, like themselves, had just moved out of winter quarters.

That evening the whole band started south. As the hours went on, one by one their guides dropped out, exhausted by their efforts but two of them kept up the pace and they led the band back to Etruria.

They found the farm deserted.

There was a hasty war council. The warriors who had stayed had left clear trail signs showing which way the soldiers had gone. They were only hours behind. The strongest were for pushing on immediately. Others urged retribution on the farm, looting and an overnight rest. In the end they compromised. In a wave of destruction, they rampaged through the farmstead, smashing everything that came to hand, piling together everything that would burn in the house and buildings so that fire would find all the fuel it needed to do its work unaided. They kindled torches and ran with them through the farmstead lighting a score of fires.

They hardly paused to watch their handiwork. They left Etruria in flames and ran on down the drive and onto the military road.

They stopped at Durocornovium and crowded into its posting house to eat the food they had with them and to sleep. The cold of the small hours woke them and, to warm themselves, they set fire to the building. When the heat had thawed their blood, they set out again.

The glow of the flames, reflected flickering on the cloud base, was spotted by Servius from the high country of the Downs as he and his men detoured to overtake Caius. He had not seen the band but the distant glow told eloquently of its presence. He smiled to himself, well satisfied with events.

The glow was also seen by Caius' sentries. Its message brought Caius from his blankets while his sleeping soldiers were roused cursing from their rest. Marcus went to join him, drawing his cloak tightly round him, shivering with cold. For a moment they stood together, staring at the flickering light.

'They didn't take long, Sir.'

'No.'

'Bloody cold, isn't it?' Marcus cupped his hands and blew into them, arms pressed tightly against his chest.

'It's going to be a long day, Optio. Make up the fires and get some food into the men. Move in an hour.'

'Right, Sir.' Marcus saluted and strode off. Caius stood, watching the distant light, impervious to the cold. He listened to Marcus relaying his orders and silently wondered how many of his men would ever eat again.

Sleep sodden and shaking with cold the legionaries choked on their meat and bread as they struggled to hitch the teams, saddle up and break camp. The wine issue warmed them and they moved more quickly in the firelight to pile their kit and the wounded into the wagons. Marcus called them onto the road and they took post to make their dash for the sanctuary of Calleva Atrebatum.

With drawn swords Valerius silently led his rearguard to a hilltop half a mile back along the road. Satisfied that the road was empty they sheathed the swords, dismounted, and stood cold and silent, huddling close to their horses for warmth. They watched the glow of the distant fire and listened to the night, wondering what the day might bring.

Caius' column moved slowly in the darkness. They led the wagon teams carefully, holding them to the crown of the road. Guides walked on the edge of the paving to mark its limit lest the wagons lose the camber and slip off into the soft grass of the verge. They had moved perhaps three miles before the dawn gave them enough light to quicken their pace and to see, not far away, where the treeline began at the edge of the Downs. Aulus and his men moved on ahead. Caius urged the Century forward, away from the open, coverless danger of the hills.

Tension quickened in the little knot of men grouped round Valerius as the light grew and the grey ribbon of the road became visible. Automatically they slipped their fingers under their horses' girths and checked the fastenings on their bridles. If daylight showed anyone on the road there could be no moments lost in frantic adjustments.

'Well, thank the gods for that.' Valerius relaxed with a sigh. In the colourless dawn the road seemed empty. 'Where's the wineskin?'

The men rubbed their hands and gathered round as one of the troopers untied the wineskin from his saddle. They all drank, passing the skin from man to man, wiping their mouths with the back of their hands and eyeing the skin as it was passed around.

'Come on, mate,' Faber held out his hand. 'You'll finish the bloody lot.'

The trooper next to him took the skin from his mouth with a wide grin and handed it on with a deep belch. 'That's better,' he said.

Faber tilted his head back as he lifted the wineskin, and suddenly he froze. Wine ran in a red stream from both sides of his mouth. He gulped, and as the others cursed him, he lowered the skin.

'Tesserarius,' he said, 'See there!'

They were a long way back up the road, like a dancing black shadow in the bad light. The wine forgotten they all turned to look.

'What in Mithras' name is that?'

'Well, it's not the garrison tarts, that's for sure.'

'Them bloody buggers 'as gone an' brought their big bruvvers. Must be a bloody 'undred of 'em.' The speaker's voice was tight with awe.

Valerius said quietly: 'I do believe you're right.'

The shadow had disappeared down a hidden fold in the hills. They waited. No one spoke.

'There they come!' There was something ominous about the oncoming runners. They were too far for any sound, too far clearly to distinguish who or what they were. They were like some shapeless, black, swaying reptile.

'It's them Scots, right enough. I can see that red 'air.'

'How many, d'you reckon?' Valerius' voice was taut.

'Four score, maybe.'

'Yea, something like that, I'd say.'

'Come on.' In a flurry of cloaks and flying legs they gathered their reins and vaulted onto their horses, kicked the cold, protesting mounts and rode at a gallop to warn Caius.

The Chief Centurion saw them coming. He wheeled his horse and cantered back to meet them. He nodded as Valerius reported, then glanced over his shoulder towards the edge of the Downs and the sheltering trees.

'Take four men back, Tesserarius, and watch them. You others, come with me.'

He put his horse into a fast canter, shouting to the men as he rode. 'Don't stop at the column. Get on ahead and tell the Tribune I want a good defensive position as soon as he can find one. Look for the first side road he can find in amongst those trees. Find somewhere we can get out of sight. Report back to me when he has found somewhere. Right? Get moving.' And, as they came up to the column: 'Wake it up, Optio. At the double! We've got company.'

The teams strained into their collars as the whips cracked. They broke into a lumbering trot which set the wagons rolling and bouncing over the paving. Inside them, the wounded soldiers grabbed for handholds and cried out involuntarily. In front and behind the legionaries doubled to keep station.

Ahead of Caius there were two other watchers. Aulus had reached the trees. He had stopped to look back and had seen Valerius' galloping troopers and then the wagons quickening pace. He galloped back to meet them.

Had Aulus but known it, Servius was not far from him. He had chosen a spot in the trees from which he could see well back onto the Downs and a fair way down the road into the woodland. He was alone, judging both that the mounted troopers would be concentrating on the road ahead and that he could hide himself well enough to be invisible. He had sent the rest of his band along the treeline to hide themselves several hundred paces away. He had covered himself with dead bracken and was lying motionless.

Aulus listened briefly to Caius' orders. 'Let's go!' he shouted and they galloped into the trees and on, searching for a track. They were not long in finding one, leading obliquely off into the woodland. They swerved off the road and raced along it. It was grassed over, little used. It dipped and wound across a gravel bedded stream running from the Downs. On the far side it rose gently up a slope from which charcoal burners had sometime cleared the trees. Deer or sheep had cropped the grass short here, leaving a meadow-like clearing.

They pulled up at Aulus' signal. 'This'll do fine.' he shouted over the blowing of the horses and the curses and encouragement of their riders as they controlled the excited animals. 'You four, get back to the Chief at the gallop. Tell him we've found a good place to make a stand. You two' – he indicated two of his Contubernium – 'Back down the track slowly to the road. Make sure no one else is using it. Sing out if you see anything unusual. You two, scout to the left along the tree-line and you two, same thing to the right. I'll go on ahead up yonder. Get back here as quick as you can .' With Baldur and Lucian Aulus galloped on across the open ground up the slope. The trees grew thickly at the top. The track had petered out into a winding game path that was quickly lost in the undergrowth. Nothing moved except a small deer that had watched this invasion in petrified fear, a tuft of grass sticking half eaten out of its mouth. Catching their scent, it crashed away through the trees, sending the riders' hearts into their mouths and hands flying to their swords.

'Damn thing. It be only a deer,' Lucian laughed. 'We'll not harm thee.'

'No.' Aulus swore under his breath at his sudden panic. 'There's been no one here lately then, that's certain.'

They rode back to the others. The reports were all the same, of startled wild life, confirming that no human being was there except themselves.

They galloped back to the military road to meet Caius as the first men of the Century came running from the Downs and into the trees.

'Can we hide the tracks where we turn off the road?' Caius was as cool as though he was on the parade ground.

'Men and horses, maybe. The grass is thick and overgrown and it hardly marked. I particularly noticed. If we cut some bracken and scatter it where the wheels leave the paving, the wheel marks may not show.'

'Good.' Caius jogged steadily beside the wagons. He looked at Aulus with the ghost of a smile. 'You're beginning to learn. Get to it.'

At the turnoff the troopers dismounted with drawn daggers. Marcus joined them with some of the legionaries and they ran to cut bracken to throw it down on the verge where the grass track began.

The drivers took the turn at a swaying trot. The wagons bounced lurching onto the grass.

'Keep' em going! Keep' em going!' Marcus yelled. 'For Mithras sake, don't stop.' They watched in an agony of suspense as the wheels crushed the bracken and sank into the springy turf. The drivers stood on their boxes, whips lashing. The horses strained forward, eyes staring, heads tossing, and one by one the wagons pulled over the verge. Firmer ground beyond held their weight and they disappeared jolting into the trees.

The soldiers ran to gather up the muddied bracken. Dismounted, Caius watched them work. 'Not bad,' he said. 'Not bad.' There were only slight depressions in the grass. They might go unnoticed. Beside him Aulus said: 'I'll take the men back a bit and gallop up the roadside over the marks and carry on for a while. I'll circle back through the wood and join you.'

'Right.' Caius nodded and swung into his saddle. 'Post a man here to guide Valerius in.' Then Caius and the legionaries were gone, running through the trees to catch up the wagons.

From his hiding place Servius had seen the wagons leave the road. Military approval fought with personal anger. There was still no sign of the pursuers. The road ran empty over the first skyline. The presence of a solitary cavalryman waiting on the grass track beside the road confirmed his guess that Caius had left a rearguard to cover the Scots' approach. He frowned and turned his attention back to the skyline.

Suddenly, Valerius and his men appeared. They came over the brow, stopped and wheeled to look back the way they had come. They sat for a while, unmoving, then turned and came cantering down the road, presumably anticipating that the vanished column would have stopped somewhere to form up and fight. He heard a shout from the waiting trooper. Together they disappeared up the track. The road was empty.

'Right, you black-hearted renegades,' Servius stood up and brushed the bracken off his uniform. 'This is where we earn our keep.'

He signalled to his band to join him. They left their hiding place and ran to the military road. On the paving they stopped, standing just above the treeline so that anyone coming over the brow quarter of a mile away must see them.

The first of the Scots appeared over the skyline. Immediately Servius started shouting. He ran to the trees, signalling to an imaginary column and back into the open, arms waving wildly. The figure on the skyline stopped. It stood motionless then leapt in the air and swept its arms over its head in encouragement to the unseen followers.

Servius waited long enough for a crowd of figures to appear, then they started running. At the turn onto the track they stopped, eyes riveted back to the spot where the Scots would appear. They had gained and had time to recover their breath before the first runner appeared and yelled in triumph at the sight of them.

'Come on, then, you red bastards. We'll show you where they are.' shouted Servius. He turned and he and his men raced along the track into the trees.

Caius had had plenty of time. The wagons negotiated the hard gravel bed of the stream, but quickly lost impetus and began to labour heavily up the slope. He let them struggle on until, judging that he was approximately in the centre of the clearing, he halted the first wagon and pulled the second and third up to the right and left of it, axle to axle.

'Unhitch. Get the teams into the trees and out of sight. Hobble them tight and get back here fast.'

He drew up his men in two lines across the track, their backs to the three wagons. They were painfully few to fight off a strong attack but Caius was confident. These were the best veterans of the army, men of steadiness and battle experience. He watched approvingly as they moved into line; anticipation shone in eyes grown suddenly fierce. Jaws thrust forward. Teeth were clenched. They squinted along the hafts of their javelins and tested their sword blades with their thumbs. They loosened the daggers in their sheaths and checked the lacing of body armour and helmet strap. Spare javelins were brought from the wagons and handed out. They stuck them into the ground ready to hand beside their own. They propped their red painted shields in front of them, to be snatched up and locked into a wall when the javelins had gone and the fight closed to a hand to hand struggle.

Judging that he had time enough Caius ordered the sharpened stakes to be thrown down from the wagons and had them set, slanting outwards, three deep, in front of his little force. They would not help much but would serve to check some of the impetus of the Scots' rush at the crucial moment of impact. He had the stake palisade curved round at either end of the line, thickening it on the ground as it passed his unprotected flanks and swung it in to meet the parked wagons.

He viewed the preparations with a critical eye. Valerius had reported upwards of eighty Scots. 'Please the gods, they'll come straight at us.' he thought. 'Things will get difficult if they use their heads and surround us. It would be out of character, I think, with the javelins to prick them on.'

Aulus and his troopers appeared from the trees and cantered across. He called 'With a bit of luck they'll go straight past the turning. Our hoof prints cut up the turf quite nicely.'

Caius nodded. 'Don't count on it, lad. Same tactics as on the farm. They know we've got horses, but they won't know whether you're still mounted or fighting on foot, nor which side you'll hit them from. Now, listen. This fight may depend on you. You must hit them at the right moment. Maximum impact.' He thumped his clenched right fist into the palm of his left hand. 'Remember your training. Keep the men together. Clear the trees at a trot, then charge. Hit them in a solid phalanx, knee to knee at top speed.' Again, his fist smacked into his palm. His eyes bored into Aulus' eyes as he looked up at him. 'This time your timing is vital. There'll only be one attack – once we're engaged there are too few of us for either side to draw off and regroup. Either we'll hold them and start to push them back or they'll be too strong for us. If they are, you'll likely see the line waver. That's the moment I want you here.' He stabbed a finger at the ground in front of the waiting legionaries. 'Got it? Good. I'm taking the right flank. Get yourselves out of sight on that side and be sure you can see me. If I can, I'll signal you. Off you go.' And under his breath he added: 'Mithras ride with you,' as he turned away for a final inspection of his battle line.

Again, the waiting: again, the feeling of unreality. Across the clearing Aulus watched the waiting legionaries, standing quietly, hardly moving, eyes fixed on the track down at the stream. He could hear its rippling murmur in the stillness. Somewhere a thrush started to sing. Beside him, Valerius touched him with outstretched fingers. He looked round. The Tesserarius had a hunk of bread in his hand. He raised his eyebrows and pointed at it. Aulus shook his head. Valerius smiled and shrugged and tore off a mouthful.

Suddenly, they heard them – men running in the trees across the stream. Aulus braced himself for the Scots' appearance.

Incredibly, it was six Roman soldiers who materialized. Running hard, they cleared the trees and were through the stream before they checked and stopped. For a moment they stood still, chests heaving, staring up the slope towards Caius. One of them raised an arm in a mocking greeting then they spun round and made off down the stream, cascading the water in silver showers around them before disappearing up the far bank and away into the trees.

For a moment there was silence, then a howl of execration along Caius' line as they recognised Servius and his followers. Momentarily the legionaries were unbalanced. Then hands tightened on javelin and sword hilt.

'If it's the last thing I ever do I'll have that treacherous bastard nailed up so tight he'll pray he'd never been born,' Marcus swore loudly through clenched teeth.

'All right. Steady down.' Caius' voice cut above the muttering. 'We've plenty of time to catch those traitors when we've dealt with these Scots. They'll be here soon.'

There was a ripple of approval. 'Well done, Chief,' Marcus nodded.

Like a charged thunderhead, the tension rose. Silence – and then, somewhere below them in the trees they heard a shout taken up and repeated and a sort of sigh whispered along the line.

There was not long to wait now. Although they could not know it the Scots had stopped at the turn off to let the stragglers catch up. For a while they milled excitedly beside the military road, shouting encouragement to each other and laughing at the fight to come. Then, elbowing and jostling, they plunged into the wood.

In a body they burst from the tree-line and splashed into the stream. At the foot of the slope they paused in a crowd which swelled quickly and bellied outwards as the warriors at the back ran to either side to see their quarry. The sight of the armoured line waiting motionless half way up the slope sobered them and their yells faltered and died to a murmur. Then the howl of their war cry started, swelling and rising until it was a high- pitched scream. In a mass, they charged up the slope.

'Wait for it!' On right and left flank Caius and Marcus shouted simultaneously. A small pile of stones on the track in front of them marked the limit of javelin range. The first of the Scots reached it and passed it.

'Now!' Front rank, back rank, strong arms hurled the javelins. As the weapons left their hands the legionaries reached for another and again they threw, front rank, back rank, and again; the muscles of their right arms putting every ounce of strength into the throw. The Scots checked, then came on again, but Aulus, watching in the detachment of imminent action, saw with a thrill that many dropped or were spun sideways by the impact and staggered on towards the Romans on limbs that were suddenly old.

He looked back to the line. The legionaries were reaching for their shields. They swung them up in a solid red wall in front of them. They stood braced, left leg in front, crouching forward to take the impact of the rush. Then the Scots were at the stakes – there was a check in their wild run as they tore at them and pulled them aside, and then they were through and onto the defending shield wall.

The line recoiled, then checked, and held steady. Aulus realised that he was shivering with tension – 'Ye gods. How long can they take that pressure?'

He saw men fall in the Roman ranks and the men of the second rank step forward to take their place. He saw the towering figure of Caius surrounded by a mob trying to reach him through the protecting stake wall. Without conscious thought he waved his troopers forward. They came to the edge of the trees and silently formed into line, knee to knee, himself in the centre.

He drew his sword. He heard the rasp of metal on both sides of him. The horses snorted and danced and threw their heads.

He thought: 'That line can't hold much longer.' And aloud. 'Walk!'

'Yes, by the gods, they're wavering.' And aloud. 'Charge!' Without realising he rose in his saddle to shout the order, then down into his seat leaning forward over the withers, sword arm straight.

He had timed it perfectly.

The solid knee to knee phalanx hit the flank of the Scots, scattering men like chaff. He saw the white, blurred faces ringed by red hair, mouths open like black caves and white rimmed eyes staring up at him. He smelt again the rancid fat and sweat and the nauseous tang of blood and fear. Then he was through and on the open ground. He sat back in the saddle to pull up, to turn and reform. Valerius was there and most of the troopers.

'Re-form!' he shouted and heard Valerius repeat 'Re-form! Re-form!'

They hurtled back into the Scots, slashing and chopping, then the marauders were breaking and turning to run and the legionaries were cheering. It was all a confusion of hitting and slashing until he realised that the splashing water under his hooves was the stream and he looked up and drew breath.

It had become a massacre. Behind him, Caius had his men well in hand. In a single line they were coming down the slope behind him, sword arms swinging as they finished off their attackers. Around him his troopers were chasing the fleeing warriors, riding them down, revelling in the blood lust of victory.

'This time,' he said it aloud. 'I think we really have fixed them.'

The excitement of battle was still on him as he washed his sword in the stream and dried it on his cloak. The grassy slope was a shambles. He watched as the soldiers moved among the bodies, making sure there were no survivors, finishing the day's work with their bloody daggers. There were horses there too, some standing riderless, some thrashing on the ground, some lying still.

'Valerius!' he called. 'Valerius!' He felt the excitement drain from his body. He turned to the man nearest him, a grizzled warrior, blood splattered from head to foot.

'Where's Valerius?'

The man nodded back up the slope. 'He copped it.' His eyes were expressionless.

'Oh, gods, no! No!' He was suddenly cold, frigid with cold, the sweat icy on his body. For the first time he looked around him with seeing eyes. Dead? Valerius? Who else? How many? 'Did we rescue you from Corinium for this? My own men – Baldur. Gratian Lucian. Where are they?' He heard his own voice shouting: 'Rally on me, troopers! Rally on me!'

How many would come? 'Please the gods, more than this handful. Where are Baldur and Gratian?' The faces looked down at him as he stood beside his horse. 'Are you all that's left?'

There were seven mounted troopers. One of them, Naso, said: 'The boy's all right, Sir. He's up there.'

Lucian was crying shamelessly over the bodies of his friends. He had straightened their limbs, even wiped the blood and mud from their faces. Slowly, Aulus led his horse over to the boy and put his hand on his shoulder. Lucian looked up, his eyes blinded by the tears that ran down his cheeks. He bent his head again and sobbed. Aulus shook his head and turned away.

Again, the body count. More than sixty Scots were certain kills. Almost certainly, others had disappeared into the trees with wounds that would probably kill them. There were no known survivors. But at what a price. There were thirty-one dead legionaries, including Valerius and eight of the troopers. Miraculously, neither Caius nor Marcus were touched. They had taken the positions of danger on the exposed flanks, but their skill and experience at arms had not failed them. They moved now amongst their men, restoring routine, directing preparations for fires and a meal, blankets and bandages for the wounded, and for the dead a hasty mass grave.

They had fourteen wounded now. They laid them beside the wagons and put the blankets of the dead under them to ease the chill of the ground. They bound their wounds and fetched water from the stream to slake their thirst.

When it was dark, and the fires burned brightly in the little camp, Aulus wept. Caius stood up and came around the fire and shook his shoulder in a rough, impatient gesture that was half affection, half irritation, then turned and went off into the darkness

Chapter XI

Quintus Polybian Epaticus was a most important man. As Senior Magistrate of Calleva Atrebatum in this time of crisis he was responsible for the safety of the city and well-being of its inhabitants. The grandeur and responsibility of the position suited him well. Unlike the wealthy of Britannia's old established families he had sought the post and he welcomed its duties. That the offices of magistrate brought their holders little but unpopularity mattered not one jot to him. The percentage payment that he exacted on every commercial enterprise in the city more than compensated for any discomfort in that direction. That the appointment made him a target of hatred against the ever unpopular and mounting imperial taxes was immaterial. A genuine bustling efficiency coupled with a happy knack of disassociating himself from unpopular decisions while adopting popular ones as his own had brought him from humble origins to this position of power and importance. A compulsive speech maker, it mattered little to him that the flowing phrases which rolled resonantly from his tongue were old when the wolf was suckling Romulus and Remus. They sounded good to speaker and audience alike, satisfied all but the intelligent and endorsed his stature as leader and politician.

Under his jurisdiction the city ran as smoothly as could be hoped in a time like this. He delegated unpleasant duties wherever he could and firmly placed responsibility for shortcomings on the heads of his subordinates. His own time he divided between sweeping attacks on the details of his work, civic banqueting and the business of keeping himself in the public eye on all appropriate occasions.

Seated in his private office in Calleva's basilica he shifted his portly frame to a more imposing position in his favourite basketwork chair and nodded to his secretary to bring in his unexpected visitor.

The Centurion who entered, saluted and stood stiffly to attention on the threshold had done well in securing this interview. Quintus did not like the army. Their straightforward, crude manners and blunt speech aroused a deep antipathy in him. He hated the way the Roman officers treated him and smiled secretively when they spoke to him. To have one politely and respectfully requesting an audience emphasised the Magistrate's stature and the responsibility of his position.

He waved the man forward and signalled for wine to be poured for them both. He eased himself from the chair and picked up both goblets from the table.

'Please relax, Centurion. A chair? It is not every day nowadays that senior officers visit me.' He handed one goblet to the Centurion and resumed his seat. 'May I ask what this visit is about? By all accounts you and your men have caused quite a stir turning up here.'

Servius raised the goblet, tilted his head back and drained the wine in one draught. He looked ruefully into the empty cup, then at the wine jug and back at Quintus.

'Help yourself.' Quintus studied Servius as he refilled the flagon. Why did soldiers always have this effect on him? The man's uniform was dirty and stained as though he had slept in it for days. The man was both greedy and ill-mannered. He felt anger beginning to bubble in him as he waved his hand towards an empty chair.

Servius remained standing. 'I need your help, Sir.' – That was better. - 'If you can spare me some minutes of your time I have a strange and terrible story and I'd like to tell you the full facts.' He picked up the wine jug again, refilled his goblet for the second time and sat down.

'Yes, I am a busy man. I trust these facts will not take long to relate?'

'I think you'll find them of interest, Sir. My name is Servius Cenric. I am a Centurion in the field army of the North. Or I was, while the army existed.' He smiled ironically. 'You'll have heard what has happened up there?' Quintus nodded. 'Well, last autumn when the troubles got out of hand I was detailed by my commanding officer to escort a convoy of the army's treasure chests to Londinium.'

Servius' blue eyes gazed into Quintus' eyes, gauging the reaction. He had the Magistrate's full attention. A spot of colour had reddened his cheeks. The brown eyes had flashed with greed.

The fish was nibbling!

'The field army was rich, Sir. We had gold and silver in our vaults with precious stones and jewellery.'

Quintus was sitting forward.

'I came south with an escort of legionaries and the treasure hidden in three wagons.' Servius paused.

Quintus leaned forward again. 'Go on.' His voice was thick.

The fish was hooked! Inwardly, Servius laughed.

'Well,' he said. 'We ran into trouble near Corinium...' He described how the treasure had arrived at Etruria. He told of the arrival of the deserters, the dawn attack and the casualties. Only the roles of the protagonists were reversed. 'I was wounded in the attack.' – There were plenty of scars under his armour if proof was needed – 'What with our casualties and the depleted force, I had no option but to stay there over the winter. As luck would have it the ringleader of the deserters, himself a Centurion of many years standing, was not accounted for. Of course I didn't know it at the time, but he kept the remains of his traitorous gang together. Worse, over the winter he must have scoured the countryside for other deserters to join him.' Servius shook his head in wonder at the treachery of human nature. 'He got together as desperate a bunch of criminals as I've ever seen. His name is Caius Martius. He's a cunning and resourceful man. He didn't dare attack me in my winter quarters on the farm. I had fortified them too well. But I have no doubt he had me under observation.

'I left camp three days ago.' He broke off and dropped his eyes. Quintus was sitting very still, looking fixedly at his goblet with a show of disinterest. Servius dropped his head between his knees and spread his hands in a gesture of despair. 'He was waiting for me. He ambushed me as I came off the Downs. Somehow – the gods know how – he had got together more men than I had and some cavalry – about twenty five horse. We didn't have a chance. When I could see it was hopeless I...' He broke off again. His voice choked. He shook his head as if to clear it of the memory. He looked up at Quintus, the blue eyes clouded with anguish.

'I'm a soldier, you understand. I've served Rome all my life. When I saw it was hopeless I knew my duty was to get away and get help.' He stood up and began pacing backwards and forwards. Quintus watched him with narrowed eyes.

'You lost this treasure?'

Servius nodded miserably. 'I've got to get it back. I need your help.'

Quintus' voice was as smooth as cream. 'I don't quite follow, Centurion. I have no army units under my command. We are hard put to it to maintain the defences of ...'

Servius cut him short. This was the difficult bit. 'He's no fool. When he saw I'd got away he put his cavalry out to find me. He guessed I'd head for Calleva. Like a soft-headed idiot I took two wounded men with me when we broke from the ambush. They slowed me down and were so weak from loss of blood that I had to leave them by the road. I can see now how stupid that was. His cutthroats will have found them and they'll know by now that I'm in the city. My guess is he'll follow me here, bold as brass, to finish me off. My five loyal legionaries and myself are the only people alive who know the truth. Silence us and no one will ever know what happened to the treasure.'

Quintus was silent. What a story. Could it be true? Why not? The Centurion looked anxious enough. The anguish in Servius' eyes was indeed not entirely false since the success of his scheme depended on the Magistrate swallowing his story. Even to himself it sounded unlikely despite being in many respects true.

'Go on.'

'I may be wrong, of course. It would take a cool brain and a strong nerve to try it. I may be over-estimating him. But remember, he's got his wounded with him and he'll want shelter and help for them. If he does try it, you must be ready for him.'

'And how do you suggest I do this?'

'I've had plenty of time to think about it.' Servius laughed, a short, bitter laugh. 'Play him at his own game. Bluff him. Let him in. Billet his men in small numbers around the city. Lull his suspicions and when he's off guard arrest him and his men with your civil guards.'

'Y-e-e-s.' Quintus sat absolutely still, his face blank.

'Damn this bastard.' Servius swore to himself. 'What in hades name is he thinking?' He decided to raise the tone of his appeal. 'Can you imagine the dishonour of what's happened? Roman soldiers have turned on themselves in lust and greed.'

Quintus nodded. That, at least, did not surprise him. He had never thought anything of the military other than that they were a greedy, brutal and rapacious lot, capable of murdering their own mothers if it suited them.

Encouraged by Quintus' nod, Servius went on: 'In the name of Rome, I ask your help. This money is desperately needed to push the barbarians back into the sea. I must get to Londinium. I must exonerate my name and see just vengeance on these traitors. Rome demands it.' Unused to voicing such stirring sentiment he paused, wondering what emotion he could attribute to the Emperor other than the obvious one of wanting the treasure in his own voracious hands.

Quintus held up a hand. 'I understand, Centurion. You and your men would like lodging in the city for a few days until we see whether these renegades do indeed try to follow you in. Presumably if they don't turn up within that time you'll carry on to Londinium yourself to enlist the help of regular troops?'

'Of course. It's only a chance that they'll come here, but naturally I must take it if I can.'

Quintus summoned his secretary. 'The Centurion here has become detached from his unit following some fighting towards the west. He is naturally most anxious to rejoin it. I want an immediate report if any other army unit is seen or seeks admission to the city. They may possibly have some wagons with them. - Oh, and keep this strictly confidential. We don't want to spread alarm through the populace that the barbarians are on the rampage again.'

The man bowed and left.

'The Imperial Posting house at the south gate is at your service, Centurion. It has been empty over the winter, though I have, of course, kept it ready at a moment's notice for any Imperial visitor.'

Servius frowned. 'D'you think it would be wise for us to billet there? It'd spread the news through the city like wildfire.' He sat for a moment, concentrating fiercely. He looked up, his face eager. 'No, by the gods, I have it. Billet us out quietly in the town. If Caius Martius comes let him go to the posting house. Once he's inside you'll have him bottled up where you want him.' He started to pace up and down, shaking his fists in front of his chest. 'That's right, Sir. That's the answer. Please Mithras, let them come and let Rome be avenged. They must all die. Crucifixion would be too good for them.'

Quintus held up his hand again. 'I take your point, Centurion. Let us arrange for rooms to be made available to you in the town. I know of a suitable place which I occasionally have cause to use. The proprietor is a most confidential and trustworthy citizen. Then we'll see what happens.'

'Thank you, sir. Rome will not forget your action.' Servius kept his face impassive as he fitted his helmet over his fair hair and saluted smartly, but the vulpine grin which took control of his features as he walked out so terrified two clerks that they cowered before him.

Quintus sat on for a long while, deep in thought. This curious story worried him. He had no desire to become embroiled in army affairs of which this was demonstrably one. On the other hand, if the story was true, there could be great honour and advancement in restoring this treasure to the officer commanding the army in Britannia. There might also be a lot of unpleasantness should he refuse to help. Then there was the Centurion's interesting assertion that only he and his five men knew the whereabouts and full story of the treasure, apart, of course, from the traitors who were at present in possession of it. If, indeed, the story was true. It hardly seemed credible that this traitor – this Caius Martius and his men –would really risk coming into the city. Surely they would divide the spoil and scatter.

And yet ... sometimes the truth is incredible. If the Centurion thought the possibility existed, then maybe it did. Or maybe not. Why should a desperate criminal gang – because that's what it must in effect be – come into the city?

Quintus found himself hoping that nothing would happen and that the Centurion would go in a few days to seek help from his own kind. But, against this, it was not every day that large sums of money lost their rightful owner. He wiped his hands down his tunic. The palms were sweating and his stomach felt taut. If indeed the Centurion was to be believed. There was a wild, desperate look about him, like a hungry wolf. A dangerous man: a hard case. A deeply unpleasant man. But perhaps his life would be of little consequence if he really had lost this treasure. Perhaps all his wild talk of honour merely hid a natural reluctance to fall on his sword, since that would possibly be the least troublesome answer to his problems.

'No,' Quintus said aloud. 'Let us wait and see.' Without a doubt he was doing the right thing: keeping all options open. Without final commitment he had given the Centurion full support. He sighed and stood up. He brushed the folds of his tunic into place and wondered whether he would be able to concentrate on the mundane details of sanitation and water supplies while possibilities, however remote, however unlikely, of diverting the treasure to his own possession, were on his mind.

They came to Calleva by the West Gate. The countryside was heavily wooded and it was with relief that Aulus and his two companions came out of the trees and trotted through the fields and farmlands surrounding the city. He was surprised at the size of the place. The solid West Gate reared up above them, topped by crenelated battlements. A wide carriageway passed through it while on either side, massive walls stretched away for hundreds of yards.

'It must be as big as Corinium' he thought as they came close and he saw the helmeted guards on the battlements. 'I never thought I'd be so pleased to see a town.'

The adventure had turned sour. He was thoroughly relieved to reach this sanctuary. The deaths of Valerius and his troopers and of Baldur and Gratian had thrown him into a guilt racked gloom. He could not look at Lucian's grief-stricken face, though the boy did not seem to blame him - rather the opposite, for he had hardly left Aulus' side since it happened – but the sight of him was like the personification of his conscience. Even the battle at Etruria and the burning of the labour lines had not affected him like the death of his comrades. It had been a shattering nightmare that had left him silent and withdrawn.

He longed to see Flavia, for physical contact with her, to talk and explain everything. Nagging fear gnawed at him that Corinium might be besieged and fall to the barbarians or that she might stupidly decide to go back to Etruria and fall into their hands. Constantly he wondered why he had let Caius talk him into this business and whether he had betrayed Flavia and his people by leaving. Repeatedly he contemplated telling Caius that he had gone far enough and must now go back. Sullenly, he knew that he could not conceivably do that.

He felt bewildered by Caius' veterans. They seemed unmoved by the loss of so many of their comrades. Caius and Marcus behaved as though nothing had happened, Caius dour and stern as always and Marcus bright and cheerful; both apparently oblivious to their losses and the danger they now faced.

Hourly Aulus had expected some sort of attack from the Scots. Some must have got away, just as they had at Etruria. If they were still around they must have seen how weakened Caius had been. What had they to lose from a sudden rush in the night? And what about Servius and his men? Caius had dismissed the possibility of an attack by them with a savage shake of his head: 'That pack of dogs? Let them try it. Nothing would give me greater pleasure than to take that traitor to Londinium spread-eagled round a waggon wheel.'

They had stayed at the scene of the fight only long enough to bury their dead. The Scots they left for the crows. In the morning five of the wounded were staring glassy eyed at the sky. When they had buried them they loaded the others with rough gentleness into the wagons and moved out.

It had rained in the night, enough to make the grass slippery. The wagons took four hours of sweating and cursing struggle to pull up out of the stream and through the woodland back onto the road. Exhausted, the little column had marched only ten miles in the day and had had to camp for a second nerve-racking night in the wooded country through which they were now passing.

Never had city walls looked so inviting. For the first time in two days a flicker of a smile cheered Aulus as he hailed the guard on the gate towers.

To his surprise the sentries seemed almost to be expecting him. Aulus supposed vaguely that it must be because they had been visible for some time as they came along the road.

The gates were swung open immediately. An officer came clattering down from the battlements to greet them. Aggressively, he said: 'All military are ordered to report immediately to the Chief Magistrate on arrival.'

'All right. Where?' A good idea.

'Is this all there are of you?' The officer seemed surprised. He looked at Aulus suspiciously. 'Well, go on. Can't stand here all day. You! Escort the troopers to the Basilica.'

The streets were as crowded as Corinium's. The same pathetic lost chaff of humanity stood white-faced and empty-eyed as they passed. Tents and hovels overflowed across once empty spaces that must only recently have been paddocks or gardens. There seemed to be less stone built houses than in Corinium but everywhere the city was cluttered with the makeshift shelters of the refugees. In front of them the towering bulk of the Basilica dominated the city. Their guide pushed purposefully through the crowds towards it.

'The gods help them,' Aulus thought as the people fell back, apathetically clearing a path. 'They'd have died outside, and they'll die inside just as surely if plague breaks out.'

He was taken straight to a room in the Basilica where a large, fleshy man in a flowing toga was dictating to a clerk. Aulus stood for a minute, half listening, surprised at the pomposity of the language, irritated by the man's rudeness in ignoring him.

'Sir, if I may interrupt.' The man looked up. His eyes were hostile. For a moment they stared at each other then the man waved the clerk away. He looked Aulus up and down. Finally he said 'Ah!' with the same purposeful innuendo as the guard officer.

Aulus' irritation rose. 'I am the advance guard for a column heading for Londinium.' He spoke aggressively. 'Chief Centurion Caius Martius of the Northern Field Army is commanding. We ran into trouble with a warband of Scots just this side of the downs. We've got ten wounded with us.'

Again, Quintus said 'Ah'. This time, there was a hint of satisfaction in his voice.

Aulus ploughed on: 'The Chief Centurion requests the use of the city's facilities. He understands there is an Imperial posting house here.'

Quintus nodded. He was puzzled. The soldier before him did not look like a hardened deserter. His face was tired, strained and angry but it was basically open and honest. It certainly showed no trace of guilt or villainy. But on the other hand the man did not talk like a legionary. His speech was educated and correct, despite the plain chain mail armour that he wore. What was more, he was talking as if to an equal.

'Is it not normal for legionaries to salute the Civil Administration?'

The soldier looked surprised, then faintly amused. Quintus' eyes narrowed. A surge of excitement set the pulse hammering in his throat. 'Servius Cenric is right then,' he thought. 'This man is an imposter.'

Aulus eased his helmet with one hand and scratched his hair with the other. 'I'm not a legionary. I'm not really a soldier – just a temporary one. I'm a landowner and farmer. I live just this side of Corinium.'

Quintus frowned. Surely no desperado would be as naïve as this? 'Please explain yourself.'

'Look. I'd be delighted to explain some other time, but it's a long story and I don't know that it would make much sense to you. The column will be here any time now and some of the men are badly hurt.' He thought to himself: 'What in hades name does it matter to this fat idiot who I am?'

Quintus picked up the wine jug and a goblet. He filled it slowly, pointedly omitting to offer a cup to Aulus. He was thinking: 'This man's got a nerve. He admits he's not a soldier and he's challenging me not to ask questions. Who on earth is he? Who are these people? What on earth is their game, this man and that Centurion. I don't like this business at all.' He forced himself to laugh lightly. 'Very well. There'll be other opportunities, no doubt. You want to bring your column in? Good. Bring them here first, will you. I must meet your commanding officer while I make the necessary arrangements for your stay. I shall, of course, be pleased to put the posting house at your disposal.'

And as the door closed behind Aulus he added venomously: 'And if you are the impostor the Centurion says you are I shall be pleased to arrange your execution. It will be painful, I can assure you.'

Aulus met the column at the gate. He and Caius went ahead to the Basilica. Caius saluted Quintus. 'Caius Martius, Chief Centurion of the Northern Field Army, on special Imperial duty to Londinium.'

Quintus inclined his head. 'I gather you had some trouble with a Scots warband? My condolences. It's the first I've heard of a warband in these parts this year. Certainly no reports have reached us.' The Centurion's closed, grim face did not alter one muscle. The hard eyes continued to outstare him. Quintus dropped his eyes.

'Maybe you haven't. This warband followed us across the Downs. I'd advise you to be ready for them. With the spring they'll be on the move again and there's nothing that I know of to stop them going wherever they like. Is the posting house empty?'

'Yes. May I ask you the nature of your business? It is some time since I last heard of the Field Army and naturally in times like this one likes to know what is going on. This fellow here, for instance, informs me that he is not, in fact, a soldier at all.'

'That's none of your business, and neither is my mission.'

'I see. And have you any more – ah – outsiders like this man?'

'This man, as you describe him, is in command of my scouts. Now, if you please, I've got ten wounded men in my wagons. I'll thank you, Sir' – he emphasised the word pointedly – 'to guide us to the posting house.'

Before the stare of those uncompromising eyes Quintus temporarily surrendered. He hid his fury in a show of importance as he swept through the Basilica to inspect the waiting wagons. It was always like this with the military. Frustration boiled in him at the Centurion's lack of deference.

The wagons were drawn up in the street outside the Basilica. The legionaries were posted round them with their javelins in their hands, keeping the curious bystanders at their distance with good natured firmness. On Caius' appearance a tall, useful looking officer called them to attention, and they moved smartly to obey.

Quintus frowned. These did not look like deserters. He had not risen to be Chief Magistrate without mastering the arts of probing and exploiting the human weaknesses and guilts of those around him. He sensed no such secrets here. He walked slowly round the wagons. The men were mud stained and the black discolouration on their tunics and breeches could only be blood. Three or four of them had fresh looking, angry cuts on arms and faces, but this, together with the riderless horses tied to the back wagon only confirmed their story of a battle. He peered under the canvas of one of the wagons. White, bearded faces, exhausted and pain racked, looked briefly back at him with dull eyes.

Perplexed, Quintus watched as they set off down the street to the Imperial Posting house near the South Gate. The mounted troopers rode ahead and behind to clear and keep a path and the legionaries marched close beside the wagons. It was inconceivable that such a company of men would be such consummately good actors. He sent for a junior official.

'I want those soldiers watched closely and discreetly. I want all their movements and actions reported to me immediately.' The official looked mildly surprised. 'These are difficult and uncertain times,' he explained. 'This city is my responsibility and its security is in the hands of the civilian administration. A regular army unit could quickly cause friction and bad feeling by its presence.'

Caius had no intention of causing friction. He grunted with satisfaction at the sight of the posting house. Built round three sides of a square it had a good sized central courtyard closed on the fourth side by a high stone wall with stout gates. In the outer stable yard was a respectably sized bath house which reminded Aulus, perhaps alone of the whole party, that his hair was beginning to itch and he stank of sweat.

The place was empty except for the caretaker and his wife and family. He was a grey haired veteran who, after twenty five years' service, had achieved the rank of Tesserarius and had opted for this pleasant caretaking job as an alternative to taking up a small plot of land. Life had been very quiet over the winter, with no visitors. He apologised profusely that there was almost no food to be had.

'What with all them refugees and that, the authorities say they haven't had any spare to keep us stocked up. Suppose that's been right enough – there's been no one here to eat it anyway.' The old man grinned, displaying empty gums. He was delighted to see and be among soldiers again. It reminded him happily of old days and good companions. He bustled busily about, scolding his wife to hurry and light the fires and sweep out the winter's dust.

Chapter X11.

Behind the impassive mask of his features Caius studied Aulus. There was no doubt that the impact of his well-timed charge had saved all their lives. There was also little doubt that it had been more by good luck than judgement. He could hardly expect twenty years' battle experience from a recruit.

But Aulus had taken the deaths of his men badly. His uncertain status as a volunteer officer did not help. It put him apart from normal army discipline. It had been so many years since Caius had ceased to be moved by violent death that he had genuinely forgotten how these things can affect an undisciplined man. He reflected impatiently that he had seen shock on a recruit's face after his first battle, and horror, but the iron framework of discipline and punishment kept such weaknesses firmly under control.

The worst of it was that Aulus had let his personal feelings cloud his military judgement. Unnerved by the killing he had let it show that he was nervous about another attack. Of course he was – everyone was – they had no real idea of how many Scots or Saxons or indeed renegade soldiers might be gathering against them. Caius himself had lived every moment of the past two days in dread of a sudden rush from the trees surrounding them, or a frantic call to arms in the darkness. All too clearly he could picture a hopeless resistance and a back to back ring of desperate defenders falling as exhaustion defeated them and their shields slipped or swords parried too weakly.

'But you can't show it,' he thought savagely. 'You can't let the men see you're worried.' He adjusted his sword belt minutely. 'It's time I told that young man a thing or two about life.'

Equally, Aulus was concerned about Caius. 'Inhuman bastard,' he thought. 'You've forgotten that men have feelings.' He found himself hating that hard face. In his imagination it seemed to be made of the same steel as the helmet that framed it. Mixed with his resentment he nursed self-pity and injured righteousness that his humanity for his comrades had cut him off from Caius' respect. The Centurion had treated him with a cold contempt since the battle.

He gazed miserably round the courtyard. Marcus was supervising the unloading of the wagons. Javelins, bent on impact in the recent fight, were being piled ready to straighten the soft metal shaft behind their heads. The sharpened stakes were being sorted, ready for their points to be trimmed. The last of the soldiers' kit was being carried away and the stack of spare weapons was being taken for cleaning and oiling. Marcus' step was springy, his back straight, and he joked with the men as they worked.

'Why in hades name can't I be like that?' Aulus thought morosely. Consciously he drew back his shoulders and jerked his head up. 'Damn you, Marcus, I'm as good a man as you.' He strode angrily through the gateway to the outer stable yard. The troopers and drivers were busy with the horses. They had them hitched outside the timber buildings and were brushing them down. Dust enveloped them as they swung the brushes in long sweeping strokes under the horses' bellies. The seed of an idea struck him. He stopped, staring unseeing at the troopers. There was a gust of laughter among them at some unheard joke. He spun on his heel. 'By the gods, yes' he said aloud. He ran back to the inner courtyard and onto the portico just at the moment that Caius was leaving to find him.

'Caius!' he shouted. The Chief Centurion appeared immediately, frowning.

'Well?'

'I've got an idea.' Aulus stopped close in front of him. Caius bit back the attack that was on his lips. The truculence had gone from Aulus' face. It still looked strained and tired, but his eyes were alive again and he was smiling.

'I'll go on to Londinium. It all fits. With the wounded and the few men we've got left, you're bound to stay here for a while. Let me take some of the troopers and make a dash to Londinium. I can get men to come back with me and escort us in. What d'you say?'

Caius turned to stare out across the courtyard. Anger still burned in him and with it a sudden exasperation at himself that he had not already thought of this obvious solution. He supposed that it must have been because he had lost confidence in Aulus. But coupled with these emotions was a sudden lifting of his heart, as though the burden of his responsibility had somehow lightened. He watched the soldiers, armour discarded, with buckets and brushes, now clambering aboard the wagons to clean them inside and out. So few were left. How many more good soldiers must be sacrificed?

'Good thinking, lad. Should have thought of it myself.' A quick smile lit his face and was gone, but the unexpected pleasure of it warmed Aulus' heart like a bright shaft of sunlight.

'I could go tonight.'

'Yes.' A sudden image of Flavia's face rose in Caius' mind. She had trusted him to look after Aulus. He was under no illusions about the dangers Aulus would ride into. The country to the east of Calleva might well be inundated with Saxon warbands. The chances of running into one were rising daily as the winter drew out. Would Aulus have the resourcefulness to get clear? He visualised the remaining troopers. Aulus would need the best. Equally, he must keep good men with him in case Aulus did not get through. But he would have to take the risk. 'Take Faber and Naso with you,' he said. 'And you'd better have Lucian as well.' To himself he added: 'At least he'll die for you.'

Together, they walked towards the stable yard.

'Londinium is always heavily garrisoned. Go straight to their commanding officer. Tell him the full story. He should have some cavalry under his command or at least know where to get hold of some. Impress on him the absolute necessity for an escort of cavalry.' They went through the courtyard gateway. 'Detail the men now, then get some rest. Leave after dark and ride all night. Hide up by day and, above all, get out of the way of trouble. You should be there in two nights. I'll give you a week to get back here. Then we'll move. Come what may.' And to himself he added: 'Because if you're not back by then you'll likely be dead and I must take my chances with the few men I have left.'

Quintus Polybian Epaticus was red with rage. Roused from his bed, he listened to the apprehensive messenger with explosive fury. Four of the troopers had left the posting house well after dark and had demanded that the East Gate be opened to let them out. From what Quintus could gather their leader had been the well-spoken farmer from Corinium.

Quite properly the guard commander had refused. The gates were never opened after dark. There had been an argument. The farmer had threatened frightful penalties if the guards dared to stand in the way of the Imperial Army and its business.

Quintus shook with rage. Instead of sending for instructions the commander had let himself be bullied and cowed by the farmer's arrogant domineering attitude. He had compromised and taken them to the Northern Postern Gate and the soldiers had vanished into the night.

It was typical of the army! The now terrified messenger watched like a hypnotised rabbit as Quintus danced with passion. How dare they flout his authority. The messenger's flesh crawled. Wisely, he held his tongue and when Quintus demanded to see the commander of the Basilica police 'on the instant' he bolted out knocking over a chair in his haste to be gone.

Orders were issued for the guard commander of the East Gate to be arrested. Quintus mollified his anger with the promise that he would personally supervise the man's flogging the next day. The thought gave him a vicious pleasure. In slightly calmer mood he ordered the posting house caretaker to be brought to him in the morning and retired back to bed.

The sight of the slave girl warmly curled up under the covers brought the anger irrationally back to flashpoint. He pulled her roughly out. A dozen satisfying full bodied blows to her naked buttocks made her dance and squeal with pain. A well aimed kick at her stinging backside sent her flying from the room.

He felt better. Perhaps he should have treated himself to a dozen more. Or bent her over for other purposes. Her quivering reddened bottom was pleasantly titillating. He opened the door and shouted 'Come back here!' The portico was dark and still. She must have bolted. He imagined her hopping along, hands clasping her smarting hide. He chuckled. There would be other times. He slammed the door shut. A pity, though. Her bottom would have felt deliciously hot. And he always loved it when they squirmed. He flung his head onto the pillows and pulled up the covers.

Quintus had completely recovered his composure when the greybeard was brought to him in the Basilica the next morning. Dressed in freshly laundered robes he looked every inch the senior Magistrate. He ignored the man for several minutes, busying himself with a scroll, until the old soldier began to shuffle and cough, scratching his head and running his hands up and down the sides of his tunic.

Quintus put the scroll down and stared at the man. He had decided to be magisterial and severe, but changed his mind, intuition telling him that he would gain more by taking a fatherly line.

'Well, caretaker, you know who I am? – The old man nodded – 'I am the city's senior Magistrate. I have sent for you because, for the good of the city, it is necessary that I should know everything that is going on. Four troopers left Calleva last night - a most dangerous precedent, involving opening the gates in the hours of darkness – strictly, as you know, against all regulations. Now, these men will have talked amongst themselves and no doubt they will have mentioned their destination – where they are going, that is.'

He paused expectantly. The man looked thoroughly miserable. 'I'm not a spy, Sir.'

'No, no, of course not.' Quintus looked suitably shocked at the idea. 'I wouldn't dream of asking you to spy. You are, after all, an old soldier yourself. The idea would be unthinkable.'

The old man did not entirely understand the flowery longwinded Latin that Quintus spoke but the charming smile and the dismay on the Magistrate's face at the suggestion of spying combined to set him at ease. Besides, there could be no harm in telling the gentleman such a straightforward and obvious bit of information.

'Gone to Londinium they have, Sir. To get help from the garrison there.'

'Londinium? To get help?'

'That's right, Sir. They'll be back within the week with a squadron of cavalry.'

'Really?' This was amazing news. 'Are you sure? Why should they want a squadron of cavalry?'

'Escort, Sir, of course.' – as though it was the most natural and obvious thing in the world.

'Why should they need an escort?'

'Ah, you've got me there, Sir. Maybe to help with all them wounded.'

'Maybe. Tell me. Do you notice anything – ah – unusual about these soldiers?'

'Yes, Sir.'

'Ah.' Quintus sat forward. 'You can tell me.'

'They're good, Sir, the best I've seen for many a year. Almost as good as my own unit. Saxon Shore Garrison we was, Sir, back in...'

Quintus cut him short with a raised hand. He smiled indulgently. 'Quite. Another time, maybe.'

He dismissed the caretaker with a kindly smile and a fatherly warning not to repeat this conversation with anyone, least of all the soldiers themselves. 'It would never do for them to feel that the civil authorities disapprove of their actions. You understand me?'

The old man left, grinning toothlessly, feeling important at this high ranking confidence, relieved that nothing unpleasant had been demanded of him.

Once again, Quintus sat frowning. There was only one explanation that could possibly make sense. He looked up as a secretary knocked discreetly and announced that the centurion Servius Cenric was outside, requesting an audience.

'Show him in.'

Servius had discarded his uniform for the anonymity of civilian clothes, bought, had Quintus but known it, on a promissory note written in the name of the Magistrate. Servius' hair had been cut, he had bathed, he looked urbane and civilized. Without introduction he said: 'They're here then?' He settled himself in a chair.

'They are indeed. You have seen them?'

'Yes, I watched them come in. Twenty four or five of them, I reckon, including the ringleader. You met him? Impressive, isn't he? His nerve beats anything. You've given no hint that you know who they are?'

'I know who they are. The question is, who are you?'

'What d'you mean?'

'Four troopers left the city last night. They are riding to Londinium for reinforcements from the garrison there.' Quintus appeared to be studying his fingernails. 'Hardly the move of deserters, I think you'll agree.'

Servius was silent. As though rubbing his leg he ran his hand over his thigh. He was reassured by the feel of the dagger strapped there under his tunic.

'What makes you think they've gone to Londinium?' His tone was scornful. 'I expect they've left some of their friends outside and these renegades have gone to contact them. What are you trying to say?' If the worst came to the worst he could have the dagger into the fat politician's guts within seconds, before the man could raise the alarm.

Quintus was convinced now. He was watching Servius' eyes. He had seen the alarm that had briefly flared and then seen the merciless killer glare of the wild leopard. Aware, and frightened that he could be close to death, he smiled reassuringly.

'I think we should understand each other, Centurion. I am aware that Chief Centurion Caius Martius is not a deserter and that he and his men are more or less what they purport to be. I assume that you are also a genuine

196

soldier, but that you have reversed the roles – you, in fact, are the renegade – hear me out' he added quickly as Servius tensed in his chair. 'It crosses my mind that we could be of some mutual benefit to each other.'

Servius sat still. Quintus involuntarily wiped the sweat from his palms on his tunic. The gesture was not lost on Servius. It gave him a sadistic stab of pleasure.

Quintus went on. 'Since you do not trouble to deny my accusation I presume that I am correct?' No reaction. 'Come, come, Centurion, it is essential that we understand one another.'

The merciless blue eyes held his steadily. There was now a hint of amusement in them.

'You are thinking that you could kill me with the dagger hidden about your person and be out of Calleva before the alarm is raised?' Quintus laughed a fat little chuckle that he was very far from feeling. 'At least do me the courtesy of not underestimating me. My guards are not regular soldiers I grant you but I fancy the men waiting next door at this moment would effectively overpower you and prevent your escape. Your colleagues are, of course, under observation and their arrest and execution would follow as a speedy matter of course.

'I hold the cards, Centurion. I control this city. One call from me and you are a dead man.' He watched Servius closely. Used to violence, this was the sort of thing Servius would expect to hear. He would have acted like this himself in similar circumstances. To Quintus' enormous relief Servius relaxed and sat back in his chair with an easy laugh.

'Very well, Magistrate. What are you proposing?'

'I assume we may take it that the substance of your story is correct in that the Chief Centurion is in fact escorting treasure chests to Londinium?'

Servius nodded.

'Good. I have no doubt that the troubles affecting Britannia will shortly be resolved. With the coming of spring the Emperor will send sufficient reinforcements to restore order. The question will then be asked: what happened to the treasure of the Northern Field Army? It will be known that it headed south under the Chief Centurion's command. It will be remembered that soldiers came here with three heavily laden wagons; the timing does not appear to fit, but I have no doubt it will be correctly assumed that the column ran into trouble and had to go to ground somewhere over the winter. If this farmer and his men'- he noticed the sudden raising of Servius' eyebrows – 'You know this man then?'

'I've met him.' Servius smiled faintly.

'Yes, well, as I say, if he and his men get through to Londinium the facts will be corroborated and troops will in all probability be sent to escort the wagons.' He paused and studied his fingernails once more. He did not look at Servius. 'If, in the meantime, the wagons have left again, under the Centurion's escort as they arrived, the matter passes out of my hands. If they were never seen again it would of course be unfortunate and a grave loss, but a loss which indubitably would be attributed to the Saxons or Scots or whoever. There would be no opprobrium or blame.'

Servius said quietly: 'Go on.'

'You understand me so far, Centurion? One soldier after all looks much like another. There is a slight discrepancy in numbers to be accounted for. How many men have they got? Twenty something? Less four: you have five.' He pursed his lips and scratched the back of his neck thoughtfully. He sighed. 'Regrettably, the city is full of refugees and desperate men. A brawl, perhaps, or a fire at the posting house? It would, indeed, provide the excuse for your early departure.'

Servius smiled. This sort of thinking had his full approval. 'In return for which I presume you want a share of what's in the wagons.'

Quintus shrugged his shoulders. 'Correct, Centurion. There is considerable risk to myself in carrying out this deception. There is also the risk that you or one of your men may be captured and tortured. I would then have some very awkward explaining to do. Two thirds would be appropriate, I think.'

For a moment the enormity of this demand failed to sink in. Then Servius leapt to his feet.

'You treacherous, thieving bastard. That's my treasure.'

'Please yourself. Consider the alternatives, deserter. And sit down. I dislike you standing over me.'

Servius crossed to the wine jug and poured himself a goblet. 'A quarter,' he said.

'Consider your position once you are outside the gates. There are six of you in all. You would be well advised to scatter. I suspect there is far more in any one of those wagons than six men can carry.'

Servius drank the goblet in silence. Since he had no intention of sharing the contents of the wagons with anyone there was a certain logic in the Magistrate's argument. There were also two further possibilities. Quintus would be at a distinct disadvantage when the time came to divide the contents of the chests, as he would hardly wish anyone else to be present. If, as was likely, he thought his way round that one there was always the possibility of blackmail at some future date. But the villainy of it! In sudden rage Servius threw the goblet across the room.

'May the gods smite you, politician. May they damn you and curse you and yours for all eternity. Mithras, do you wonder why the world abhors a politician? Look at you. All the vices of the world rolled into one fat carcass.' Despite his anger Servius was careful to control his tirade to an approximation of the outpourings of an honest heart. Only the greed and duplicity of the Magistrate had saved him from arrest. If he overstepped the mark at this stage it might ruin everything.

There were, Quintus considered, two problems. The first was disposing of some twenty legionaries who, by all accounts, were extremely good soldiers who had survived a number of attacks in getting this far. The second was to prevent this wild eyed traitor from cheating him and to ensure that he did indeed get a sufficiently large portion of the treasure to warrant the risks he was about to take.

That, at least, should be possible. He would issue strict instructions that no military wagons leave the city unless he himself was there at the gate to authorise their departure. The bloody back of the erstwhile East Gate guard commander would ensure that this order would be rigidly obeyed. With a stirring of pleasure in his loins he remembered that the man's punishment had yet to be carried out. The wagons could be driven to his private house and his share unloaded quietly in the privacy of his courtyard. Only Servius would be allowed in with it. The other soldiers could be held under escort until he was ready for them to go. Two slaves would be enough to hide the boxes. Their lives might have to be a necessary expenditure for so great a return.

No, the first problem was the difficult one and highly dangerous. Under no circumstances must any breath of participation be attributable to him. He eyed Servius. The man was an animal but a resourceful and unscrupulous one. Obviously he must be responsible for this preliminary work and contingency plans made for his immediate silencing in the event of his failure.

'Please, Centurion.' He held up his hands. 'You have made your point. I am not a horse trader. I will agree to split the treasure fifty-fifty with you. You may take it or leave it as you wish. We are agreed? Good! Come back this afternoon. I will have a purse of coin here for you. The arrangements for the disposal of the soldiers will be in your hands. Hire your own men for this work. There are plenty of ruffians in the city at present for you to choose from. That farmer fellow can't possibly reach Londinium in under two days. If he does bring an escort back with him he's bound to be at least another three or four days. So you have perhaps a week in which to act. I think we should assume that he will succeed in getting back, even though with luck he will never be heard of again.'

Chapter XIII

The hiring of a gang of cutthroats gave Servius little trouble. In a tavern close to his lodging he had found a girl after his own heart. She was the daughter of some African auxiliary; Pedra was a dark skinned whore of statuesque appearance and bearing. She was tall and full hipped with breasts and buttocks that richly filled her apparel. Her face was beautiful with the beauty of the leopard and framed with long, thick black hair that fell about her shoulders. Like Servius, she enjoyed her pleasures spiced with violence. A vein of sadism made the infliction of pain as amusing to her as the masochism that enflamed her lust as the thong curled succulently round her body. She was old enough to have experienced and relished every dissipation, not so old yet that it showed in her features.

They recognised each other as kindred spirits the instant their eyes met. She had been sitting at a table in the candlelit taproom, the centre of a laughing knot of tough, unshaven ruffians. Abruptly, she broke off her conversation and pushed them aside. In the sudden silence she stood up and walked round the table to stand provocatively in front of Servius. Her feline eyes smiled their invitation.

Behind her there was a sudden protest.

'Hey Pedra, you're with us!'

'Whatcha playing at, Pedra? Come back 'ere.'

And then, more threateningly: 'Who the hell's this? Throw him out.'

'Yea, let's get 'im. 'e's no business 'ere.'

Pedra turned on them like a whiplash. 'Shut up, the lot of you! I do what I bloody like and if I want a change from you bastards that's my affair. Not yours.'

Behind her, Servius had not moved. He stood relaxed, smiling, his blue eyes gazing over her shoulder at the men. 'That's right, boys. You heard what the lady said.'

In the smoking candlelight they faced him for a moment, then, muttering, turned their backs and sat down again. Without a word Servius and Pedra left the taproom.

Now he unhesitatingly took his problem to her. 'I need some men.'

'How many?' There was no need to ask what sort of men.

'A score. Ones I can rely on to strike fast without any questions.'

'What are you paying?'

He laughed. 'Enough. There'll be a lot in it for you.'

'In gold?'

'Or silver maybe.'

She pouted, looking up at him from lowered eyes. He gripped her chin and raised her head. 'Can you find them, tigress?'

She laughed back at him. 'Of course I can.'

'Go to then, love.' He pulled her to him and as her stomach pressed against his he slapped her bottom and dug his fingernails into the full, round buttocks.

Within hours she had contacted a ferret-faced convict called Knifehand, leader of a gang of verminous gutter rats that plagued the city; young men who had come into Calleva as refugees with nothing and had nothing to lose. They met Knifehand that night in Pedra's lodging. Servius poured a trickle of coins into the man's hand as he explained what he wanted. Knifehand understood perfectly. His men would appear when Servius asked. No questions asked, they would do his bidding and vanish again into their ratholes when he had paid them. Knifehand's eyes glittered in the candlelight. For Servius was gambling: gambling on the experience of many years of army life.

The day after Aulus left Caius' men were cheerful and in good spirits, relieved to be in the safety of the posting house.

The second day they were restive.

The third day they were sullen and a fight broke out, stopped with bellowed anger by Marcus. He sought out Caius. 'The men need a break, Sir. If we've got to sit here for another three or four days they'd do better for a skinful of wine.'

Caius had already come to this conclusion himself. He nodded. 'Won't do them any harm. D'you want a night on the town?'

Marcus grinned. 'Wouldn't mind one, Sir.'

Caius gave a rare smile. 'Right, Optio. Town passes for yourself and eight men this evening. Draw lots for it. I'll have the hide of any man who gets into a fight or makes trouble. Any trouble and there'll be no passes tomorrow night. Clear?'

Caius smiled bleakly at the cheer from the men's quarters as Marcus relayed the order. The black mood lifted instantly. They set about polishing uniforms and weapons with ribald laughter and boasts for the night ahead.

Servius, watching from the anonymity of a refugee shelter, smiled also as the gate opened and the legionaries came out. He recognised Marcus, striding confidently behind them. He drew back and turned away. 'That's them Knifehand.' He looked back over his shoulder and jerked his chin towards the soldiers. 'It's tonight, then. Let them enjoy themselves a while. Wait for them to split up a bit and get a bellyful. No bungling. None of them's to get back.' He drew his forefinger across his throat with a quick chopping flick. 'Strip the bodies and hide the uniforms. When you're done get back to Pedra's like I told you. Got it?'

'I got it, boss.' Knifehand smiled, showing teeth pointed like a rodent's. Then he was gone, disappearing miraculously into the evening.

The streets had more or less emptied. The refugees had drifted back to the relative safety of their encampments and the warmth of their camp fires. The soldiers made for the centre of town. Their pay was solid and heavy in their purses. Eager and good-humoured they turned as a body into the first tavern they came to. Marcus shook his head as they called to him to join them. He strolled on towards the centre. He had his evening planned out. He passed the colonnaded forum and walked on until he found a well-lit, bustling tavern. He stood for a minute in the doorway, assessing it, taking in the curtained off passage at the back of the taproom, sizing up the girls who sat around the tables. He nodded to himself and went in. He signalled to one of the girls to join him.

'Hello, lass.'

'Hello, soldier.' She smiled easily at him, flattered perhaps that he had picked her out. She was about his own age, a simple peasant girl.

'Got any good wine?'

'He'll find some for the likes of you.' She indicated the apron-clad proprietor standing at the casks.

'Good lass. Get a couple of jars and come and join me.'

She was obviously pleased. 'Not every day we get an army officer here, love.' There was a gleam of cunning in her eye as she looked up at him. 'I'm good. You won't be sorry.'

She left him, swinging her hips jauntily as she crossed the room. The proprietor nodded as she spoke to him, looking across at Marcus speculatively. The girl vanished and reappeared a moment later with two wine jars clasped to her bosom and two pewter mugs.

'It's expensive, mind.' She smiled as she put them down in front of Marcus. 'Best he's got. Don't let many customers have it.' There was admiration in her voice and a calculating shrewdness.

'Forget the cost. Come and sit here beside me.'

The jars emptied, they went through the curtained doorway to her candlelit cubicle. The wine had done its work. Her eyes sparkled and she laughed as she loosened the clasp and let her dress slip to the floor.

They went back at last to the taproom. For the hour there was warmth between them and a tenderness.

'Get another jar, lass.' Marcus settled himself comfortably with his back to the wall, at peace with the world. 'We'll drink to each other and the next time I pass this way.'

Across the town the eight soldiers drank hard and fast. The winter's thirst demanded it. They moved on then, seeking the nearest brothel. There, they split up. Five of them decided to stay, the woman smell holding them like bulls to the cowherd. The other three, desire slaked, shouted their farewells and wandered on, looking for another tavern.

The streets were empty now. Knifehand attacked the three wine seekers first. Relaxed by the mixture of cheap liquor that they had drunk, their reflexes were too slow when the shadows in a dark alleyway moved. Their bodies were stripped naked and left for the dogs to sniff and lap the blood.

Knifehand's gang converged on the brothel. They were waiting when, for the third time, two of the legionaries went through its curtained doorway with new girls. In the dimness of the cubicles they were knocked unconscious as they concentrated on the bodies under them. Half naked, they were dragged from the couches, bundled from a back entrance and knifed in the darkness of the alleyway. In the cubicles Knifehand's lips were bright and wet as he stood over the horrified girls. He twisted the knife in his hand. It caught the candlelight and flashed dully.

'You ain't seen nuffing, my lovely ones.' The words were soft and caressing. 'Nor you ain't heard nuffing neither. Mute little sparrers, that's what you are, 'cos you knows what 'appens to songbirds as sings too loud.' He paused, letting the words sink in, holding the knife close to the candle, waving it gently to and fro. 'We wouldn't want no 'arm to come to sich lovely little creatures as you, now, would we?'

Fascinated, the two girls stared at the knife. One sobbed. She thrust her fingers into her mouth trying to stifle the sound. Knifehand laughed. 'You'll remember my face then, my lovelies. And at the same time you'll forget it, eh? That's my lovely girls. Now, we'll settle down nice and quiet, see. Not a word. Not a word.'

In the taproom the three remaining soldiers grew tired of waiting. 'They can't be at it still. Not for the third bloody time. Go and see what they're bloody doing.' One of the men got up with a grin and sauntered through to the dark cubicles. Unseen hands grabbed him and he was knifed immediately. His blood left a deeper river of blackness on the dark earth floor as he was dragged out. One of the girls screamed.

In the taproom the two soldiers came crashing to their feet, suddenly sober. All eyes turned to the curtained doorway. The buzz of conversation was cut off dead. In the silence that followed the soldiers drew sword and dagger. The rasp of steel was loud and menacing.

'Get lights!'

'No trouble, gents, if you please.' The hard-faced landlord came hurrying forward. 'We don't want no authorities in here. It's just one of the girls playing up a bit. Don't make no trouble.'

'Get lights.'

The landlord read the look in the soldiers' faces. He did not argue. He sent two of the girls hurrying for lanterns. He took them without a word, staring murderously at the soldiers, his face livid. With a jerk of his sword one of the legionaries indicated the doorway. The landlord went ahead, holding the lanterns above him one in each hand. Save for the dark, wet trail on the ground the cubicles were empty.

They backed into the candle-lit taproom. In their brief absence it had emptied. Only a frightened cluster of girls stood huddled together by the casks.

The soldiers were not articulate men. Their comrades had disappeared. Suddenly they were in danger. They did not waste time on questions that would not be answered. Caius must be told and fetched back here as soon as they could get him. They moved cautiously across the taproom, sword and dagger ready.

'Open the door.' One of the girls scurried across and threw it wide.

On the threshold they hesitated. The street seemed empty, the black mass of buildings on each side menacingly quiet. They stood for a moment, watching the shadows, waiting for their eyes to get accustomed to the dark.

'What's the quickest way back to the posting house?' The girl was still gripping the opened door, staring at the weapons. She did not answer, just looked dumbly at the speaker. He repeated the question over his shoulder to the landlord. The man came forward, lanterns still in his hands. He said: 'Right out of the door: third left and straight down past the Basilica. You can't miss it. Then keep going. And don't come back.' He exhaled in relief as the soldiers nodded to each other and went through the door at a run. He turned to the girls.

'Don't just stand there, you stupid sluts. Bolt the doors. There's work to be done.'

The soldiers ran in the middle of the street. There was enough light from moon and stars to throw the paving under their feet into relief against the black rectangles of the stonework joints. Shuttered windows and doorways were blacker squares in the dim light on walls and roofs.

They passed one crossing and an alleyway and turned left down a broader street. A late traveller was being trotted home in a litter, escorted by his jogging, torch-carrying slaves. Otherwise, the street was empty. They sheathed their daggers and ran on, boots ringing on the paving. They passed two of Calleva's gridiron blocks before one of them swore.

'We should've been at the Basilica by now. Where in hades is it?'

'That poxy bastard's sent us wrong. D'you think he meant that alleyway as a turning?'

'We're not bloody far enough over. We ought to go right here.' They chose a broad street and turned into it. At the far end of the block they stopped. The crossing was totally unfamiliar. They both swore and panted in consternation. They had expected to see the bulk of the Basilica looming up as a landmark and guide. The gutter rats following them pressed themselves into doorways as the soldiers stood peering into the night. Two armed and angry legionaries were a very different proposition to the unsuspecting victims they had dealt with so far.

'Buggered if I know which way to go.' One of the soldiers spat furiously. 'Perhaps that bastard was right and we just haven't got to the Basilica yet. Not as how it greatly matters. We only have to go on going that way'

– he pointed with his sword – and we'll end up somewhere handy to the posting house.'

'Yeah. Buggered if I like fucking about this bloody town in the bloody dark. Sooner we get the chief out the better.' They peered around in the faint moonlight. 'We'd best go back to that other bloody road.'

They turned and started back. Halfway along, hidden at the corner of a house, one of the assassins tensed and drew back his throwing arm. As the soldiers passed he hurled his cudgel. The heavy stick twirled through the air, struck one of the men behind his knee and sent him sprawling to the ground. The force of the fall knocked the sword flying from his hand. It slithered across the paving into the gutter in a flash of reflected light. His companion pulled up and turned back with a curse. In the instant that he stood still, looking down at his winded companion, Knifehand threw his weighted knife at the small pale target of the man's neck. The soldier crumpled, collapsing like a gashed wineskin. As the second man struggled to his knees, gasping for breath, reaching for his dagger, the cutthroats were on him. His cry was a single scream in the darkness.

Behind their shutters the citizens stirred and strained their ears but all they heard was the thudding of their own hearts.

Alone of the nine who had set out to enjoy their evening on the town, quick wits and a sixth sense warned Marcus of his danger. In the street outside the tavern the three assassins set to watch him grew cold and impatient. As the evening wore on they began to wonder whether the officer had left without them knowing. The warmth and light of the taproom beckoned. They decided to go in.

Marcus was talking to the girl, sitting close beside her, enjoying the female company. He watched the door open with detached interest and came instantly alert as the men shuffled in and peered around in the candlelight. Beside him, the girl started. He felt her body tense. One of the trio saw him and nudged his companions. They all looked in his direction, then quickly away and walked with too little concern to the casks.

'Who're those men? He spoke conversationally, without looking at her. She whispered 'Knifehand's gang.' Her voice was frightened.

'Who's he?'

'They're trouble, bad trouble. They shouldn't be here. They must be after someone. They're evil...' Her voice faltered and Marcus felt her body tremble beside him. His stomach was suddenly taut. He watched as, backs towards him, the trio ordered drinks from the girl at the casks. Her expression was nervous as she served them and shocked, as though their presence was alien. The men drank quickly, shoulders hunched and heads down. They spoke briefly as they set the cups down and laughed suddenly together. They tossed the girl a coin and turned away. At the door none of the three could resist a quick glance in his direction.

Marcus said: 'Quick, lass. Go see if that girl heard what those men were saying.'

She was back in a moment, her face ashen. She sat down beside him.

'Well?'

'One of them said; "Hurry it up, you army bastard. We can't wait all night," and they all laughed. They're waiting for someone.'

Without looking at her he said 'Why would they do that?'

'I don't know. I'm frightened. It's what they do. People hire them to get rid of people and things like that. They beat people up and kill them. It's bad trouble to see them. They don't come here. Someone's in trouble.'

'Yes,' he paused. 'Me.'

'You! Why?' She was shocked.

'I don't know but it's me right enough they're after.'

'Why? Why should they. What've you done?'

He did not answer. It made no more sense to him than to her. Perhaps his uniform had attracted them and the prospect of a full purse. The girl's distress was genuine though and he had seen their type too often to doubt the probability of what she said.

He asked her: 'Will you do something for me?'

She looked doubtful.

'Go with one of your friends and stand in the doorway as though you were getting a breath of fresh air. See if you can see those men outside.'

'You're sure it's you they're after?'

He nodded, and smiled at her. Her face relaxed, a mixture of relief and compassion. 'All right, then.'

He watched as she went, calling to a friend 'It's hot in here. Come and get a breath of air.' They opened the door and stood on the threshold, drawing in deep breaths of the night air, chatting and leaning against the doorpost. When she came back her cheeks were flushed with excitement. She said: 'I think there's one waiting in the doorway opposite. I can't see the others. They could be watching the back.'

'There's a back way out, then?'

'Um, past the rooms.'

'Show me, lass.'

She looked doubtful again. 'They're bad. They're killers.'

He stood up and smiled at her. 'So am I.' He put his arm round her. 'Come on.'

They went through the curtained doorway. She felt the tension in his body and as they passed her cubicle she stopped. 'Shall we? D'you want... ?' He chuckled, shook his head and squeezed her hand. She took him past the cubicles and through a second door. A passage led on ahead of them, doors opening off on either side.

'Keep hold of my hand. I'm putting the candle out.' They moved slowly down the corridor, feeling their way past the doors. She guided him round a corner, down a short leg of passage. 'The door's just ahead,' she said.

He groped past her and felt for the bolts. Behind him, she whispered 'It leads into the yard. Go straight across and you'll see the archway onto the street. Go straight down it as far as you can and you'll come to the posting house.'

Marcus nodded. He had remembered the route of his evening stroll and had visualized the town layout. The tavern stood on a corner, its main entrance in the street running at right angles.

'Thanks, sweetheart,' he said. 'Here.' He felt in his purse, took out several coins and put them into her hand. 'I don't know what's there but thanks again.'

She reached up in the darkness and kissed him. 'Come again, love. You're fun to have around. I'll stay and bolt the door after you. Good luck.'

Marcus drew his sword and slid the bolts back with his left hand. He inched the door open. After the blackness of the passage, the night was light and silvery. He stood silently watching the yard and the open curve of the archway leading to the street, trying to probe the shadows. Eventually he was rewarded. A figure materialised suddenly from the blackness beside the archway and stood looking into the street. Apparently satisfied that there was no one in sight it slipped through the opening and turning towards the front of the building, vanished.

Marcus slipped through the door and ran lightly across the yard. He pressed himself close to the wall at the spot where the figure had appeared. He looked around. Nothing stirred. He concentrated on the street opening, and waited. A figure materialised suddenly, darker than the night. It paused in the archway, looking up and down the street. As it turned to enter the yard Marcus stepped forward. He struck hard and fast, arm straight, the weight of his body behind the blade driving the weapon deep into the man's throat. With his left hand he caught the falling body round the waist as he twisted and jerked the sword clear. He pulled it into the yard and lowered it to the ground. He straightened up and stood listening. Still nothing moved. He knelt quickly on one leg and felt the body. As he had expected a long double-edged dagger was sheathed on the man's belt. He drew it and balanced it in his hand. It would serve as a secondary weapon if need be.

He stood up. Probably the second man was on the street corner, watching both front and back entrances, ready to signal up either of the two other watchers. Marcus took off his helmet. He tied it to his empty sword sling and slid it round into the small of his back. He drew his cloak round his armour, hunched his shoulders and bent his knees slightly, imitating the silhouette of the dead man. He moved into the archway and stood looking out, up and down the street, then slouched out towards the street corner, slinking beside the wall, furtive and shuffling.

A voice ahead of him in the darkness hissed: 'What'cher bloody doing?' A dozen paces ahead a shadow detached itself from the wall and faced him. He slunk towards it with a stage whispered, 'Ssshhh' and pointed back to the yard with his left hand. The figure came quickly towards him.

Three paces apart Marcus drew himself up and sprang forward. The man said 'What the ...' and Marcus was at him. He struck again for the throat and his body weight drove the blade home. The body crumpled with a whistle as the man's breath hissed from his severed windpipe. The sword jerked free and Marcus felt the blood hot and sticky on his hand. He dropped into a crouch and peered round the corner. He saw the third assassin immediately. Alerted by the noise, the man had started forward from the doorway in which he had been standing. The white circle of his face was turned towards the sound, a dark hole showing his open mouth and hanging jaw. He saw a glint of light from Marcus' breastplate. As his slow brain registered this unexpected sight the figure sprang from the ground and came flying towards him cloak billowing darkly behind him. The man turned to run, fear suddenly engulfing him, legs rubbery with panic. Marcus caught him before he had gone a dozen paces. His right arm swung from the shoulder in a wide circle and slammed into the man's neck. He pitched headlong into the gutter.

Marcus did not wait to check that he was dead. He began to run, light-footed and fast, towards the posting house.

Chapter XIV

Aulus smiled to himself. The expression on the guard commander's face as he led them to the postern gate had been a picture. The threats of Imperial retribution had obviously frightened him. They had passed the great black bulk of the amphitheatre and rounded the corner of the city's wall to meet the Londinium road. In the half moonlight it stretched away arrow straight in front of them. They set off along it at an easy jogging trot.

Illogically, Aulus felt cheerful. Surprised, he realised that he had not felt like this for weeks. He cast back in his mind: 'Since I don't know when,' he thought. 'Perhaps since Caius came. I suppose it's because I'm on the last leg of it all now. Londinium in two days, then back home – or Corinium maybe, and at last I'll take charge of my life again.' His heart warmed as he thought of Flavia. He pictured her asleep in her old childhood bedroom safe behind the Corinium walls and himself lying warm and close beside her. 'Here!' he thought suddenly, 'This won't do. If I'm not careful I'll end up staked out by the Saxons.' He pulled his mind back to the present and to the dimly lit road in front of him.

He trotted his little troop quietly along the verge. They made almost no sound. All the metalwork on bit and saddle had been carefully wrapped in strips of cloth. Apart from the creak of leather and the breathing of the horses they moved like shadows. As they had done with Valerius when they had been watching the

Scots they had dulled armour, helmets and equipment. Their movements gave no tell-tale gleam of light on metal to warn of their approach.

Around them, nothing stirred. Once, after an hour or so, they smelt woodsmoke and later a dog barked somewhere off into the night. They quickened their pace but the barking raised no alarm.

They stopped for a while in the middle of the night to ease the horses and to stretch their limbs but the cold of the night air soon bit into their tired bodies and they led the horses on for a while to get their circulation going and to keep warm. As they mounted again Aulus decided that he would repeat this tactic through the night. He rode for what he judged to be an hour then whispered the command to dismount. For a few minutes they stumbled over the tussocky grass of the verge. After that the effort seemed too great.

Despite the danger and the cold Aulus kept nodding off in the saddle. Repeatedly he had to snap his head upright as it fell forward onto his chest. Glancing round he saw that the others were in the same condition. Faber and Naso, like him, were fighting it, but Lucian was riding asleep, hands steadying him on the pommel of the saddle, body lolling and head on chest.

'The only consolation,' Aulus said it aloud in a sleep slurred murmur, 'is that everyone else must be asleep as well.' He peered up the road. 'It'll only be if we actually bump into anyone that we'll really be in trouble.'

The night became an eternity of cold and aching muscles. The horses plodded slowly, often stumbling so that their riders came briefly awake with a quick curse and grab for the reins. Fingers numb, legs frozen, Aulus fought to keep his eyes open and his brain alert. The road danced and floated in front of him, hazy and dreamlike in the dim light. The weight of his helmeted head seemed too great and the effort of keeping it erect too painful for his neck muscles. The creak of leather became a constant rhythm, like breathing, that lulled his brain, whispering "Go to sleep - Go to sleep - Go to sleep." The warm smell of horse and sweat and equipment filled his nostrils, contrasting sharply with the cold, clear smell of the night. Beside them, beyond the verge, the black bulk of trees and the grey veil of open country merged into a dream of endless, forgotten patterns as the road unfolded like an endless treadmill.

It was with dull surprise that Aulus noticed that he could see further ahead down the road and that they were passing a countryside of trees and scrub. The night had given way to a misty, indistinct and grey dawn. He had been more asleep than he had realised. His horse walked on slowly as he wondered where he was and what he was doing. Then he jerked guiltily awake. The imminence of danger in the growing light set his blood going. He pulled his horse's head up sharply. Lucian was riding beside him, slumped in the saddle. The boy's horse stopped thankfully as Aulus drew rein and the change in movement pitched him forward and awake. Behind them the two troopers' faces were dull and blank. Their horses stumbled half-abreast of Aulus before stopping.

Naso looked up, grey and unshaven. He shook his head, years of training automatically taking over.

'Time we got off the road, Sir.'

Beside him Faber's voice was slow with sleep. 'Too bloody right.'

They moved towards the scrub. It was mostly birch, with an undergrowth of bracken and brambles. It seemed to stretch away all round them. They walked on until they found a little valley running away down from the road. They dismounted and led the horses in amongst the trees. Aulus stayed back, making sure there were no hoofmarks to show their trail in the sandy soil. Then, satisfied, he hurried on after them. They moved slowly down the slope, brushing aside the branches and trampling down the dead undergrowth.

The valley opened out into a clearing. An underground stream must have run down the slope and the water now bubbled through and ran sparkling across the ground before disappearing into tangled bushes on the far side. The ground was boggy but sweet, green grass grew around the stream edges. The horses' ears flicked forward and they quickened their stride, suddenly desperate to drink.

The four men stood silently watching as the animals buried their muzzles in the bright water and sucked greedily for long minutes before raising their heads and letting the last mouthful spill back into the stream. Then, immediately, thirst forgotten, they put their heads down and started to tear at the grass.

'Glad someone's hungry,' Aulus said. 'I suppose we'd better eat something too.'

They held the animals as the tired men chewed their bread and meat and washed it down with water from the stream. Wearily they unsaddled and hobbled the horses. Aulus detailed the guard rota, taking first shift himself. He watched his companions wrap themselves in cloak and blanket, scoop hollows for their hips in sheltered, hidden spots under the trees and lie down and fall instantly asleep like dead men.

He pulled his cloak more tightly round his shoulders and sat down with his back to a tree, watching the horses pulling the grass. His eyes glazed. He fought to open them. 'Keep awake, idiot,' he said. 'I'd better keep walking around.' He thought about it. The effort of getting to his feet seemed enormous. Abruptly, he was asleep.

The cold and the cramp in his legs awoke him. Again, he wondered where he was and he looked stupidly around the clearing for several seconds before he remembered. Two of the horses stood nearby, heads down as they dozed on their feet, their hunger satisfied. The other two were out of sight. Aulus groaned. He struggled agonizingly to his feet. The sleeping horses raised their heads at the movement, eyes alarmed, ears back. He yawned, stretching his arms high above his head. 'Ugh,' he said. He was shivering with fatigue and cold and felt like death. He looked up at the sky. It was grey, a uniform grey that gave no hint of the sun's position. He sighed heavily and went to retrieve the two horses that had moved off with little hopping steps in search of sweeter grass. He removed the hobbles, led them back and rehobbled them. Then he went to wake Faber.

The trooper woke easily and sat up, rubbing his face. He, too, glanced up at the sky. He grinned. 'You've taken a long shift, Sir.'

Aulus grinned back. 'Yes. No harm done, I'm glad to say.'

Faber got to his feet. 'Nice, comfy spot, that.' He pointed to where he had been lying.

'Thanks.' Aulus stretched out. The ground was faintly warm under him. In a second he was asleep.

They slept through the day and woke cold and stiff as the evening came on. Aulus would not allow a fire and they stamped their feet and swung their arms to set the blood going and work out their cramp. They ate again, hungry after the first mouthfuls, enjoying the taste of the bread and meat, savouring the spring water as if it was wine.

They resaddled the horses and made their way back to the road. Aulus went on ahead, moving cautiously as he approached the edge of the trees. The road was as empty and the surrounding woodland as grey and dead as when they had turned off in the morning. He stood listening. Nothing stirred. 'Not even a bird,' he thought and waved his companions forward. They tightened their girths and mounted stiffly for the second night's ride.

At first they rode half asleep, tongues and teeth furred and rank behind clenched lips. But slowly the jogging rhythm of the horses brought them awake and eased the chill and stiffness from their muscles. They came alert, listening to the night, eyes probing the country around them. The half moon showed that the scrub woodland was thinning, giving way to open pasture and cultivated farmlands.

'We must be getting close to Pontes,' Aulus whispered over his shoulder. Caius had warned him of this settlement where the road crosses the great Thamesis river that is the main artery of Londinium's trade. It had been a nagging worry. 'Be careful,' Caius had said. 'The bridge is an ideal spot for an ambush.'

Suddenly they could smell it – a combination of wet, long dead wood ash and decay. They gathered their reins and walked the horses more slowly. Automatically, they checked their sword slings and loosened the swords in their scabbards. The night was very quiet. They caught the gagging stink of death: it wrinkled their nostrils and drowned their own familiar smells.

There was nothing much left of Pontes.

So far as they could judge it had once been a long, straggling township, ranged haphazardly beside the road. But someone – Saxons maybe - had razed it. They passed odd shapes in the dim moonlight - mounds of sodden wattle and daub and charred thatch, the skeletons of timber framed buildings and, as they moved closer to the river, the occasional jutting empty walls of gutted stone buildings. Nothing moved. The ruins in the gloomy light were ghostly and menacing. The four men rode close together, overawed, peering round, fear prickling at their shoulder blades.

Abruptly, they were at the bridge. As Caius had said, it was masonry built. There were huge squared blocks of stone set solidly at the start of its parapets. Miraculously, it seemed to have survived. The river flowed black on both sides below them but the bridge stretched unbroken as far as they could see. Aulus muttered a prayer of thanks to the river gods and to the Roman masons who had built it.

They stopped and sat bunched together, looking at the bridge. The silence around them was absolute, heightened by the quiet river noises, the click of the water as it ran, the swish as it parted at the bridge piers. Aulus willed his eyes to pierce the gloom but the double line of its parapets grew fainter as they stretched away and then became indistinguishable from the night. He looked down at the water. Its surface was highlighted by clouded silver darts of light. Somewhere out in midstream its deeper black mingled with the night. Try as he might, he could not see the farther bank.

He sat irresolute, thinking: 'Maybe it's ominous that the damned thing is still standing. Like a baited trap.' He shivered, imagining Saxon warriors crouching in the darkness at the other end, waiting for the horses to cross. Perhaps the Saxons were behind them as well, grinning in the darkness as they waited for the horsemen to pen themselves onto the narrow carriageway before springing forward to close the trap. Briefly, he wondered whether to cross it himself on foot to test the lure. The feel of his horse under him was too solid and comforting, a chance for escape where a man on foot had none. Should he send one of the men across? He dismissed the idea stillborn. But the longer he sat the more the darkness danced and wavered, the heavier the gloom and the closer the evil of the ruined settlement menaced their backs.

One of the horses tossed its head and pawed the roadway. The sudden noise was terrifying. He felt the sweat break out cold on his body. 'Keep your bloody horse quiet. Draw swords.' The metal grated and flashed dully in the moonlight. 'Line abreast. Come on.'

The bridge was just wide enough to take four horses. The troopers moved out to either side: knee to knee they walked the animals forward. Almost immediately they left the solid road, and their hooves rang hollowly on the paved causeway of the bridge.

Once committed, the fear was gone. Aulus felt the elation of action. His fingers tingled. The sword felt heavy and powerful in his hand. He revelled in the tension of his arms and body. The blood beat hard in his throat but his heart was high and light. He peered ahead, straining his ears for any sound from the further bank, isolating the ring of the hooves and the creak of leather. Beside him he smelt the acrid tang of sweat and fear as the troopers pressed close, buffeting knee to knee.

The gloom moved ahead of them, retreating at their advance. The world narrowed to the carriageway and the parapets and the silvered moving blackness of the river glimpsed below them. He looked back over his shoulder. The big cornerstones at the start of the bridge had disappeared. All around them was empty darkness and the gloom mockingly creeping in behind them as they rode. And then, faintly, he saw the twin cornerstones of the far bank, two blacker masses in the murk ahead. Five paces more and they were solid and square. The end of the bridge! Involuntarily he squeezed his knees into his horse's sides and quickened his pace, and then the hoof beats no longer rang hollow but thudded on firm ground.

The walls of a stone building rose up on his right, a new threat looming out of the night. The urge to set spurs to the horses and gallop from this haunted place was strong. 'Steady, lads.' He said. 'Keep it steady.'

'Halt there!' The voice cut like a thunderbolt out of the night, harsh and strident, urgent in its immediate command.

'Gods!' Aulus' heart leapt to his throat. His reaction was fury. Blood flooded red behind his eyes. He snarled, the deep growl of the hunting bear. His left arm jerked the horse's head. His sword arm straightened. He drove his boots hard into the horse's flanks.

The voice shouted again: 'Don't try it! You're surrounded. Move and you're dead.' The shout was in Latin – good Latin, well spoken, without an accent.

Aulus checked the bound of his horse, so that it reared and flung its head. 'Who are you?' he yelled. 'We're Roman soldiers.'

Silence. He stared about him. Men had risen silently on a hidden catwalk of the wall above them. Armour and helmets glinted, throwing the men's faces into black hostile voids. They stood poised, right arms above and behind their shoulders, the heads of their javelins catching the moonlight. There was movement on his left. He looked round. Shadowy figures were running to form rank beside and behind them, forming ranks with legs apart, bodies oblique to their targets, left arms held forward and right poised to throw the javelins they carried. The voice from in front of him shouted: 'Drop your swords. Dismount. Your leader come forward.'

They sat rigid, staring at the surrounding soldiers.

Aulus shouted: 'No. We're Romans.' He would not part with his sword. The solid metal in his hand was his only hope.

'I'll count to three. Then you're dead.' The voice was unhurried now, confident that the trap was sprung and the prey at its mercy.

'No. We're Romans.' The javelins would skewer them before they could move.

'One.'

'For the love of the gods, who are you?'

'Two.'

There was a pause. The voice came again, half impatient, half coaxing. 'Come on. Drop them. We're Romans.'

Aulus unclenched his fingers and jerked his wrist forward. His sword caught the light and clattered onto the paving. Immediately, his three companions followed suit. He swung his right leg over his horse's neck and slid to the ground. He pulled the reins over its head and handed them to Lucian. He glanced up at the boy. His face was very white, but his jaw was set. Aulus turned and walked forward, back erect and head held high.

Figures materialized in front of him, all with javelins in hand. A short, square figure stepped forward from amongst them. His sword was sheathed and his hands empty. His dark cloak was thrown back showing the moulded body armour of an officer.

They stared at each other.

'I'm riding to Londinium with an urgent request for an escort.'

There was a short bark of laughter. 'Aren't we all? Prove your identity.'

'Caius Martius, Chief Centurion of the mobile army of the North is commanding the detachment I'm with. I can't prove my identity other than that.'

The man grunted. 'Come over here.' He called over his shoulder. 'Bring a lantern.' The order was relayed into the darkness and a moment later a door opened in the wall and was framed by the warm yellow light of a lantern which bobbed from side to side as its carrier ran up.

The officer walked up to Aulus. 'Let's have a look at you.' He was a hard looking veteran with a pugnacious square face and jutting jaw. He surveyed Aulus in silence, then walked round him and back to stare up into his face. Aulus returned the stare. The man's voice was hard. 'Don't you know to stand to attention when an officer addresses you, soldier?'

'Oh, Hades, not again.' Aulus swore under his breath. 'I am not a legionary. My name is Aulus Aurelius. I joined Caius Martius at the end of last year when he got stranded on my land near Corinium. I am scouting for him as a Tribune, commanding what is left of his cavalry escort. We didn't have any officer's armour.'

The Centurion did not reply. He grunted again, signalled to the lantern carrier and walked forward to scrutinize Aulus' three companions. Aulus walked with him. The three troopers had dismounted. He felt a flash of pride as they sprang to attention, Lucian included, at their approach. The lantern ducked and rose as the Centurion inspected men and horses. Its mellow light played on the carefully bound metal work of the horses' bridles, took in the regulation saddles with their polished worn seats, and rose over the blackened armour of the troopers to hang motionless in front of their grimed faces.

Abruptly the Centurion bent and picked up Aulus' sword. 'Here,' he said briefly, handing it hilt forwards to Aulus.

'Thank you.' Aulus took it gratefully and sheathed it.

'Pick up your weapons.' Wide smiles showed as they bent quickly to retrieve their swords. They stiffened to attention again.

The Centurion nodded. 'Hum.' There seemed to be a hint of approval in the sound. 'Into the posting house with those horses.' He turned and snapped orders at his silently waiting men. The menacing javelins were lowered. He said: 'Come with me, let's hear what this is all about.'

He led the way through the doorway into the yard of the building. Behind him, the legionaries relaxed. Their voices were full of grim, soldiers' humour.

'You were lucky, mate. Another step and you'd 'ave been dead duck. What a way to die.' There was a loud chuckle with this remark.

'Thought the Field Army 'ad been cut up. Poor little buggers, they should 'ave joined us down 'ere. We'd 'ave showed 'em how to look after theirselves.'

'Get stuffed.' – Faber's voice.

'What's been 'appening up there, then?'

'We've not heard nothing from the Field Army for bloody ages. You been having a nice easy winter with your feet up?'

'Listen, mate.' Faber again. 'You bastards down here don't know what fighting's about.'

Aulus passed out of earshot as the Centurion led him into the patched up ruin of one of the rooms. Evidently the building had been fired. The plasterwork of the walls was smoke blackened and crazed. In places the heat had burned it off, exposing great patches of the stonework. Charred timbers, obviously salvaged, spanned the roof and above them the reed thatch was still honey brown and fresh. Candles flared smokily on the table which, apart from a narrow bed in one corner, was the room's only furniture.

The Centurion studied Aulus again. When he spoke it was to an equal. 'You'd better put me in the picture.'

'We didn't think we'd find the army here. We thought the Saxons had overrun everything between Calleva and Londinium.'

The Centurion laughed shortly. 'Those vermin. They've yet to better the Londinium garrison. The road from Pontes to Londinium has been in our hands all the time except for a few weeks at the beginning of the trouble last summer. That's why this place is like this,' he indicated the room with a wave of his hand. 'It took us just that little time to sort 'em out. But enough of that. I want to hear your news. There's been no word from the north all winter, not since we heard that the Field Army had been cut up along with the border garrisons. What's happening, eh? How come you've survived and got through to here?'

Aulus told the Centurion how Caius and his Century had been detached from the mobile army and had come to Etruria. He spoke of Servius and his treachery and

231

the Centurion stared silently at him, his eyes fierce and hard. He explained how the events of the winter had culminated in the fight with the warband at Etruria and the dash to Calleva. The Centurion nodded approvingly as Aulus recounted the vicious battle on the edge of the Downs and he pursed his lips and shook his head when he heard of Caius' losses.

'So you see,' Aulus summed it up, 'we're desperate. But now that we've run into you we can be back in Calleva tomorrow and have the wagons safe in Londinium within days.'

'Some story.' The hard eyes in the tough face were unfocused. The Centurion hoisted himself onto the table and sat, arms spread beside him, swinging his boots, staring blankly at the wall. Aulus watched him with a sudden stab of alarm. Was this another Servius? A deserter? Was this the remnant of a decimated unit that had turned to marauding? Had he escaped one enemy only to fall into the hands of another? Instinctively he looked towards the door, his hand seeking his sword hilt.

'Not so fast.' Without shifting his gaze the Centurion raised a hand that was both conciliatory and warning. 'You're among friends here.' He looked at Aulus. 'But I can't help you. Half my Century are patrolling north. Reports have been dribbling through for days of a Saxon warband or bands on the rampage somewhere up there. My auxiliaries are out as well, trying to find the bastards and get a proper report on them. I've forty men here, and my orders are to hold Pontes. It'd be more then my life's worth to send my men back with you. Besides, the amount of men I could spare would make precious little difference if you ran into a strong warband.' He suddenly swung his compact frame off the table. 'No. You've got to go on to Londinium. See the Legate. Get him to detail you a full Century. Those wagons sound too valuable to take any more chances.'

'But...'

'No "buts"' The Centurion jerked the door open and shouted into the darkness for an orderly. 'I'll give you an escort of a Tesserarius and two men.' He smiled. 'You're honoured. They're all the mounted troops I've got left here. The road's clear enough, of course, but you never know. Besides, they know their way round Londinium.'

'But...' Words failed Aulus.

'Look, son, I can't help. Your wagons are safe enough at Calleva. I've heard of Caius Martius and he's the best. See the Legate. Get a proper escort. Hell, man, you'll be back here by evening tomorrow and at Calleva with eighty men before you know it.'

For a moment they stared at each other in the smoking candlelight. Aulus shook his head. 'Well, we've got this far...'

The Centurion's face relaxed. 'Good lad,' he said. He clapped Aulus on the shoulder with a comradely blow that sent him staggering. 'Ah, orderly.' He started giving orders to the soldier who stood rigidly waiting in the doorway. 'There. That's fine.' He turned back to Aulus. 'Your horses look in fair order. What about food?'

Aulus shook his head. He was bone weary with disappointment. 'All right, thanks. The sooner we go the better.'

Chapter XV

They left within minutes. They rode in pairs, the escorting Tesserarius taking the lead with Aulus. There was little inclination to talk. The Tesserarius pointedly informed him that he'd been patrolling the whole of the previous night and half the morning and lapsed into a gloomy silence that matched Aulus' own mood.

The miles passed in the now familiar pattern of cold and fatigue, aching muscles and jarring bone, creaking leather and the warm animal smell of men and beasts. Sometime during the night it started to rain. The rain ran in cold unseen droplets down their necks, the more uncomfortable for the charcoal grime that it carried with it. It drew the warmth out of their cloaks so that they cursed miserably and pressed forward faster. But in the small hours of the morning they were rewarded by a shouted challenge, and before the wet dawn broke they were trotting past Londinium's walls and through the western gateway of the city's military fort.

The Tesserarius took them straight to the headquarters' complex. Aulus' spirits lifted slightly as he took in his surroundings. The building was spotlessly clean, the sentries immaculately turned out and the duty Centurion, an alert, intelligent looking man who listened quietly to the Tesserarius' report, then stood up and motioned for Aulus to go with him. 'Legate always wants to be the first to know what's going on.' He strode buoyantly beside Aulus, his boots ringing decisively on the stone flagged floor. 'I'm taking you over to his quarters. It's normal practice when there's something unusual to report.' They went through a courtyard into the imposing hall of a grandiose building.

'Wait here.' The Centurion spoke to a sentry and together they disappeared.

The hall was pleasantly warm. Beneath its fine mosaic floor a hypocaust was blowing hot air luxuriously through the mansion. A score of mellow candles burned. Aulus felt faintly surprised that the emergency had so little affected the Legate's life-style, but he shivered gratefully, thankful for the heat. His cloak began to steam. The rainwater made a sodden black puddle around his boots. He looked at his hands. The rain had streaked the charcoal paste into a filthy black mess. He examined his cloak and armour. The same. He looked as though he had rolled in a bog. He wondered what his face looked like. He ran his fingers along his unshaven cheek and looked at them but it was impossible to tell whether they were dirtier than before. He shrugged his shoulders. A door opened. Two soldiers came through carrying heavy candelabra. Behind them a magnificently dressed officer appeared. Aulus smartened to attention, saluted and waited.

Pontius Livius Varro, Legate of the Londinium garrison, was a professional soldier. He was a Roman and a patrician; a man who owed his command to a well-placed private fortune and a blood relationship to the greatest in Rome, rather than to military brilliance.

He was a martinet. His mind revolved around the intricacies of the drill book and a passionate attention to detail and cleanliness. The wide-ranging broad mentality of the strategist was alien to him as well as being somewhat suspect, curtly dismissing it as an adventurer's approach, a dangerous and foolhardy shortcut to the Oak Leaves and Victor's triumph. He commanded an immaculately smart parade ground garrison. Apart from his fourth Cohort, on detachment at Rutupiae, which had been overrun in the first unsuspected moments of the Saxon attack, his men's well-drilled steadiness had withstood the shock of the barbarian invasion, had thrown the raiders back to the limits of the ground that Pontius Livius considered he should control and had kept them warily at bay ever since. The thought of a counterattack did not enter his mind and he dealt coldly and severely with any hot-headed officer who suggested it.

Instinctively Aulus realised something of this mentality in the arrogant face and coldly disdainful eyes. He drew in his breath somewhat nervously, supremely conscious of his own unmilitary appearance and of the beautifully made and decorated uniform that perfectly fitted the Legate's tall and erect figure.

Pontius Livius' first reaction was one of disgust. He sniffed: his eyes sparked as he scrutinised the muddy figure, the tarnished chain mail, the filthy, travel-stained uniform and the steaming cloak. His eyes moved downwards, noting the black streaks on the soldier's legs and the damp oozing from the sodden boots.

'I trust you have some urgent news, soldier, to dare to appear before me in such a disgusting state?' His voice was as icy and scornful as his eyes.

'I have, Sir.'

'We have a way, here, of dealing with soldiers who do not know how to dress themselves, do we not, Centurion?'

The duty Centurion braced his body, eyes pointedly fixed ahead. 'Yessir.'

'Very well. Proceed.'

For the second time in twelve hours Aulus launched into his story. Despite his fatigue he spoke firmly and decisively, the shock of the Legate's warning lending clarity to his brain. At first he had no idea whether he had the officer's attention. Pontius Livius crossed without a word to a chair and sat down, his eyes on Aulus' face. He nodded briefly when Aulus explained how he had come to join Caius. It explained the cultured voice and the face that, despite its grime, was fine featured. As he listened Pontius Livius imagined what Aulus would look like properly cleaned up and dressed. 'Quite presentable,' he thought. 'He's tall and he carries himself well.' He visualized Aulus in gleaming body armour: possibly as a member of his own personal bodyguard. The thought gave him a flicker of pleasure. His gaze softened slightly.

Aulus noticed the slight relaxation of the stiff figure. Encouraged, he embarked on details of the fight with the Scots and Caius' move to Calleva. He finished his story: 'Chief Centurion Caius Martius requests, Sir, that an appropriate escort may be detailed to Calleva to accompany the special century to Londinium.'

Pontius Livius nodded his acknowledgement. He was not particularly impressed. The story was too melodramatic. It smacked of vulgar showmanship. He had never liked the Northern Mobile Army. He had never seen eye to eye with its aims and means. There had never been sufficient emphasis on the parade ground and the drill book. Their Legate had been an unorthodox fool. Well, he had paid the price. The Mobile Field Army had failed: disgraced itself and endangered Britannia, while he had survived with honour. What a vindication of his military philosophy! The thought gave him satisfaction. He could afford a magnanimous gesture now – a final twist to the knife of their humiliation. Their treasure would be escorted and brought safely to Londinium by his men – Yes, the thought gave great pleasure. He got up and crossed to the central table.

'The day's muster roll and duty roster, Centurion, if you please.'

The Centurion saluted and hurried out. Pontius Livius sat down. There was silence. Aulus' muscles were beginning to stiffen from the wet and the night's ride. Pontius Livius ignored him. He sat stock still, staring fixedly across the room. Aulus wondered whether he had sufficiently explained his position as a temporary Tribune and therefore an officer like the Legate himself – albeit a junior one – to risk speaking again. Should he ask what reinforcements the man proposed to send? Could he relax? The cold, withdrawn face was discouraging. A drop of tepid rainwater formed on his soaking neck scarf and ran uncomfortably down his back. He shivered. Surreptitiously he eased his position.

Abruptly, they heard running footsteps in the courtyard. A shouted word to the guard was followed by a quick, heavy knock and the duty Centurion burst in.

'I beg your pardon, Sir, for the intrusion. A messenger has just arrived this minute from Rutupiae. Count Theodosius landed three days ago with reinforcements. There are urgent dispatches for you.'

Pontius Livius rose pushing his chair back with a strident squeak across the mosaic floor. 'What? Is this true? Where is this messenger? Bring him in immediately.'

The Centurion was smiling broadly. Aulus' brain, muzzy with warmth and fatigue, struggled to cope with this sudden change of mood. Both the officers were looking triumphant, almost dancing with excitement. There was shouting outside. Someone was yelling 'Reinforcements have landed' over and over. Somewhere a group of voices raised a cheer. Aulus was completely forgotten.

Count Theodosius' messenger hurried in. He was a dark-skinned man, a junior officer with broad shoulders and bold, self-confident eyes. Despite his muddied and dripping appearance and his obvious exhaustion he swaggered as he entered the hall and saluted with an exaggerated flourish.

'Dispatches from Count Theodosius, Sir, personal to the Officer Commanding the Londinium garrison.'

'Yes, yes. Give them to me.' In the excitement of the moment, Pontius Livius seemed to have also forgotten that this was the second time in twenty minutes that an improperly dressed soldier had been brought before him.

'Very good, Sir.' The officer pulled at a broad leather strap running across his breastplate and slewed it round to bring the dispatch pouch to his front. In dramatic silence he unbuckled the flaps and drew out a rolled parchment wrapped in oilskin. Pontius Livius held out his hand impatiently as the soldier unwrapped the covering.

'Give it to me, man. Give it to me. Hurry up.'

The duty Centurion stepped closer. The tension of the moment caught Aulus. Involuntarily, he moved nearer. With an 'Ah' of pleasure Pontius Livius took the parchment and sat down, motioning for the candles to be brought to his side. The three men hurried to obey and they stood, the duty Centurion on one side, the two mud stained messengers on the other, as the Legate started to read.

Again, there were running footsteps. The door was thrown open. The garrison's senior officers were congregating. To a man they were properly dressed in armour and helmet. To a man they came to attention as they entered and saluted and paused a second before marching smartly to the table. Not one spoke a word. Pontius Livius read the parchment through. He glanced up briefly, a smile on his face, then, deliberately, he read it again. At last he raised his eyebrows and looked up. His face was triumphant. His gaze slowly swept the assembled men and they stiffened like wooden toys under his stare.

'Gentlemen, Count Theodosius has landed at Rutupiae with the expected and promised reinforcements. He has been placed in command of all forces in Britannia with orders to quell the incursions with the maximum of speed and efficiency. All available troops are to march immediately to join him in his advance.'

There was a sigh round the table. Fascinated, Aulus watched the Legate's face. The cold eyes were roaming the waiting officers. Vindictive malice shone nakedly from them as he spoke again.

'Well, Sempronius. Well, Junius. You wanted me to avenge my fourth Cohort in a premature counterattack? You dared to question my judgement? You know nothing of soldiering - nothing, do you hear? Count Theodosius shall hear of your unreliability. It will be noted in your records. Here is full confirmation of my strategy.' He slapped the parchment with his left hand. ''Ah, yes, Calpurnius, I see that you skulk back. How would we have looked now if my garrison had not held Londinium? Answer me that, man! Answer me!'

The officer dropped his eyes. 'You were right, Sir.'

'Right? Of course I was right! Some of you men are not fit to command a brothel. You would have thrown my men away like that imbecile in command of the Fourth Cohort. As it is,' he smiled round the room and his voice was triumphant, 'we will march as a proud unit, intact, to meet the Count. We will go down in history for our steadiness in this adversity and our defence of Londinium when all else failed and fell. We have kept the bridgehead for the Empire. We have kept the honour of our Eagles untarnished.' He paused and cleared his throat. When he spoke again his voice was cold and remote. 'You will have your orders this morning, gentlemen. Put all troops on immediate marching alert. Detailed planning starts immediately.

All staff officers will report now to headquarters. That is all, gentlemen.'

He rose, and in the silence as he adjusted his tunic Aulus heard himself say 'Sir.'

Pontius Livius turned. His face showed surprise and outrage. There was no recognition in his icy eyes.

'Sir, my escort to Calleva?'

In the taut silence the Legate's gaze travelled from Aulus' tarnished helmet to his sodden boots. Anger flared in his eyes. 'Ah, yes. The messenger from the Mobile Army. Look at him, gentlemen. You see before you the dishonoured survivor of a disgraced army. Why did you not fall on your sword, soldier, before you brought your shame here?'

'Sir.' Aulus' jaw snapped shut. The fury in his eyes matched Pontius' cold stare.

'You heard my orders, soldier.' His voice was as menacing as a lash. 'I will not be interrupted. You have the impertinence to appear before me in that disgusting condition. You are lucky that your status prevents me from dealing with you as you deserve. All uncommitted troops are to march to Rutupiae. I do not dissipate my strength on sideshows. Inform your Chief Centurion that if he is afraid to march he is showing a pusillanimous disregard for orders that will not go unobserved. You are dismissed.'

No one looked at Aulus. The officers said nothing. They ignored him as though contact would taint them. In a body they followed Pontius Livius from the room and he was left alone, staring in disbelief after them.

The duty Centurion reappeared in the doorway. 'Whew!' he said. He walked back to the table, grinning.

'Good luck and bad luck that was, I'd say. Good luck he didn't order you flogged. He was within an ace of it. Bad luck you didn't get your escort.' He shrugged his shoulders. 'I advise you to leave it. Don't try him again. Just go back to Calleva and tell your chief what's happened. I know this one.' He pointed over his shoulder with his thumb. 'You'll end up with a bloody back. Come on. I'll get you and your men fixed with a meal and somewhere to dry out and get some sleep. We'll get the horses done first. You can start back this evening.'

Humiliated, Aulus allowed himself be led to the stables. The three man escort from Pontes had vanished but he saw that his own men had watered and fed their horses and bedded them down in the stalls. Blankly he returned to find his small troop in the barrack blocks and he sat down with them to the thick hot meat soup with bread that the Centurion had provided. Fatigue and failure swirled in his head and leadened his limbs.

'It seems we have come all this way for nothing.'

'Never mind, Sir. Us can always say we've been to Londinium.' Lucian smiled.

'Yes, I suppose we can.' Aulus tried to smile back.

'No good to worry, Sir. That's life. You can't win 'em all. Anyway,' Naso's voice was scornful, 'these 'ere ain't proper soldiers. Bullshit and parades! Wouldn't know what to do if they saw a Saxon or a Scot, I'll be bound.'

They relapsed into gloomy silence. The heat of the soup warmed their bodies and filled their stomachs. Lucian pushed his bowl away and cradled his head on his arms. His breathing came deep and heavy. Aulus looked at the two veterans. Their elbows were folded on the table, heads hanging.

'Come on,' he said thickly. 'A few hours sleep'll do us all good. Let's get Lucian onto a bed.'

Dimly, as he slept, he was aware of excitement and movement in the fort. Sometimes it was shouted orders, sometimes running or marching feet, sometimes wagons or urgent horses' hooves. He was finally wakened by cheering and then, a minute later, came the first strains of an unfamiliar marching song shouted from many throats. Underlying it came the steady rhythm of marching feet. He lay and listened. From across the room Naso said sourly: 'Go on, you fuckers. I hopes you've polished your bloody mess tins.'

Aulus swung off the bed. With returning consciousness his stomach had knotted into angry frustration. Bitterly, he cursed the Legate as he bent down and laced his damp and stiffened boots. 'By all the gods,' he said, 'I'll not leave without trying again.'

The three of them worked at the tarnish on Aulus' mail while he sought out the ablutions and cleaned himself up. They rubbed the worst of the dirt from his damp cloak and tunic, and he left them to prepare a meal while he went back to the headquarters.

The attempt was short-lived. The building was a hive of activity. Everywhere soldiers were hurrying backwards and forwards. Officers and clerks were working at a row of tables, their faces tight and closed with the concentration of deploying the entire garrison at a moment's notice. Aulus was ignored and then waved impatiently aside as he tried to explain who he was to one officer after another. There was a tap on his shoulder. He turned around. It was the duty Centurion of the previous night. He grinned at Aulus. 'You're wasting your time. Get out of it before the Legate sees you. He's jumping about like a scalded cat. Look, man. You can see for yourself. You haven't got a hope.'

'I can't just go with nothing!'

'Yes, you can. You'll get nothing here.' He took Aulus' arm and led him to the door. 'We've heard a bit more since this morning. There are not many men landed yet – sounds like just an advance party. Not many men, not much equipment. I'd act independent, was I your chief. Sounds to me your army's funds will be more than welcome in Rutupiae. I'd head straight there.' They reached the door. The Centurion held out his hand. For a moment his eyes were bitter. 'Don't judge us by what happened this morning. I served with the Field Army as a recruit. Good men, good comrades.' They shook hands. 'See you again, eh?'

Aulus went. They left Londinium in the late afternoon, a silent and sullen party. They ignored the Cohort that was forming up with its standards thrusting bravely over the heads of the assembling soldiers. They took the fort's southern gate and passed into the streets. The news of Theodosius' landing had obviously spread. The people were euphoric, laughing up at them, calling blessings and exhortations. To Aulus' jaundiced eye the faces were hysterical and brutish. 'What're you laughing at?' he shouted. For some reason they thought his words were funny. They pointed at him and clutched each other's sleeves in their amusement. 'Fools!' he shouted. 'This business isn't over yet!' He pushed his horse roughly and humourlessly through the press of bodies so that the citizens fell back and their humour turned to angry curses.

They ignored the solid, stone built houses, whitewashed and red tiled with the upper stories of finer and more grandiose buildings rising magnificent and stately above them. They ignored the shops and the excitement of Britannia's capital city. Thankfully they left Londinium through one of it's huge fortified western gates. It took an hour's riding through the quietness of the cultivated farmlands surrounding the city to work the resentment out of them. Their spirits began to recover and Aulus realised that in his anger he had overlooked the importance of the news. He smiled. He turned to the troopers.

'What in hades name if we haven't got an escort? In three months we'll have driven the barbarians into the sea. Come on, we've got news for Caius Martius,' and he clapped his legs to his horse's flanks. Illogically cheerful, the four of them broke into a canter.

The nondescript day had long since died when they reached Pontes. The news had preceded them, carried back by the Tesserarius who had gone with them to Londinium and had arrived back some time before them. It was giving the Centurion no comfort at the moment. His pugnacious face was worried as he greeted Aulus in his candlelit room.

'All my men have fallen back here. There's no doubt there's a big warband in the area. There's no pattern to their movement but they're drifting more or less south across our front. We're fortifying the bridge as a precaution, but it's anyone's guess...' He left the sentence unfinished and hoisted himself onto the table. 'I'm not getting any reinforcements either. Sounds crazy to me, sodding off to Rutupiae when I've reported there are Saxons in this area. Fat lot of good they'll do there when we've got problems here. If we're not careful we'll be cut off and have the bastards between us and Londinium.' He swung his legs furiously. 'Anyway, my orders are to stay here and keep the bridge. Well, hold it I bloody well will'

There was silence, both busy with their own thoughts. The Centurion sighed. 'Still,' he sounded resigned, 'that doesn't solve your problems. My advice to you is to spend the rest of the night here. I've got a patrol out on the Calleva road. Let's see what they report tomorrow. If it's clear you can make a dash for it on rested horses. Do the journey in one.'

'What if it's not clear?'

'You'll get through. Only one warband has been reported. Give them a wide berth – ride round behind them, of course. It's a risk, but a better one than going on tonight and riding full tilt into them.' He looked up sharply. 'Have you ever come up against Saxons before?'

'No, only Scots.'

The Centurion nodded. 'Hmm. If you do, make sure you kill them or die in the fighting.'

Aulus' stomach muscles tightened. He managed to smile. 'Thanks for the advice. Can you give us somewhere to bed down?'

The Centurion's mounted Calleva road patrol clattering into the courtyard woke Aulus the next morning. They were auxiliary cavalrymen, dark men with dark eyes, black hair and beards. There was a lot of waving and pointing and gabbled argument as they reported to the Centurion. He smiled faintly as he dismissed them and strode across to Aulus. 'Can't stop those fellows talking. They're from the Ordovician mountains. It's just a natural impossibility.'

Over a spartan breakfast he explained to Aulus: 'The Saxons have crossed the river to the north west and they seem to be going west. On the face of it, that's good news for you. They're not getting any closer to the Calleva road and with a bit of luck they could turn north again. There are rich farmlands up that way. The trouble is that that land was overrun last autumn and the best pickings are gone already. My guess is that when they realise this they'll turn south and then the fun'll begin. Chances are it won't be for a bit yet, though, - should give you plenty of time to get through. I'm surprised in a way that they haven't attacked us already. It's luck probably. They don't put out any scouts and they go the way of the wind. I don't suppose they know we're here. Ah, well,' he sighed. 'I'm getting too old actually to welcome a fight but there are plenty of scores awaiting settlement.'

'When d'you suggest is our best time to move?'

'Afternoon, for sure. You can safely go ten or fifteen miles in the light. Unless they've doubled back, the road's clear. Even if they have, I doubt you'd be far enough along to meet them in daylight and over that sort of distance with fresh horses you'll be able to make it back here. When it gets dark, well, that's more a matter of luck.'

Aulus nodded. 'So long as we go carefully we should see or hear them. They won't be expecting us.'

With the Centurion, Aulus crossed the bridge to watch the soldiers fortify the western approach. Stripped to their tunics they were building a semicircular wall round the bridgehead, its ends running down the bank on both sides towards the water. They were working swiftly, taking the stone from neatly stacked piles of dressed masonry that they had obviously collected and laid ready for just such an emergency. In front of the wall the ground had been cleared and levelled for thirty paces. Aulus looked around him curiously. Coming to the bridge as they had two nights ago they had missed these precautions. A group of legionaries were busy setting a thick screen of sharpened stakes in front of the wall. These, too, must have been long prepared. They looked a formidable obstacle.

The Centurion confirmed his thoughts. 'You'll be wondering why we've left it till now to do this. Several reasons – it's been an odd campaign, this. There's no plan or coordination to the Saxons, no idea of taking land and holding it. Maybe they'll attack – maybe not. If they had, we might not have wanted to defend the bridge – not, in any case, if the Londinium road had been cut behind us. There's less chance they'll try and destroy it if they've not had to fight for it. We've been waiting for reinforcements and a counterattack, for which we'd need the bridge, of course. So we've taken precautions. Everything's to hand' – he indicated the masonry and stakes – 'My patrols can be relied on to give me a day or two's warning. It's all I need.' He surveyed the growing defences with grim satisfaction. 'Not the easiest thing to defend, a bridge. It can only be a question of time before it occurs to them to swim the river. We'll hold 'em, though. With the posting house at the other end they'll not get past us.'

'How am I going to get out?'

The Centurion laughed. 'Don't worry. I'll wait till you're gone to close it. What the hell's that man doing? With a bellow of rage he hurried away to reprimand one of the soldiers. Aulus wandered back across the bridge. 'Funny,' he thought, 'how different it all looks in daylight.'

He walked on past the posting house into the ruins of Pontes. The settlement was as sorry a sight in the daylight as the other bank had seemed at night. The timber framed buildings were sodden mounds of ash and the black skeletons of their framing stuck through like the bones of ribcages. Depressed, Aulus turned back.

Opposite the posting house the ruins had been skilfully built up into a continuous wall and peering over it Aulus was not surprised to see a thickly bristling forest of sharpened stakes. Only the actual carriageway of the road was clear and beside it lay enormous tree trunks ready to be dragged across to complete the ring of the Centurion's defences. He sighed and turned away.

As the day wore on his impatience to be off increased. He began to wonder whether he had delayed too long. He stood leaning on the bridge parapet looking upstream, watching the water glide past below him, going over the events of the past few days in his mind. He picked a piece of moss from the stonework and flicked it into the water. 'It's like a dream,' he thought, 'or a nightmare, all this.' He pictured Etruria and shook his head. 'I wonder if life will ever be the same? It would have gone though, just the same, whether I'd joined Caius or not. Perhaps worse. We might have been caught there.' He contemplated the thought for a moment, remembering the screams of the Scots' prisoners. 'It could have been us. Flavia or me. At least I'm ready now. I've learned more this last few months than I ever could have learned without Caius. I wonder what will happen? I suppose we'll drive these warbands out.' He sighed. 'They'll come again.' He flicked another bit of moss at the river. It scarcely rippled the water and was immediately carried away out of sight below the bridge. 'Maybe that's my fate,' he thought. 'What's to stop them coming again? Will Rome send enough men to replace all our losses? Not a chance. Some sort of auxiliaries maybe. There's too much blood-letting across the empire as it is for the Emperor to send his good troops. Perhaps Rome is dying.' He contemplated the thought for a while, watching the river flow on towards him. His trend of thought changed slightly. 'It'll take some time to get over all this. The damage is so immense. So many people killed. So much stock gone.' He shook his head. 'One day we'll have to look to ourselves for our own defence. Rome'll stop sending troops. What then?' He felt the seeds of a new purpose stir suddenly in him, as yet unformed. A spark of excitement gripped him and set his blood racing. 'And then,' he said aloud 'it'll be up to me and men like me. Britannia will be our responsibility.' He glanced up at the sky and turned and strode towards the posting house. 'Lucian,' he shouted. 'Get saddled up! We're leaving.'

Chapter XVI

The Centurion made no effort to stop them. He was on the far side of the river, explaining something to one of his men, one eye fixed bleakly on the working legionaries. He paused as Aulus led his party across the bridge and glanced at the sky. He shrugged and went on talking until Aulus came up to him.

'You're too early, of course.'

'I know.'

'Well, can't say I blame you. Waiting's difficult when there's work to be done. You'll learn.' He held out his hand. 'Mithras go with you. I hope we'll meet again. Go down by the bank. We've left it clear for you.'

'Thank you. Thank you for everything.'

The Centurion nodded and stood aside. He watched as the four walked their horses down the bank and squeezed round the unfinished wall at the water's edge. As Aulus passed through the Centurion raised his arm in farewell and the fierce face lit up in a smile. Aulus waved back. A narrow path had been left through the stakes. As they passed two legionaries ran across. They stood waiting, crowbars and stakes in their hands. They smiled as the men passed and nodded in comradely greeting.

'Hope you don't change your minds,' one said. 'Your horses'll have to be hellishly good jumpers to clear this lot.'

They all laughed. They checked their girths and mounted. Aulus looked at his men, 'Ready?'

'Ready, sir.'

'Come on, then'

Fortune favoured them. They rode in daylight for several hours, for the most part through a scrubby heath country of birch and gorse. They met no one. The occasional cleared fields of farmland were deserted and unworked, already looking ill kept and forlorn. The few houses they passed, on or near the road, were all in ruins bearing, as in Pontes, the blackened scars of the fires that had gutted them.

Without recognizing it they passed the place where they had slept two days ago. Already it seemed an age since their outward journey. Aulus did his best to spot it, to gauge the distance they had come, but the country all looked much the same and all equally unfamiliar. Eventually he gave it up. At dusk he halted them, judging it safe to dismount. They rested the horses awhile and ate, washing the meal down from a stream that ran through a culvert under the road.

When it was dark they mounted up. They were silent now. The primeval fear of darkness weighed on them, peopling the gloom with shadowy ghosts. They rode two abreast, bunched close together, drawing comfort from each other's bodies. The last leg of the journey seemed the longest and the hardest. The dangers pressed on them. The security of Calleva's walls seemed remote and unattainable.

Perhaps two hours later they spotted the warband. Aulus judged that the country must have changed from scrub heath to open farmland. They smelt the Saxons first, a faint whiff of woodsmoke and roasting fat and, almost simultaneously, away to their right, they saw the orange twinkling spark of a fire some way off in the night. Instinctively, they drew rein. Floating, almost lost with distance, its harshness muted to the warming murmur of human companionship, they heard shouts and laughter and broken snatches of song and cheering.

Aulus whispered: 'How far d'you reckon?'

Naser said uncertainly: 'Well off the road, Sir.'

Lucian spoke. 'They'm be a long way off, Sir. They'll not see us nor hear us.' He spoke with a countryman's certainty.

'I think you're right.' Aulus felt the tension ease from his body. 'For the love of Mithras, no noise, now.' Gently he urged his horse forward, and they walked their mounts quietly on. As they rode more camp fires came into view, until there were a score of twinkling lights dancing in the night. Above the soft tread of the horses' hooves and the quiet creak of leather the sounds of the Saxon camp came muted like a far off conversation in a crowded room. The campfires began to disappear. Somewhere between them and the Saxons, wooded country or the shoulder of a hill must have screened their view and the far away sounds of the camp were cut off. Aulus breathed a quiet prayer to his gods. He wondered how much further they had to go. He felt exhausted. Under him his horse was beginning to stumble and hang heavy on his hands.

'Can't be far now, he whispered. 'Just keep it going for a little while more and we'll be safe back in Calleva.'

The road seemed interminable. There was no sound save their own, and no movement but their own faint shadows. The moon shone pale and misty on the road and merged with the cleared verge into indeterminate darkness on either side of them.

Lucian saw Calleva first – a pinprick of light that vanished and came again. Excited, he whispered 'Look!' and gripped Aulus' arm. They halted. The town was still some way off, across the farmland they remembered from the outward journey. The pinprick showed again, moving slowly.

'Looks like a lantern on the wall.'

'By the gods, we've made it. Thank Mithras, we're back.'

With a burst of new energy they pushed forward and minutes later the black bulk of the Eastern Gate materialized solidly in front of them.

'That's close enough, Sir.'

'You're right, Faber.' The walls were perhaps a hundred yards from them, well out of accurate bowshot in the darkness. Aulus cupped his hands to his mouth. 'Hail Calleva!'

There was no reply. Somewhere on the ramparts a light appeared and moved swiftly, swinging in the dark. It vanished into the dimly seen gatehouse.

'Hail Calleva!' He stood in his saddle to get the full force of his lungs into the shout. 'We're Roman soldiers. We're coming up to the gate.'

The answered shout floated back to them. 'Stay where you are! Identify yourselves!'

'We're here to join Chief Centurion Caius Martius of the Mobile Field Army who's camped in your imperial posting house.' Remembering the argument at his departure Aulus had decided against too personal an introduction. There was a long pause.

'Are you the escort he sent for?' The voice sounded surprised.

'Stupid bastard, who in hades name do they think we are?' Aulus was in no mood for this shouted conversation.

Beside him, Faber cupped his hands to his mouth. 'Reinforcements is landed at Rutupiae.'

Aulus shouted 'We're his cavalry escort.'

There was silence again as the unseen guards digested this news. Light flared in the gatehouse, silhouetting a window. It vanished and came again at ground level, briefly framing the outline of the gate. It faded quickly.

'Come up to the gate.'

'About bloody time,' Faber muttered. They kneed their tired horses forward. The mass of the rampart rose enormous above them. From above a voice shouted: 'Why are there only four of you? You said you were reinforcements from Rutupiae.'

Aulus called up 'We're the men who went to Londinium. Come on, for the gods' sake, open this bloody gate.'

On the rampart above them the guard commander swore. His promotion and the fate of his predecessor were not yet a week old. The flesh on his back crawled. Flogging was a fine thing for others – another thing when it was your own hide involved.

'It's you four bastards, is it?'

Behind him there was a snigger from one of the guards. 'Let the bastards freeze.'

'Come on, open up!'

'You wait there till I get my orders from the Basilica. You've caused enough trouble already.' Around him the sentries laughed their approval. They leant over the crenellations and greeted the profanity which floated up to them with delighted mirth. In the darkness the new guard commander smirked. His runner was already on his way to the Senior Magistrate with the news that reinforcements had arrived in Rutupiae and the escort for the Chief Centurion had reached the city. He tucked his thumbs comfortably into his sword belt. 'Curse yourselves hoarse,' he shouted down. 'You don't come in till I get my orders.'

Quintus Polybian Epaticus was preparing for bed. He had been working late on matters of civil administration. He was enjoying a final cup of wine, relaxing in front of the brazier, his mind drowsy with the contentment of a good day's work behind him. No harder decision faced him now than whether to have intercourse with the slave girl waiting in his bed or to send her back to her quarters. He greeted the arrival of the panting East Gate messenger with an annoyed sigh of impatience. He pursed his lips querulously, his ample cheeks puckered in protest. 'Well, man, what's the trouble?'

'Soldiers have arrived at the East Gate, your honour. They're a cavalry escort for the Chief Centurion at the posting house, and they're from reinforcements that's landed at Rutupiae. Guard commander asks what's to be done with them?'

'What? For a moment the hand holding the wine cup shook violently. 'Are you sure?'

'Yes, Sir, certain, your honour. They hailed us from the Londinium road. Reinforcements is here from

Rutupiae, they said. We're the cavalry escort. Guard commander sent me straight along to report.'

'Wait outside.' Quintus clenched his buttocks, fighting a sudden desire to rush for the latrine. The spasm passed. He set the wine cup down. It rattled as it touched the table. 'Reinforcements!' he breathed the word. It hung in the air like an executioner's axe. 'So they got through – and found fresh troops in Londinium. How could they be here so soon? They must have met them on the road. They must have been advancing anyway'. What now of Servius and his plans? How much time did he have? Already it might be too late. The palms of his hands were damp with sweat. Again and again he wiped them down the side of his toga. Thank the gods that Servius had not struck before. But did he plan to tonight? Quintus began to pace up and down. The bulky toga-clad figure swirled backwards and forwards throwing great agitated black shadows across the room. Servius must be stopped. He must be arrested, killed before he could talk to anyone – all his men with him. Immediately.

'Keep a cool head,' he said aloud. 'Messenger!' – he called the man back into the room. 'I want the commander of the Basilica police here immediately. He is to turn out his men and have them ready and armed to move as soon as he has my orders. Then get back to the gate and let those men in.'

'Let them in, Sir?' The man stood uncertain.

'Let them in, you fool. D'you hear me? In! In! In! Go on, get out.'

He barely noticed as the man saluted and ran out. He looked at the wine cup and bit his nails. He fought down the temptation to refill and drain it. A clear head would be needed now. He bellowed for a slave and when the man came running he ordered his litter and escort to be ready in five minutes. 'Now bring my cloak.' His voice was shrill with impatience. 'And help me dress. There's not a moment to be lost.'

The litter was waiting in his courtyard, surrounded by a dozen yawning, armed, torch-bearing slaves, as the commander of the Basilica police came running to answer his summons.

Quintus received him booted and cloaked, his composure recovered. 'Are your men ready?'

'Twenty men ready to move now, Sir.'

'Go at once to the posting house. Double march there. I have this minute heard reports that there is a dangerous renegade in the town, a deserter from the army with an infamous gang of cutthroats at his command. He is planning to attack the soldiers there. His name is Servius Cenric. Put all your men on alert and scour the city for these criminals. Use all your men to search. He is to be killed immediately. He has been lodging above the shop of Fabian the Weaver. Send men there at once. No prisoners, you understand? The men may be dressed as soldiers and armed. Take no chances. Strike first. I will follow you to the posting house.'

'How will we know these men, Sir?'

'Their leader is fair-haired with blue eyes. The others I don't know. They're armed, they look like soldiers – use your initiative.'

The man saluted and ran back through the courtyard towards the Basilica.

'Dear Jupiter,' Quintus prayed silently, 'let me be in time. I will raise an altar in your name.' He strode from the house to the waiting litter. No decent citizen would walk the streets at this time of the night and he planned to arrive at the posting house in the style befitting the Senior Magistrate of Calleva Atrebatum.

Had Aulus known it, at the same time as the suddenly subservient and deflated guard commander was apologising for the delay and ordering the gate to be opened, Marcus was tackling his would be assassins outside the tavern. Aulus wasted no time on the sentries. He was speechless with fury. As soon as the gate began to move he drove his horse up to it and with the combined weight of horse and boot sent it crashing open. It caught one of the sentries full in the face and sent him flying. They glimpsed blood gushing between the man's fingers as his hands flew to his shattered nose and they heard his shrill scream as the horses barged past, scattering the guard before them. They bounded from the gatehouse and on into the city at a gallop. At the forum Aulus pulled up to get his bearings. He turned left-handed and clattered on past it towards the posting house.

Marcus heard them as they turned. He was running ahead of them, his bloody sword in his hand. He swore, assuming that his fight had been witnessed and someone had raised the alarm. He quickened his pace, imagining the horsemen to be a mounted patrol. There was a break in the building walls beside the street and he slithered to a halt and turned into it, crouching into the blackness, tensed to defend himself.

A minute later the four horsemen passed him. Marcus drew in his breath and whistled sharply as he recognised the uniforms and silhouettes of Aulus and his companions. He leapt from his hiding place and sprinted down the street after them.

Servius and his men were waiting in the shadows on the portico of a small shrine close to the posting house. Around them crowded the tents and huts of the refugees. They blocked Servius' vision of the street but he heard the horses pass and savagely stilled the whispered queries of his men. A moment later the lookout – one of Knifehand's men - materialized from the jumble of huts.

'Who was that?'

'Four soldiers, goin' to the postin' 'ouse.'

'What?' He caught the man's tunic and jerked him close. The face was lined and unshaven. Servius gagged at the reek of the man's breath as he growled 'Take yer 'ands off of me.' He thrust the man from him. 'Shut up, you damned fool.' For a moment he stood frowning, then he smiled. 'So the ploughboy's back. So much the better. We'll get the lot then.'

It could only be Aulus and his men. Probably they had gone some way along the road and run into a warband. Perhaps they had hidden up for a day or so and were now back with their tails between their legs. Presumably they had failed to get through to Londinium and failed to find any reinforcements. Servius' smile broadened. He glanced down at the oil-soaked rags bundled beside the temple wall. Now there would be no survivors from the fire that Knifehand's gang would start and no one except the treacherous Quintus Polybian Epaticus would know that the six soldiers who would gallantly rescue the wagons were not the last of Caius Martius' Century.

In the moonlight Servius' teeth showed bone white. The smile was a snarl now. He was still in two minds whether or not to kill the Magistrate when the rescued wagons were unloaded in his courtyard. The fat politician had planned it well. What could be more natural than that he should offer the hospitality of his own house to the legionaries and their cargo after the destruction of the posting house. Quintus could not have chosen a more obvious or more private place for his pillage.

But perhaps, Servius reflected, he would let the Magistrate live. Such duplicity deserved a longer retribution. He should sweat with the fear of exposure sitting like a death's head on his shoulder and Servius would prosper at his expense. Things were going well. Servius glanced round. Most of Knifehand's gang were waiting in the shadows. Caius' eight soldiers were accounted for, dead and stripped and it only needed the last of the gutter vermin to report in with the news of the Optio's death.

Unseen and unheard, at that moment Marcus passed their hiding place. The intervening hovels masked the sound of his boots and the affronted lookout had sulkily sworn that if the Centurian was like that he could watch the street himself. Servius could not know it, but Caius barely had time to greet Aulus before Marcus too was in the posting house.

But Servius did hear the approach of the Basilica police. They were running, twenty armed men, pounding along at the double, making no attempt at quiet or concealment. In the darkness Knifehand swore hideously. Servius slipped from the shadow of the shrine and was in time to see the police pass. He had been in Calleva long enough to recognise the spears and leather uniforms of the Magistrate's men. Something had gone wrong. He watched them pass, fury swelling in his heart. He ran back to the shrine. His own men stood grouped together like a pack of cornered wolves. With drawn swords they faced the shadows. One shouted: 'What's up? The gang's run.' There was panic in his voice. Servius cursed. Knifehand and his gang had indeed vanished. The six of them stood alone.

'Pull yourselves together.' There was no hint of fear in Servius' voice. 'Something has gone wrong. By Lucifer, someone's going to pay for this. Move it.' Despite his fury his brain was clear. They must get away from the vicinity of the posting house before the place erupted like an angry hornet's nest. In a body they weaved through the hovels into the street down which the police had come, pelting along the paving towards the centre of Calleva.

A minute later, coming towards them, they saw the torches of Quintus' litter escort. They were too far away to see details. All Servius could distinguish were the torches bobbing and swinging as their carriers trotted towards him. Logically he assumed that these were more town police. He stopped. His men collided with each other as they came to a halt behind him. They were beginning to panic, starting at the shadows, seeing enemies in every doorway.

'Scatter! Meet on the Londinium road two miles out of the city at dusk tomorrow.'

A moment later he was alone, standing staring up the street towards the advancing torches. He looked about him. He was abreast of a narrow lane leading to unseen buildings set back from the street. Cat-like, he disappeared into its darkness and vanished into the recess of a doorway. He waited silently, controlling his breathing until the reflected light from the torches lit the opposite wall and flickered down the track. A moment later the litter passed. He glimpsed the slaves holding its carrier poles shoulder high, jogging in unison, and the surrounding escort of armed men. But what caught his eye and brought a curse to his lips, was the figure in the litter. Sitting craning forward, urging the slaves to greater efforts, was the ample bulk of his erstwhile ally, Quintus Polybian Epaticus.

He waited until the litter had passed and the light had faded from the walls, then he relaxed and moved cautiously from his hiding place. As he turned back into the street he smiled the smile of a man who has made up his mind on a difficult decision.

He move carefully through the sleeping city, pausing at every corner, making use of every shadow. Once he froze, hearing shouts somewhere close and pounding feet but his street remained quiet and empty. He waited for the noise to die to nothing before he crept on, like a prowling leopard, towards the sanctuary of Pedra's lodging.

At her lodging he stopped, probing for any movement in the dim light that would betray a trap. Satisfied, he crossed to her door and roused her with a persistent soft knock.

Recognising his voice she lit a candle and pulled a cloak round her naked body as she went to let him in. The cruel eyes lit up and the candlelight danced in them as she smiled at him.

'Are you alone? Servius pushed her back as soon as the door opened, stepped inside and shut it quickly behind him.

'Trouble?'

'Yes. No customer?'

She smiled. 'Not with you around.' The thick black hair tumbled over her shoulders, framing the feline beauty of her face.

He smiled back and turned to drop the bar into its brackets across the door. When he looked round she had discarded the cloak and stood naked before him.

He leant back against the door and eyed her appreciatively. She backed away from him, moving fluently, writhing her hips. She set the candle down on the table and moved behind it. Its light emphasised the dark triangle of her pubic hair, shone yellow on her stomach and thighs, and merged her silhouette into shadow. Deliberately she thrust her groin towards him.

Servius laughed out loud, a delighted bark of mirth. He had not planned for this. He had needed sanctuary and time for the bees' nest of the posting house to subside, but her flaunted invitation whipped the fury in him to sudden, thrusting desire. What better way to fill in the time than with Pedra's body?

Their lovemaking was primitive, full of fire and lust. In the yellow candlelight their bodies met and entwined, came apart and locked together again like wrestlers in some strange combat. The shadows danced black on the walls. Her cries were animal noises of pain and pleasure. Their breathing came deep and fast as they moved to their climax.

When at last they were done and lay spent Pedra's dark soul remembered that this was her dangerous time of the month. Servius' unexpected arrival had given her no time to take precautions. Desire slaked, she cursed herself for her impetuosity. If the gods were vindictive she might conceive. She thought about it. Servius was a man among men. To reproduce him might not be such a bad idea. Reflectively she put her hand on his genitals. With velvet fingers she massaged the moist skin.

Beside her Servius lay relaxed, considering the details of his next move, the voluptuous body beside him temporarily forgotten. He tolerated the bewitching coaxing of her fingers for a pleasant while, then pushed them away.

'Bastard,' she laughed at him and raked her nails deep into his thigh.

'Hell cat,' he returned the insult with a grin, reached over and grabbed her hair. He twisted his hand as he jerked her head towards him. He kissed her open mouth and as she responded his fingers in her hair relaxed and he caressed the back of her head and slid his arm down and around her shoulder in protective affection.

'Tell you something,' He propped himself up on an elbow. She nodded. 'You're the sexiest lay I've had in Britannia.' He laughed delightedly as she struck out at him and swung off the bed. 'Wait for me, lass, eh? I'll be coming back for you.' He reached for his tunic and began to dress.

'Where are you going?' She lay back, squeezing her thighs to relive the pleasure as she pulled the covers over her.

'Never you mind,' he replied absently. He was thinking: 'No armour on this raid. Just the dagger.' He drew it from its sheath and tested the blade. Watching him, Pedra's heart began to pound and saliva filled her mouth. She sensed the violence in him and sat up, her face eager.

'Blood thirsty little bitch,' he laughed down at her.

'Can I come with you?'

'Not likely. I told you. Stay here and wait for me.'

Suddenly in the street outside they heard marching feet. Servius snuffed the candle. The footsteps passed the door, then halted. They heard the mutter of voices and the ring of a single pair of boots returning. Someone hammered on the door. From the bed, Pedra's voice sounded sleep sodden. 'Who's there? Go away. It's too bloody late and I'm asleep.'

There was a guffaw from the other side of the door. 'Pedra?'

'Push off, you randy bastard.'

'It's me, Allectus.'

'I don't give a fuck who it is. Fuck off.'

'Are you all right? Are you alone?'

'Course I'm all right, fathead.'

'Seen anything of a fair haired legionary? Blue eyes? Tough looking?'

'There was one like that a few days ago. Something to do with the posting house I think. Not seen him since.'

'We're looking for him. Let us know if he calls on you. Sweet dreams.' The man guffawed lewdly and his footsteps echoed as he rejoined his companions. A second later they heard the patrol move on. The footsteps faded into the night.

'Good girl.' Servius' voice was warm with approval. 'Who's Allectus?'

'One of the guard officers. I do quite a lot of business with him.'

Servius laughed. 'Keep my armour here for me, will you? Got somewhere to hide it?'

She relit the candle, stretched up and tapped the wall behind her head. 'I keep my special things in here. I'll put it in when you're gone.'

He nodded approvingly. There was no sign of the hidden cupboard behind the wooden planking of the wall. He threw armour, helmet, sword and cloak onto the bed. He buckled the dagger round his waist.

'Let me out, tigress, then. I'll be back soon.'

The city was quiet as he slipped from Pedra's house. The moon had vanished, leaving scant starlight to guide him through the streets. But it was enough for his purpose. Already, by daylight, he had memorized the way to the Senior Magistrate's private house.

Quintus Polybian Epaticus' residence lay towards the city's North Gate. It was built four square to the junction of two streets. On its western façade its double gatehouse flanked the ornate doors which led into the courtyard. A high blank wall closed its southern face, behind which rose an imposing and pleasant L-shaped house occupying the northern and eastern sides of the square. Servius studied it quietly. In the small dead hours of the night it gave no sign of life. He waited, listening for the sound of a patrolling watchman in the courtyard. None came.

Satisfied, he judged his distance, ran lightly across the street and jumped with outstretched arms to catch the top of the southern wall. He pulled himself up and a moment later dropped quietly into the courtyard. Again, he waited, crouching on all fours in the shadow of the wall until he was sure that the noise and movement had disturbed no one. The sleeping house was silent. Noiselessly, he began his search, moving onto the dark portico, stopping at every door, listening, concentrating all his senses.

Quintus Polybian Epaticus was sleeping noisily, the deep untroubled sleep of an easy conscience. He had been in time. Caius' anger had mounted by the second as the eight soldiers had failed to return. But the anger had not been directed at Quintus and he had used all his skill and experience to heap it onto Servius' head. True, they had not apprehended Servius and there remained a risk that he could talk but most likely he would have fled the city already. Three of the renegades had been found and despatched. They had had no chance to talk. It could only be a question of time before the remaining three were caught. Quintus' breath rose even and untroubled as Servius slipped noiselessly into his bedroom.

Servius listened in sadistic enjoyment. His body felt tinglingly alive. He savoured the moment and moved forward to the bed. He bent and laid his left hand gently over the sleeper's mouth. Quintus stirred and then was totally awake, coming up quickly from deep sleep, fear lancing through his body. As he moved Servius clamped his hand hard over Quintus' jaw and drove his knee into the Magistrate's chest, pinning him to the bed. Under his fingers Quintus' frantic cry of alarm was no more than a muffled choke. The dagger blade pricked the skin below Quintus' right ear and the sweat of terror broke out over his body. The voice that spoke quietly and conversationally to him from the darkness was unmistakable.

'Hello, Magistrate.' Servius' greeting was warm and cordial. 'I just thought I'd drop in for a little chat.' The bed heaved frantically. He pressed the dagger blade fractionally harder. 'Lie quiet, or you'll get hurt. That's better. Something went wrong tonight, didn't it? You changed your plans. The only thing was, you forgot to tell me.'

The friendly tone was horrifying. 'You double crossed me, rat. Why? Why did you do that? Tell me and I'll let you go. Had you planned it all along?' Desperately, Quintus tried to shake his head. 'Well, that's something at least. Why, then?' Under the pressure of Servius' hand Quintus struggled to speak. Servius listened to the incoherent mumble reflectively. 'Something to do with the ploughboy's return? – the four who went off to Londinium? Ah, you nod your head –they met up with other troops? I see. An escort is on its way? – So that's it – and you decided that it would be safer and more profitable to back the other horse? Don't shake your head, politician. You're lying now.'

Quintus lay paralysed with terror. His flesh cringed from the knife. Under the choking pressure of Servius' hand he began to sob, desperately fighting to frame the explanations and promises that might save his life. Servius listened with erotic pleasure. 'Magistrate,' he said at last, 'When you deal with straight men, act straight. Your twisted politician's mind is too clever by half. You betrayed me. No one does that. Now, what should I do with you, that's the question? Castrate you, maybe? Well, no, perhaps you're right. – Cut you up a bit? –the idea doesn't appeal? – Then again, dare I let you live at all? – Hardly, you'll agree. – No, sadly I must be judge and executioner. The world must learn from your mistakes.'

He drove the dagger into Quintus Polybian's neck.

An echo of Quintus' agony woke the night watchman in the gatehouse who started guiltily and looked quickly round, straining his ears to remember the noise that had disturbed him. He heard the slight creak as Servius pulled the bedroom door shut and he came to his feet, grasping his spear. He tiptoed to the door and peered across the dim courtyard. For a while he saw nothing. Servius was standing still in the shadows, listening to the night. Then the watchman sensed the distortion of familiar shapes on the portico as Servius moved.

He bellowed: 'Hey! You! Stop!' and started to run, shouting 'Watch. Raise the watch. Stop! Stop!'

Servius cursed. Whatever his adversary's skill he had no doubt that he would cope with the man. But the delay could be fatal. He sprang off the portico, ran across the yard and vaulted for the wall. As he leapt the watchman threw his spear, point blank, all his muscles concentrated in his effort to stop the intruder.

The spear grazed white hot along Servius' ribs. It ripped through his tunic and smashed into the wall. The force of its blow unbalanced him and he fell back heavily. The watchman gave a shout of triumph and stepped back to draw his sword. Servius rolled onto hands and feet and came up in a run, right hand drawing the dagger as he came, left hand tearing at the spear that was still entangled in his tunic. The night watchman's shout of triumph changed abruptly to high pitched alarm, but he was too slow. Before the sword had cleared its sheath Servius was at him and had struck, slamming the dagger into the man's stomach. For a second their faces almost touched. Servius saw the man's eyes start wide in disbelief. He twisted the dagger and jerked it free. The guard staggered back, hands clutched to his stomach. Servius pulled the spear clear from his tunic and raced again for the wall. Left handed he lobbed the spear over in front of him, thrust the dripping dagger between his teeth and leapt for the wall top. He had pulled himself up and over as the doors began to bang open behind him and a light came hurrying into the courtyard. He dropped into the street, sheathed the dagger, scooped up the spear and ran.

As he ran he felt the blood hot and sticky from the spear graze. He paused. How badly was he bleeding? There was no way of telling in the darkness. It could leave a trail. 'Besides,' he smiled to himself, 'there's been enough action for one night.' Suddenly the city seemed to press in on him like the walls of a cage. The cries of the alarm were clearly audible behind him. Pedra would have to wait. He changed direction and ran direct to the city wall. Choosing his moment he ran up some steps onto the rampart, climbed over the wall and dropped into the empty darkness beyond.

Chapter XV11.

For a moment Servius hung at arm's length from the ramparts. He released his left arm and pushed himself off the wall, so that he turned as he fell. He let his knees buckle as he landed and rolled over and over. The jarring fall was like a hot iron on the spear wound and he winced as he picked himself up and dropped into the wide ditch beyond the berm.

He ran straight out from the walls until they became hazy and merged with the night. He turned right-handed and circled round, past the amphitheatre onto the Londinium road. For a while he listened, then he set off cautiously along it. He had put several miles between the city and himself before dawn.

With the light he looked around for a hiding place. He was in scrubby country consisting of tree and bush and he soon found what he wanted. Out of the cutting east wind he chose a thicket in the lee of rising ground that gave him a long view of the military road. Once in the trees he stripped off his tunic and undertunic to examine his wound. It was painful to touch, wide and angry looking but basically no more than a bad graze. Satisfied, he dressed again. Already the bloodstains on his clothes were drying and blackening. He dismissed it from his mind and sat down, his gaze on the empty road below him.

Defeat was his companion. Without armour or sword he felt naked and unbalanced. At any second he expected to see the advance guard of the fresh troops that Quintus had said were coming to Caius' aid. Once they met up the game was lost. And what then? Order would eventually be restored in Britannia and deserters would be hunted down along with the warbands. His name would surely top the list both of the army and of the civil administration. He had always admired the army's tenacity in pursuing its renegades and had approved of its painfully public ways of dealing with them when caught. He smiled wryly. Now the boot was on the other foot!

Nor did he fancy the life of an outlaw. He had always despised them. They lived like wild animals with nerves stretched to breaking. He remembered the mad, staring eyes and matted filthy hair of those that had been brought to justice. Their existence was a wretched fight against man, the elements, hunger and the beasts. He sighed. His one good hope for a prosperous future still lay hidden in the bed of Caius' wagons.

The morning dragged on. To his mounting surprise the road remained deserted. Where were the soldiers of Caius' new escort? As the hours passed he felt a flicker of uncertainty. It fanned into a small flame of doubt. Why had the ploughboy so far outstripped the escort? Could it be that Quintus had been wrong? The doubt fanned into a blaze of hope. Perhaps, after all, the game was not lost. And if Quintus had been wrong? Servius frowned in concentration. Caius probably had under twenty men left. The odds were shortening. He wondered how many of his men would turn up at their two- mile meeting place. Could he go back into the city? Perhaps contact Knifehand again? His eyes searched the road. It was still empty.

Through the trees his eye caught a slight movement. A small deer was foraging, moving slowly, upwind and unsuspecting. He reached for the spear. His mouth was suddenly watering and he felt the empty drag of his stomach. He balanced the weapon in his hand.

'I'll risk a fire,' he thought, as he tensed his muscles. 'I don't think anyone is going to come down that road to see it.'

Servius reached the two mile post before dusk. His stomach was comfortably full of roast venison and his heart was high. No troops had appeared. He felt certain that they never would. There was no one at the meeting place. The wind blew bleakly, reminding him that he was only half dressed. Gradually his good humour evaporated. The evening drew on and the cold and damp strengthened.

It was dark and overcast when he heard footsteps approaching. Whoever was coming he was making no effort at caution. Servius waited quietly, lying hidden in the grass. The footsteps stopped at the mile post. Servius let the man wait, amused at the way he fidgeted and stamped his feet. Then, growing tired of the game, he appeared suddenly and silently beside him.

'Bloody 'ell. You gave me a scare.'

'You want to be more alert. You'll land yourself in trouble if you can't be quiet – like getting yourself nailed to a cross.'

'Fuck being quiet. I've had this lot.'

'Where are the others?'

'How should I know? You tell me. You're the officer.'

'Did you see any of them again after we scattered?'

'No, I bloody didn't. I'm bloody fed up. I've had nothing to eat since yesterday and I'm half fucking frozen.'

'Do you mean to tell me you haven't found yourself anything to eat all day? What have you been doing?' Servius' voice was incredulous.

The man's reply was indeterminate.

'Pull yourself together, scum.'

'Scum your sodding self, Centurion. I'm sick of this whole business. It's been nothing but trouble since the word go and as for your stories of gold, you can stuff them. I'm bloody hungry.'

Servius disdained to reply. Only one out of five had made it to the meeting place. If the others were not dead they must surely have deserted him. He was not surprised at this man's attitude. He was a troublemaker and a bully, loud-mouthed and arrogant amongst company, brave in the wolf pack but showing his true colours now that he was alone and frightened. Servius would be better without him. Besides, Servius reminded himself, the man was already officially under sentence of death. 'Well,' he thought, 'Never let it be said I failed to track down Rome's enemies – quite apart from the fact that I can make far better use of his cloak and sword.'

Aloud, he said: 'All right. Forget it. Let's get going. I've found a hut and I've got food in it. That way.' He pointed and as the man moved to pass him Servius crooked his left arm hard round the man's chin, jerked his head back and cut the main artery in his neck.

The cloak was warm, despite the sticky wet patch on its shoulder. The man had been smaller than him.

Servius wondered whether to squeeze into his armour. But from now on it would hardly pay to advertise his links with the army. Better without it: helmet also. It felt odd without armour. It was like a second skin. With his fair hair he would look like a Saxon now. He adjusted the sword belt round his waist, still thinking about the Saxons. There was a germ of excitement at the back of his mind. He drew the sword and tested its balance. And then he stood motionless, the enormity of his new idea holding him riveted. 'Not bloody likely.' he said aloud. 'I'd do better to turn myself over to Caius.' He laughed. 'It's an idea, though.' His mind went back to his early childhood days. 'I wonder if I could do it?' The idea was terrifying, even for his bold and ruthless courage. He thrust it to the back of his mind. 'Let's see what's happening in Calleva,' he said.

'Easier out than in!' he concluded two hours later. The walls were high and the watch reasonably alert. With rope it would be easy. A noose tossed over one of the crenellations as the sentry reached the far end of his beat and he would be in. Without a rope, scaling the wall might be possible but it would take far too long and be too risky.

He had walked almost round the city. The Londinium road must be just ahead of him. Baffled, he stopped at a stream that ran across his path flowing blackly into the night away from the city. He glanced down at it. There was refuse in the water, rubbish that caught on the banks and moved reluctantly with the current. He swore. 'Why in hades' name did I waste my time going round the way I went last night? If I'd just turned left instead of right I'd have found the answer straight away.'

Cautiously, watching the walls for any movement, Servius moved upstream. The watercourse ran in a deep cutting through the earthworks of the city's surrounding ditch. He walked slowly through. In the ditch itself the water spread out into a marshy lagoon. Across, it ran again in a cutting through the berm, and, at the base of the wall he made out the deep, black silhouette of a square culvert. The water was gushing through from under the wall.

Very cautiously he crossed the ditch and berm and stood under the wall. He crept along to the culvert. There was a gap of nearly a foot between the water level and its roof.

'Neck or nothing.' He smiled to himself. 'I'll warm up on Pedra when I'm in.' Carefully, he retraced his steps back downstream. In a little copse beyond the old outer earthwork he stripped off. Shivering in the cold he rolled up his tunic and undertunic and wrapped them round with his dagger belt, making sure that the hilt of the weapon was clear and easy to hand. He laid the cloak and sword carefully under a tree. He went back to the stream and walked along it until he came to a place where the water ran sluggishly in a wide pool. Stooping down, gritting his teeth, he plastered himself from head to foot in mud. He straightened up. 'Here goes.'

Bundled tunics in his hand he crept back to the culvert. He eyed the black water distastefully and shivered. 'The longer I wait, the worse it'll get.' He looked up at the ramparts above his head. 'Come on.'

He stepped forward. He had to clench his teeth and concentrate all his willpower on the effort as he deliberately lowered himself into the icy water. Then, kneeling in front of the culvert, he reached down and examined the opening.

He grunted in satisfaction. It would easily accommodate him. It was too wide and deep for his body to dam the water in front of him. He picked up the tunics from the bank, ducked his head and began to crawl under the city wall. It needed all his reserves of strength and self-control. In the utter darkness and searing cold the tunnel seemed never ending and as claustrophobic as a tomb. Briefly, his body seemed to acclimatize and he felt warm but within seconds his muscles were trembling with the penetrating cold of the water. It seemed an age before a faint ripple of reflected light showed the water surface and promised that the inner end was close.

He tried to crawl faster but as the faint light strengthened his heart sank. As he had feared the mouth was barred with a thick, interlaced steel grille. On the far side refuse bobbed and tapped against the steelwork, piling back from the barrier. He scowled at it. 'It must get through somehow,' he thought.

He tucked the tunics between the bars and ran his hands down the grille. His fingers seemed to move in slow motion, almost refusing the order from his brain. But, sure enough, six inches below the surface the bars ended in splayed out barbed spearheads. Carefully, with outstretched fingers he measured the water depth underneath. There was a space of three, perhaps four, hand spans, more than adequate for a man's body. He fumbled for finger and toe holds in the masonry of the culvert, took a deep breath and lowered himself full length under the water. Immediately the current caught him. In his numbed state it plucked him from his slender handholds and he came up, spluttering, two yards downstream from the grille.

He swore viciously. The cold was beating him: his hands and feet were nearly senseless. In another minute no effort of will-power would be enough to get him out. Frantic now, he crawled back to the grating. Holding the bars, he pushed his legs out behind him, then reversed his hands and rolled onto his back. Clutching the grille just above the vicious spearheads he forced himself onto the bottom of the culvert and pulled his head and torso through, then, bracing his feet against the culvert walls, he released first one hand and then the other. Painfully he brought them behind the grille to grip it on the upstream side. With his lungs bursting he pushed against the steel and, at arms' length, sat up and gasped for air among the floating debris of Calleva's rubbish.

The sentry on the wall above was cold and bored. He heard the splash as Servius surfaced and turned to look into the stream. The day's refuse bobbed on the surface, waiting for the waterman to push it under the grid in the morning. 'Hades,' he drew in his breath. 'That looks like a face staring up at me.' He shivered and looked round for a stone to shy at the curious shape, a superstitious fear of the river gods stirring uneasily in him. There was nothing handy. 'Bugger it,' he said. 'Must have been a water rat,' He shivered and moved away.

The man's back was the first thing Servius had seen. In an agony he watched as the guard turned to stare down at him. He saw the man shiver and turn away. The paralysis crept up his body as he waited. There was no feeling in his legs. He clenched his teeth to keep them from chattering. And then, at last, the man moved out of sight. He sat up. With leaden arms he pulled his bundled clothes from the bars. He wriggled his way upstream on his buttocks until his legs were clear of the grille. As noiselessly as his tortured body would allow, he turned onto hands and knees and crawled upstream for a few yards until the bank was low enough to enable him to pull himself agonisingly out of the water.

Hovels clustered almost to the water's edge. He forced himself to crawl across to them. Almost unconscious with cold he crouched beside them and wiped the water from his body. Clumsily he began to rub and pummel himself to restore his circulation until at last he was strong enough to wring out the sopping tunics and put them on. With rigid fingers he buckled his belt and with stiff awkward steps he set off through Calleva, once again to find Pedra.

The gods looked kindly on his courage, for he met no one. Gradually with the movement some of his strength began to return.

But Pedra did not come to her door. He whispered her name frantically, and at last she called out softly 'Who is it? Go away. I'm in bed and asleep.'

'Come on, love,' he urged her. 'Open up. It's me, Servius.'

There was a long silence, then he heard the bar lifted and a moment later her face appeared. She was frowning, finger to her lips. 'S-sh. I've got someone here. He's –What on earth has happened to you?'

'Who? Get rid of him.'

'I can't. It's Allectus, the Guard Commander. What has happened to you? You look all in. You're soaking wet. You must go. He'll hear us.'

'I'm frozen to death.'

'I can see that.' His body was shuddering convulsively. 'Wait here.' She disappeared back into the room and reappeared a minute later with a blanket in one hand and an earthenware jar in the other. 'Here. Take this. And this.' She handed them to Servius 'Drink that.' She indicated the jar. It tasted like fire as he drank, flooding warmth into his stomach. She watched him, her face desperate. 'You must go! The town's been buzzing all day. They're looking for you. Where've you been?'

'Outside the city. I'd hoped you could hide me. And warm me up.' He grinned faintly.

'It's too dangerous. Perhaps in a few days, when the hue and cry's calmed down a bit.'

He accepted the inevitable with a nod. The spirits had revived him. 'What's Caius up to?'

'I don't know. They've been burying their dead. They're in the posting house.'

'Any new troops in the city?'

She shook her head. 'Servius, you must go.'

'Can you get me back into the city again?'

She was surprised. 'How d'you mean? The gates are watched all the time.'

'Have you got some rope?'

'You know I have.' She could not resist a feline grin.

'Not little bits. I don't want a sex orgy – not at the minute, anyway. I want to scale the wall.'

'Oh, I see. No, I haven't. I could get some tomorrow.'

He thought for a moment. 'All right. Do that. Then get it to me outside. Can you do that? There's a copse beyond the old earthwork where the stream runs out of the city' – she nodded – 'Leave it there. And some food. I wouldn't mind some now, either.'

He waited as she disappeared again, glancing up and down the street, shivering. He wrapped the blanket round his shoulders and took another pull at the jar. She reappeared, half a loaf of bread in her hand. 'It's all I've got. I'll leave some more with the rope.'

There was a sudden snore behind her and a man's voice called out incoherently. She pushed Servius away. 'Go on.'

He stroked her cheek in rough affection. 'See you, love.'

It was only after he had dropped over the wall again that he realised that the short lengths of rope that Pedra kept as part of the tools of her trade might, tied together, have served as well as the one long piece he had demanded. He shrugged as he slipped the sword sling over his shoulder and clasped the cloak about him.

Chapter XVIII

The coming of the dawn had been bleak for Caius Martius and his men in the posting house. There had been little sleep for any of them. Scarcely had Aulus and his troopers returned before Marcus had come running, followed by the city police and finally the Chief Magistrate himself. In the immediate urgency of the crisis Aulus' news was pushed aside and ignored. The failure of the eight to return and Marcus' story of the waiting assassins were strong confirmation that Servius was indeed in the town and leading some gang of cutthroats in another attempt on the wagons. There was no reason to doubt the Chief Magistrate's story and, although his overweight body and effusive manner were grating, his prompt action and personal appearance in the middle of the night could only have been applauded.

As the night had worn on Caius' dilemma had become bleaker. Instinct had urged him to send a rescue party into the town to find his men. Reason had told him it was too late already and his military judgement had recoiled from risking yet more legionaries from his badly weakened command.

Time and again Marcus had volunteered to go back and scour the city, holding himself responsible for what they feared must have happened. Finally Caius had turned on him.

'Shut your mouth, Optio and speak when I tell you to. Your duty is here, with our cargo. If you haven't the sense to see that you're not fit to be an officer and I'll break you to the ranks and flog the stupid hide off your back into the bargain.'

White-faced, Marcus drew himself stiffly to attention. He said nothing. Caius glared at him: 'You bloody young idiot. How many men have we got left? Not even twenty. And you want to go off on your heroics to salve your stupid conscience. What good'll you be if you're dead?'

'None, Sir.'

'None, Sir? No. None, Sir. Well, stop acting like a half-baked recruit and start thinking like an officer.' He turned away shaking with fury. Marcus did not move. Finally, Caius turned back. The passion had gone from his face, though his dark eyes still flashed. 'At ease.' he said. 'Now, sit down man and shut up.'

And so the dawn had found them, grey faced and grim, staring at each other across the table where they were soon joined by the haggard features and black-rimmed eyes of Aulus who had gone to sleep on his feet in the small hours and whose few hours of rest had seemed only to have accentuated the exhaustion of the past few days.

The dawn was grey and cold. An east wind blew cuttingly through Calleva's streets as the city stirred and discovered the bloody work of the previous night.

With the influx of refugees and the overcrowding in the city, murder had become a commonplace enough occurrence over the past months. But the killing of the Chief Magistrate and the finding of eleven bodies in their streets was on a wholly different scale of violence. Crowds formed at the murder spots, pushing and craning for a glimpse of the bodies while the city police searched on, roughly and brutally, as their tempers frayed and their efforts were hampered by the children and loafers who followed them.

Tight lipped, the legionaries thrust through the crowds to recover their own. News that three of Servius' gang had been killed was small comfort. Only Caius' iron hand prevented the eruption of their fury and the sacking and burning of the taverns where the bodies of their comrades had been found. They buried their dead that day, near the blurred remains of an old earth rampart that had once been the city's defence.

That evening they took stock of their position.

Aulus recounted his adventures again, and the story of his encounter with the Legate of the Londinium garrison. Caius grunted: 'I've heard of him. He's a good enough commander of his type. But in this case he has failed to appreciate the situation. His judgement is not worth a fig. Nevertheless, we will move out. We will join Count Theodosius at Rutupiae.'

Silence.

Marcus said nothing. Except to his subordinates he had scarcely opened his mouth since Caius' brutal reprimand. But his heart leapt. In his mind he saw the murderous faces of his remaining men. If they stayed in Calleva it would be more than Caius could do to stop them breaking out and ransacking the town. In his present mood he would lead them and be damned to the consequences. The sooner they were out of there the better he would be pleased.

Aulus said nothing. He remembered the twinkling fires of the Saxon warband but the confidence born of experience was stronger in him. He could outwit the barbarians and outmanoeuvre them. His eyes would keep the wagons in safety and his sword arm was as strong as the undisciplined muscle of any raider. He waited quietly for Caius to go on.

Caius looked at both of them with hard, expressionless eyes, gauging their reaction. Marcus' face was set and wooden, giving away nothing. He noted the thrust of Aulus' jaw. Inwardly he smiled: 'They're both learning.' Aloud, he said: 'Count Theodosius did a tour of duty with the field army. I know him. If any man can save Britannia it's him. If Aulus' information is right and he's here without a strong backing of reinforcements the army's treasure will be invaluable to him. From his orders to the Londinium garrison, he obviously plans to rally all the remaining troops to his standard. Maybe there won't be any new troops coming over. The treasure will buy weapons and pay soldiers. Nothing will give me greater pleasure now than to hand the wagons over to him and put myself and you under his command.

'The wounded will remain here with all our surplus grain and gear. We leave at dawn tomorrow with three weeks' rations. We'll leave by the southern gate and take the Noviomagus road.'

Marcus looked up with a start of surprise. 'South, Sir?' he said.

'South, Optio. We'll move south a day's march. Then we'll turn east, using minor roads. Depending upon what they're like, we'll march towards Londinium when we have circled around the warband Aulus saw and then we will make straight for Rutupiae. If their Legate strips Londinium's defences of too many of his men the Saxons may take their chance. In which case we'd do best to keep clear of the place.'

Marcus said uncertainly: 'There are not many of us, Sir.'

'I know that, Optio. Aulus, I am relying on you to keep us out of trouble. You will form two scouting patrols – yourself and four men ahead, and the remaining three men as rearguard.'

Aulus nodded. 'Of course, but Marcus is right. There are so few men left. With three of them driving the wagons, it's nothing.'

Caius did not reply.

'Why, Caius? Why risk it?'

'You farmers have a saying. When you set your hand to the plough you finish the furrow.'

'Ye-es, well..'

Caius stood up. 'We move at dawn.'

'Just like that,' thought Aulus. 'All so simple. Well, perhaps it will be. It depends on me and how well I use my men.' He got up, went to the stables and began to move from horse to horse, running his practised hand down their legs, as his mind went over the orders he would issue for the march, thinking about his men, deciding who would ride with him and who would form the rearguard.

At first light they moved out. Already they had been alert for two hours, grooming the horses, checking equipment and loading the wagons. They had eaten and rations had been issued. The wounded had been tended and given into the charge of the caretaker and his wife. They harnessed the wagons, saddled up, and paraded for inspection by Caius: three drivers, Aulus and his eight cavalrymen, Marcus, and twelve legionaries. Caius moved among them slowly, resplendent in gleaming body armour, his red horse hair crest fitted to his helmet, his medallions catching the torchlight in their harness on his breastplate. His deep red parade cloak hung from his shoulders. He spoke to every man by name, his voice quiet and confident. Then, satisfied at last, he mounted his horse and gave the order for the posting house gates to be opened and the column to march.

The sleepy night watch on the city's southern gate opened the heavy doors without question. Immediately Aulus and his advance guard spurred forward, leaving the lumbering wagons and their tiny escort to follow. Within minutes they reached the fork where the military roads split to the two south coast cities of Venta Belgarum and Noviomagus. They forked left and trotted on through the cultivated lands surrounding Calleva.

For the wagons progress was slow. The road had not been tended over the winter. Despite its camber, it was covered in a layer of mud and frequent puddles at its edge masked the limit of the paving and the start of the soft verge that could founder the wagons. Two of the drivers were nursing light wounds. They let the teams plod on at their own pace, taking no risks. The road was deserted and as the day passed they moved into country that bore the now familiar scars of the Saxon onslaught. The only living things to be seen were the birds - big, black wheeling crows circling noisily in the sky like the spirits of the dead. Not a man, not a cow, sheep, dog or animal of any kind was seen. Not a building nor a settlement was inhabited.

They passed from the heathland into a rolling landscape of big trees and wide farmlands and they camped for the night in the ruined courtyard of a burnt out farmstead beside the road. With the coming of the evening their mood became sombre. The devastation they had passed was heavy on them all. No fires were lit: they huddled grim faced into their cloaks. There was no joking amongst the men, no attempt by Marcus to cheer them. The long hours of darkness ahead were full of menace, full of the ghosts of the slain and the threat of death. Every man kept his javelin close to hand and his drawn sword stuck lightly into the ground beside him as he slept.

With the new dawn Aulus and his men went ahead, searching again for a turning that would take them east towards Rutupiae. He glanced over his shoulder as he left. To a casual eye the wagons and their escort were hidden. The ruined farmstead looked as deserted as any other they had passed.

By mid morning Aulus was exasperated. They had tried every left-handed track that they had come to. The first two had led to deserted farms, the third to a little settlement from which a network of tracks spread out into heavily wooded country. 'Charcoal burners,' Faber had said in disgust.

They went back to the military road. As they rode south the trees beside it grew closer and thicker and the tracks leading from it more devious and winding. Aulus had split them into two parties and then found himself waiting an hour for Faber and Naso to arrive at a prearranged meeting place. Half irritated, half resigned, he asked Naso where he had been.

'Following a lane, Sir. It didn't seem to go nowhere, leastwise, nowhere the wagons could go.'

Aulus clicked his tongue impatiently and shook his head.

'Funny thing is, Sir, there's people about.'

Aulus looked at him sharply. 'People? How d'you mean?'

'Tracks, Sir. Lane as we went along's muddy. There's footprints in it, and cattle tracks.'

Faber joined in. 'Aye, cattle tracks and a dog's tracks.'

'Why in hades name didn't you tell me?'

'Thought you would 'ave noticed yourself, Sir.'

'I see.' Aulus digested this rebuke. 'Well, I bloody well didn't. For the gods' sake if you see anything unusual report it.'

Naso nodded and muttered 'Yessir' with the affronted dignity of the wrongly accused.

They turned back towards the wagons, a dejected and silent party. The gloom was broken after ten minutes by a shout from Naso. 'Look, Sir! Look here!' They all gathered round. Clear in a muddy patch beside the road were the hoof prints of cattle, the outlines sharp enough to convince Aulus that they were reasonably fresh.

'Keep on the road, everyone,' Aulus ordered. 'Lucian, get off and have a look at those tracks.'

Lucian smiled and slid off his horse. He moved gingerly onto the verge, careful not to overlay the prints. After a moment he moved away into the trees beside the road. He was gone for several minutes and was smiling broadly when he returned. 'Be a herd of cows, Sir. 'Bout fourteen head. In calf, I'd say. Be a man and a youngster with'em, I'd say.'

'Are they nearby?'

'Ah, no, Sir. They'm be passed - yesterday even I'd say.'

They trotted on. Aulus wondered how he could have missed the prints. It was such an elementary mistake. 'I suppose I just assumed there was no one about. I've been looking at eye level all the time for these blessed turnings. All the same...'

Several times more they found hoof prints and footmarks. It became a game with them, something to salve the failure of the day and before they came in sight of their temporary camp at the ruined farmstead, they realized that the area still had an unseen population of men and beasts.

Caius was waiting for them. From a hundred yards he shouted: 'Where the hell have you been?'

Anger sparked in Aulus. He shouted back: 'Where d'you think I've been? Looking for a bastard non-existent road to take us to Rutupiae. There's no bloody road from here to Noviomagus that'll take the wagons.' He drew rein beside Caius. They stared at each other. Caius said nothing. His face showed no emotion, no disappointment, no anger at Aulus' insolent reply. After a moment his eyes swivelled to the three troopers bunched behind Aulus.

'Well, don't just sit there. Get in off the road. Come on, move yourselves you mud stained rabble. Smarten yourselves up.'

Grinning, the men dismounted and led the horses into the farmyard. Aulus called after them; 'Hurry up and get them to grass.'

Caius said: 'Well?'

'I don't know.' Aulus shook his head. 'There are plenty of tracks, sure enough, but nothing that'll take the wagons. They don't seem to lead anywhere, either, they just go to farms and that sort of thing. The country gets more heavily wooded as you go south and I got the impression that the side roads are fewer and the cart tracks are made by woodsmen and charcoal burners.'

'Humph.'

'What is interesting, though, is that there are people about. We spotted several places where cattle or sheep have been recently and in some places we found footprints.'

Caius nodded. 'We've found them too.'

Marcus had come from the farmstead to join them. He said: 'It probably means there are no Saxons about. It'd be a damn good thing if we could make contact with these people. They must be farm people who've been in hiding since last summer. They'd know all the local roads.' He had recovered from his subdued mood of the previous day.

Caius said: 'How far did you go?'

'Eight or ten miles.'

'Uh-huh. Only one thing for it. Try back up the Calleva road tomorrow. There was one road crossing two or three miles back that looked fairly passable.'
Unexpectedly he clapped Aulus on the shoulder. 'Don't worry, lad. You'll find a road.'

They walked back into the farmyard. Caius had kept the men busy while Aulus had been away. Behind the weakest parts of the walls they had set sharpened stakes in a triple line and a rough ladder led to a concealed lookout post in the ruined roof. The men were in better spirits, more familiar with their new surroundings and more secure behind their improvised fortifications. They were talking and laughing with his troopers as they unsaddled and tended the horses.

They settled down for a second night. Tired from the day's ride Aulus rolled himself into his cloak and blanket as soon as it was dark. Drifting, half asleep, the shout he heard might have been a dream, or imagined.

'Hello! Romans!'

Around him the soldiers sat up, reaching for their weapons. The shout came again: 'Hello there Romans!' It was a cultured voice, in good Latin.

The men were on their feet, running to their stations.

'Can I come in? I'm a Roman citizen. There's no one else about.'

'Who are you?

'I'm the owner of the farm you're camping in. You might say I'm your host. We were burned out last autumn and I've been in the woods ever since.' The voice added, almost as an afterthought: 'Deuced uncomfortable it's been, I can tell you.'

'Are you alone?'

'At the minute, yes. There are several of us about, one way or another.'

'Come up to the gateway. No tricks.'

All eyes turned expectantly to the arched entrance. The moonlight was strong enough to see across the road. On the far side a figure materialized, standing up from the ditch under cover of which it had approached.

'By all the gods,' Aulus swore softly. The man crossing the road was like something out of a nightmare. The face was lost in a tangle of matted hair that streamed over his shoulders and ran unchecked into a vast bristling beard that flowed half way down his chest. The body was a shapeless bulk of rags and skins, the feet two swollen pumpkins in the filthy strips of material and hide in which they were bound. He came up to the gateway and stopped.

'Welcome to my farm. My apologies that circumstances have prevented me from receiving you more hospitably. Please excuse my dress.' He indicated his clothes deprecatingly. 'Seen better days. I find bare feet a trifle chilly.' He lifted each shapeless foot in turn. His voice, bitter and amused, was totally alien to his figure. 'May I come in? In the past few months I have developed a strong and striking aversion to standing around in the open.'

Caius nodded. The barricade was removed from the gateway. The man came in. He stood looking round at the soldiers and the improvised defences.

'Life has its little ironies,' he laughed bitterly. 'I can't tell you how pleased I am to see you. You're the first sign of the army we've seen. I had hoped, of course, for a slightly larger show of strength but, believe me, one gets grateful for anything these days. Understandably, I trust, we are all anxious for news as well. You have no idea how trying it is spending the winter like a badger in the woods. Talking of which, don't stand too close.

The Saxons have caused a total breakdown of my bathing facilities.'

Caius gave one of his rare smiles. The man continued: 'My name is Longius Plautius, by the way. We couldn't help hearing that your cavalry patrol has been looking for a road to the east. To Rutupiae, I believe it was. Long way from here, of course – I do apologise for eavesdropping, but you did make your conversation a trifle public this evening when you and the cavalry commander exchanged pleasantries outside my gates.'

Both Aulus and Marcus laughed. There were appreciative chuckles from the men within earshot.

'D'you know of a road?'

'Not specifically to Rutupiae but, if you will forgive me for saying so, you must be strangers to the area not to know that you passed the road from Lindinis to Duvobrivae about three miles back towards Calleva. Not up to your standard, of course' His gesture towards the soldiers was graceful and courtly, despite the rags. 'But it has been in use for many hundreds of years and is more or less paved.'

Aulus felt a stab of excitement. He said: 'Damn it, what a waste of a day.'

'Would it be – ah - tactful to ask why you want to go east? There's a good road from Calleva to Londinium which most of the army usually find quite adequate.'

'There's a Saxon warband across it.'

The man fell silent. When he spoke again his voice had lost its brightness. 'Oh,' he said. 'Is that so?' It was like the sudden opening of a doorway to a dark room. 'You don't happen to know which way they are heading? One likes to be prepared for these visits.'

Aulus shook his head. 'They were moving roughly west but by all accounts they go whichever way they happen to be pointing when they wake up.'

'Quite so.' The man's voice was weary now. 'And like the wind they blow all before them. Dear gods, we've suffered.' His voice was anguished. 'Will you never move to drive them out? What's the army doing? Can't you do something?'

Caius said: 'Reinforcements have just landed at Rutupiae. They'll start to sweep the country now. We're moving to join them.'

The man's sigh was like the gentle breeze of spring after the icy winter winds. 'Aa –ah. At last.' There was silence for a moment. When he spoke again his voice had recovered its bantering tone. 'The old road to Durobrivae will serve your purpose admirably then: it will take you almost to your destination. In a humble way I can perhaps be of some slight assistance to you. You will find all this southern country in much the same state as here. A lot of people are hiding out in the woods. Although I am only in contact with those in my own immediate neighbourhood. I can pass you on. News travels amongst us almost as well as by the army's signalling system. I am surprised, in fact, that I have not yet heard of this warband. I trust it means that they are moving in some other direction. You don't, I suppose, happen to be carrying any wine with you? One tends to miss these little luxuries of life.'

When the man bade them a courteous goodnight and slipped from the gateway an hour or so later there was an atmosphere of excitement in the camp. If the gods were kind they would be able to make a quick journey across country, almost to their objective, under cover of a local intelligence system that would immeasurably improve the odds against any chance encounter with the Saxons.

Aulus pulled the cloak and blanket round him again and was immediately asleep.

Chapter XIX.

The day that Caius and his men left Calleva, Pedra failed to keep her rendezvous with Servius. The copse had remained empty and undisturbed when Servius had slipped in amongst the trees the following evening. He had accepted the disappointment philosophically, aware that she would have to pick her moment to leave the city and perhaps wait until her friend Allectus was on duty. It was a small setback compared to his satisfaction that the Londinium road had remained empty all day. Briefly he had toyed with the idea of using the culvert again but dismissed it stillborn. Only in the direst emergency could that ordeal be worth it. He could wait. A fire was safe enough in his thicket hideout and he still had food. He had known far worse conditions innumerable times on campaign.

He was careful not to get over confident about approaching Calleva. Dusk was blurring the outlook when he arrived at the copse on the second evening. He saw at once that she had been. A fallen branch, still carrying last year's leaves, had been moved. Under it, carefully hidden in the dead undergrowth, were the rope and a bundle tied up in linen. He chuckled appreciatively. 'Good girl.'

He examined the rope and grinned his appreciation. It was thick enough to climb, pliant enough to throw. He picked up the bundle. Inside were two loaves, some cheese and a leg of roast mutton. His mouth watered. He wondered how she had managed to hide them as she passed the gate. 'Up her skirt' and he grinned. He broke off a lump of bread and his lewd chuckle was still on his lips as he picked up a tablet that had been cradled between the loaves. He turned it over, mildly curious, and tilted it to catch the last of the light. Scratched in the wax in a childish and awkward hand he read: "Caius is gone. South gate. Yesterday."

He read it again. The smile faded from his lips. There was no mistake.

'Gone?' he said. 'He can't be gone. By the south gate? What in hades name is he up to?' He sat down, frowning, his blue eyes unfocused. His knowledge of this southern country was scant. He tried to visualize the map of Britannia and its road system. 'I wonder if these reinforcements have landed somewhere down there? Never heard of troops landing there. We've always used Rutupiae or Dubris. Perhaps they're in Saxon hands.' He bit into the bread and chewed slowly. 'All the same, if I was in command I'd still land at Rutupiae. It's the obvious link between Gaul and Londinium. There must be towns on the south coast, though. Perhaps there's a garrison holding out in one of them. That could fit. The ploughboy came back empty handed. Like I thought, he must have run into a warband somewhere on the Londinium road. So they go south to avoid the Saxons and look for friends. They could turn east somewhere along the way, of course. That's possible too.'

He took another mouthful. 'Yesterday, eh? He's got two days' start on me, then. But I doubt he'll move more than ten miles or so a day with those few men. If I'm quick I've still got a chance.' He stood up. His stomach was churning and his heart racing. 'Is it worth the risk?' he said aloud, and then 'What's the alternative? Lose this last chance and I've had it anyway.'

The armpits of his tunic were suddenly wet with sweat and he smelt the sharp reek of fear. He swallowed. 'I've always wondered what it feels like on the way to your own execution. Well, now I know.'

He picked up the tablet and underneath Pedra's message he scratched "I will come back." He took the food, folded the tablet into the linen and re hid it with the rope 'Pity, lass.' And he smiled bleakly as he straightened up.

He moved fast, alternatively running and walking. He took the Londinium road, sure that if Quintus had been wrong then his own conclusions must have been right and somewhere on this road the ploughboy must have seen or met a Saxon warband.

Every so often he stopped and listened, controlling his breathing. As time passed the moonlight faded and the sky became overcast. He would achieve nothing now. He move into the undergrowth, ate his fill of Pedra's food, and slept.

He searched for two days. Only the perversity of his nature kept him at it. Reason told him that even if he found what he sought he would be too late. With each hour it became more pointless to risk his life in this way. But, once decided upon, there grew in him a dogged craving for this supreme challenge. And at last he succeeded.

By chance he deviated north and crossed the path of the warband that Aulus had glimpsed in the night. Their movement had been aimless. They were living off their herds of cattle and sheep, waiting for the spring to lend them purpose. The trail was easy to follow. As the prints of man and beast showed fresher, so Servius moved more cautiously. He smelt the woodsmoke of their fires and heard the noises of their camp – the bellowing of a cow, someone shouting, someone hammering. He moved closer.

They were camped in a wide meadow, in a disorganised scattering of campfires. Underfoot the grass had been trampled to a churned up slough of mud. Wagons littered the site, their tongues thrown down in haphazard fashion where the drivers had outspanned their ox teams. Hides were stretched from their sides to form rough shelters and here and there the Saxons had pitched makeshift tents of skins slung on polework frames.

An apathetic sprinkling of women moved round the fires. They were filthy creatures, bundled in rags with long ill-kempt hair. Slaves without a doubt, they were treated like cattle, ignored or shouted at and struck with the same callous brutality that the men showed to the miserable dogs that sniffed from fire to fire. There were no children. A mob of cattle grazed across the meadow, long since grown impervious to the noise and confusion of their masters. They were gaunt, skinny animals, all rib and hip and backbone, undernourished all winter, starving now in the dead period before the spring growth. Here and there a potbellied calf butted its mother's udder in its desperate search for food, it's pathetic skeleton masked by its rough staring coat.

But it was the men, the fighting Saxon warriors, who overflowed the scene and turned Servius' blood to water. They swarmed around the campfires and wagons, talking and laughing, gesticulating, arguing, fighting and drinking – huge, bearded men with tumbling yellow hair and beards; filthy men, their hands and faces engrained with grime, their clothes stiff and black with grease and dirt. Some wore swords, long heavy weapons in hide scabbards: some carried axes or clubs, hefted from hand to hand as they moved, like extensions of their arms. They milled round with careless menace, conquerors, supremely confident in themselves and in their mastery of the land they trod. They posted no guards and detailed no patrols. This Saxon warband feared no man, no god, and no avenging army.

From the shelter of his hiding place Servius watched them. He looked at his hands. Like the Saxons' they were dark with dirt. He ran a hand over his hair and pulled a knot of it forward. He squinted at it. It was as yellow as the Saxons' – not so long, not so matted, but passable. He looked down at his clothes. After four days of rough living they were dirty – not as dirty as the Saxons' but with blackened bloodstains on cloak and tunic his appearance was just passable. He wondered whether the Saxons would realise that all his clothes were regulation army issue. His eyes roamed over the warriors. Some wore bits of armour, some chain mail coats, one or two had Roman helmets. There were plenty of army cloaks.

He wondered whether to offer a prayer to some appropriate god. He decided against it. It was a long time since he had bothered to do so, a long time since he had learnt the eternal truth that his strength lay in his own brain and muscle. Instead he drew the dagger and reversed it, holding it flat in the palm of his hand so that the blade lay hidden along his wrist.

He stepped forward from the sheltering trees and walked towards the camp. Forty yards from it he stopped. He raised his left arm in greeting and hailed the Saxon warband in the guttural, but long unaccustomed tongue of his birth and barbarian youth.

For a while no one noticed him. Then a woman by the nearest fire saw him and stopped what she was doing to stare at him. Close by, a warrior had been hectoring her. As she stood looking he raised a hand and struck her, sending her sprawling, then he turned and looked in Servius' direction. He called out to the men near him, pointing with the meat covered bone that he had been gnawing. They all looked round, hands reaching for sword hilt or slipping automatically down club or axe shaft to heft the weapon easily for full swing. They were like wary predators, like a startled wolf pack, not yet roused, but hostile, ready to kill.

Servius walked towards them, now exhilarated by this ultimate call on his courage. In this first moment he must show no trace of fear or weakness. Only supreme self-confidence would hold them back. He stopped at the edge of the camp. The Saxons facing him had bunched in a ragged half circle. They were curious, but undecided. Hands rested on sword hilts, but no one had drawn his blade nor raised his arm. Servius raised his left arm again in greeting. He nodded easily about him, smiling.

'Where is your chieftain?'

They stared at him. His native dialect was apparently unfamiliar.

He tried again. 'Where is your chieftain? Your leader. Your king.'

One of the older men in the group started talking. Without taking their eyes off Servius the Saxons half turned to listen. One spoke authoritatively, jerking his head towards him. The older man said; 'Who are you? What do you want?'

With a thrill, Servius recognised his own dialect.

'My name is Cenric. I seek your leader.'

Before the man could reply there was a shout from the back of the group. The warriors parted ranks reluctantly. A blonde giant stepped through the gap, followed by a helmeted man whose arrogant face and ferocious eyes screamed evil and power and cruelty in every feature. He pushed the giant to one side and stepped in front of his men. The gap closed behind him. Servius saw expectancy in the surrounding faces, the amusement of the Coliseum crowd as the convicted criminal faces the wild animal. He sensed, rather than saw, that all the men in the camp were hurrying to join the throng.

The interpreter was thrust forward towards his chieftain. Encouraged by his comrades he talked volubly, pointing towards Servius. As he spoke the chieftain took in the stranger, eyeing him up and down. Servius stared back, expressionless, and their eyes met and locked in unspoken combat.

The chieftain spoke briefly and the man translated. 'Who are you? Where are you from? What are you doing here?' He spoke hesitantly, searching for his words in the unfamiliar dialect, stringing them together like a child.

'I am Servius Cenric.' Servius was careful to speak slowly and simply. 'My comrades fought the Roman soldiers. They are dead.' He indicated the bloodstains on his clothes. There was a buzz of interest.

'Where? When?'

Without taking his eyes from the chieftains's, Servius pointed towards the south. 'Four days,' he said. 'I seek your help. There are many more soldiers who should die.'

Again, there was a buzz of talk amongst the warriors as this was translated. Most of them looked away to the south, as though the Romans might at any second appear. There was laughter: some of them shook their weapons eagerly.

Servius said: 'Far away. Four days. I will take you to the soldiers. You must come quickly. They march and are unprotected.'

He sensed that the Saxons now formed a complete circle around him, and that the entire band was there, hungry for diversion. But the menace of the first minutes had gone. Their bloodlust was not centred on him. As their voices rose and they laughed and pummelled each other Servius knew that he had diverted them as he had hoped and was directing them towards the common enemy.

The chieftain held up his left hand. The giant beside him bellowed for silence. The noise subsided and all eyes turned to their leader, curious and eager. The arrogant face was expressionless as he stepped towards Servius. There was anger in his eyes, a flash of cunning, even a hint of amusement. He had failed to outstare the stranger. His authority was challenged. Servius guessed what was coming.

He saw the chieftain's right hand start to move and he reversed his dagger, holding it now like a sword. He saw the two edged blade appear in the chieftain's hand. Quick as the thrust was, Servius' trained reflexes were quicker. He saw surprise in the Saxon's eyes and admiration, then the blades struck each other and the force of Servius' blow arced the man's arm in a wide circle away from his body. For a moment they stood close, faces inches apart, the daggers crossed, their deadly points thrusting towards the ground.

There was a delighted roar from the crowd.

Deliberately Servius flicked his eyes from the chieftain to the men around them and back.

The chieftain smiled, a thin lipped twitch at the corners of his mouth, but there was no mistaking the admiration in his eyes. Servius felt the pressure of the blade against his weaken and the two men stepped back. The chieftain sheathed his dagger, looking down at it as he did so. Without looking up he said to the interpreter. 'Tell him. You are welcome to my brotherhood. Join us. Eat and rest. The women are yours. Then we will talk.'

Without a further glance at Servius he turned away. The crowd parted as he walked off. Servius stood still. The crowd started to break up. Like excited children the warriors shouted and laughed, scuffled and wrestled as they went. And then Servius was left alone except for his interpreter and, grinning wolfishly, the blonde giant. He sheathed his dagger. He let out his breath in a low whistle. With care, the worst was over.

Chapter XX

Guided by their nocturnal visitor the wagons moved back up the Calleva road. They turned east onto the track that they had passed two days before. Unlike the military roads it ran like a meandering river, now following the contour, now deviating around trees or some long forgotten obstacle, now simply curving for no stronger reason than man and his beasts had trodden it this way for centuries. The track was not paved but generations of users had flung stone into the potholes and ruts, so that under its coating of mud and grass it was sound enough to take the weight of the wagons.

They were joined by a ragtag sprinkling of refugees. Word of their purpose had spread and, with contact established, bearded men appeared from nowhere and moved beside them like an escort of scarecrows. Their faces were thin and lined with suffering. The horror of the Saxon raids was still in their eyes. They walked close to the wagons, touching them. They seemed to draw comfort from their solidity; their faces lit up when they spoke to the soldiers.

'Anyone would think we were the whole bleeding army,' Marcus summed it up with disbelief in his voice.

Their cynical friend of the ruined farmstead came with them for a few miles, then bade them farewell and turned back. His place was taken by someone else but each pitiful figure was scarcely distinguishable from the others.

Aulus and his advance guard scouted slowly ahead. The land had been heavily populated. They passed deserted hamlets and farms and towards the end of the day came into an area of pottery kilns and clay pits, all abandoned. They saw no sign of the Saxons but did not now expect to. Their best defence lay in the ears and eyes of the local refugee inhabitants. As much as anything the advance guard became a matter of reporting back bad patches in the track and cutting branches and undergrowth to help the wagons over the worst spots.

Riding ahead on the afternoon of the second day Aulus saw the now familiar figure of a rag clad refugee ahead of him on the track. The man did not move as he approached. He rode up to him. Without preamble the man said: 'There's danger ahead.'

Aulus said nothing. His heart quickened.

The man smiled faintly. 'Don't look so worried, soldier. It's twenty miles off. I'm just here to warn you.'

'That's very kind of you.' The words sounded all wrong. The man laughed. 'Kindness doesn't come into it, mister. Survival does. You're not in command, are you?'

'No,'

'Let's go and see your commanding officer, then.'

They went straight to Caius. 'This man's come to warn us of some danger ahead.'

Caius nodded. His expression did not change. 'What is it?'

The man said: 'The Noviomagus road. It's about twenty miles on. A Saxon warband has been around it all winter.'

'Hmm.' Caius reined in and the wagons trundled on past them. 'Optio,' he called, as Marcus passed. 'Come here.' He dismounted. 'How big?'

'Thirty to forty. They've been camped over winter in one of the farms on the Noviomagus road. Every now and again they've been raiding around the countryside there. They attacked some Roman cavalrymen the other day. I think they may have been messengers going south to Noviomagus. Londinium's still held by the garrison, you know. I guess these men could have come from there.'

'How many?'

'Four. They hit them at night in their camp.'

'All killed?'

'Yes.'

'Hmm. Had there been troop movements on that road before?'

'No, not since all this business started. The road used to be busy, of course. There's a garrison at Portus Adurni, - or was, - as you'll know.'

'Are they likely to come this way?'

'Who? The warband?' He shrugged his shoulders. 'Who knows? They might. You're safe enough today. They seem to like the military road – like a wolf at a waterhole, they get anything that appears. You don't seem to have many men.'

'I haven't.'

'If you showed us how to do it properly we could kill them.'

'How many men have you got?'

The man shrugged again. 'If you'll lead us you'll get men. Word gets around pretty quick.'

'Now there's an idea,' Marcus spoke for the first time. 'It's about time someone had a go at them. Are you armed?'

The man's shrug was becoming familiar. 'Some are, some not. Not as well-armed as you lot.'

'No matter, we've got spare weapons.' Marcus looked at Caius enquiringly. Caius said nothing. He gazed after the wagons, stroking his chin. At last he said: 'Are these Saxons in their camp now?'

'They were when I came away.'

'Is it fortified? Do they barricade themselves in?'

The man smiled. He shook his head. 'Nowadays they don't even bother to shut the gates. They know they have nothing to fear.'

'How far off this track are they?'

'A mile, maybe,' he shrugged again.

Caius glanced at Marcus. 'Too close for comfort, Optio.'

'Yes, they'd be as dangerous behind us as in front.'

'Yes.' Caius turned to Aulus. 'Get out ahead, Aulus. I'll bring the wagons.' There was no need now for more words between them.

Caius was silent a while, staring after the wagons, frowning slightly. 'Have you got anyone watching these Saxons?'

'All the time.'

'Whatever you do, don't alert them. If they show any signs of moving or awareness warn this officer immediately.' He indicated Aulus. The refugee said nothing, but his face had lit up. Colour showed red in his cheekbones and his eyes had come alive.

'Get your men together and we'll deal with them. Get them to me – armed or not – as many as you can muster today and tomorrow. Get me enough and tomorrow night I'll clean out these vermin with you.'

A smile lit up the man's face. 'Right, he said. As Aulus mounted he looked at the refugee's eyes. Never in his life had he seen such a naked thirst for revenge.

As Aulus rode on ahead the little escorting flock of refugees disappeared. For the rest of the day, while the mounted troopers scouted ahead, the wagons trundled unaccompanied. There was little sleep for Aulus and his men that night. Fireless, they camped beside the track six miles ahead of Caius. In pairs they kept watch, cold and silent, listening for the warband. At daybreak they moved on again and two hours later came round a bend in the track and found a group of five refugees standing waiting for them. The tense faces that looked up at them mirrored their own. There were no greetings.

'That's far enough, soldiers.'

'Are they on the move?'

'No, they're in their farmstead.'

'How far?'

'Five miles. Your commander can bring his wagons this far. People will be meeting here.'

Aulus looked about him. There was a villa complex ahead. 'That villa's the meeting place, then?'

'That's right. Don't worry, soldier. We'll let you know if they move.'

'You've still got men watching them?'

'Of course. Don't worry, soldier. We'll let you know if they start moving.'

Aulus nodded. He gave the order to dismount. They loosened their girths and led the horses off the track to graze. Through the day as they waited, the refugees came to their appointed meeting place. They came singly or in pairs. Some carried swords, some only sticks. They greeted each other with nods. Not one man smiled. They talked hardly at all, but stood or sat by the track, their pinched, bearded faces devoid of expression.

The sound of the wagons' approach was like the murmur of a far-off storm, a vibration sensed through the ground. Aulus mounted and went back to meet them. 'Well?' Caius' face was bleak. There was not a single refugee with him. Aulus grinned. 'They've come, all right. They're waiting up ahead. There are at least forty of them.'

For once Caius could not keep the relief from his face. 'Thank Mithras for that.'

They drove the wagons into the courtyard of the abandoned villa. As they approached the refugees had silently fallen in around them like a rag tag mob of human scarecrows. Marcus winked at Aulus and smiled. 'Make the most of it, Aulus. You'll never see an outfit like this again.' They closed the gates behind them and unhitched the teams. Helped by the refugees they jacked the wagon axles clear of the ground and removed and hid the wheels. Only the three drivers would be left behind to guard the precious cargo and mind the horses.

Aulus said: 'We're risking everything, then? Is that right, when we've come so far with them?'

Caius' look was enigmatic. Marcus laughed. 'All these men need is someone to give them a lead. You've seen the look in their eyes whenever anyone mentions the word "Saxons." We've got surprise on our side and the Saxons are so damned overconfident they just won't believe these beggars are capable of hitting back. You'll see.'

They called the refugees together. Marcus made sure that every man was armed. He issued their stock of spare swords and, when they ran out, daggers. Weapons in hand the refugees clustered around him. There was a subtle change in them. The aimlessness of their demeanour seemed, intangibly, to have gone. Their backs seemed straighter and their faces responsive as they listened to Marcus.

'Right. It isn't every day you'll have the benefit of an army weapons instructor, so listen carefully.' He paused and grinned at them. 'It isn't every day a weapons instructor has the benefit of recruits like you lot either, if it comes to that.' It raised the ghost of a smile on a few faces. They pressed closer around him, seeming to draw strength from his confidence and courage. Marcus grinned at them again. 'Keep back, lads. Let's have you spread out around me and see if we can't teach you in one easy lesson how to stay alive with a regulation sword.'

He arranged the men in a semicircle in front of him and for half an hour he taught them the basic stab and parry of sword drill. Eventually he said: 'Right, lads, that's all we've got time for. Try to remember it tonight.'

Caius appeared behind them. He was in ceremonial dress now. The red horsehair crest sprang nobly from his helmet. The medallion harness hung proudly over his breastplate. He had buckled on his greaves and the red full dress cloak fell sheer to his ankles. There was a sigh from the refugees. Aulus saw hope in their faces, and purpose. Their eyes burned with a fierce hatred and a rising tide of lust for revenge. A refugee stepped forward. Aulus thought he was the one who had first come to warn them.

'Do you take prisoners, Chief Centurion?'

Caius looked at him. 'No prisoners.'

The man smiled and Aulus knew this was the same person. The loathing shone in his eyes like a shaft of darkness from the gates of Hades. Caius recognised him too. 'You'll lead us there?'

'Yes.'

'Good. Now come and draw me a plan of this farm where they're camped and of the country round it.'

They split the refugees into four groups and divided the soldiers between them. Caius' instructions were simple. 'Move when I tell you. Stop when I stop. Above all, keep quiet. Don't make any noise. Our whole success depends on surprise. Clear?'

Around him, the heads nodded. Someone said: 'Don't worry about that. We've learnt how to be quiet and stay out of sight this last few months'

'Good. Now, watch my soldiers when you get there. If they lie down, you lie down. If they crawl, you crawl. If they wait, you wait. Attack when I give the word and you see my soldiers start to move. I may not want you all to attack at the same time. Just follow my lead.'

The refugee spokesman smiled his slow, deadly smile. 'That's it, Sir. You give us a lead. Leave the rest to us.'

They waited till long after dark to start the five mile march to the Saxons' lair, the waning moon shining yellow behind intermittent cloud. Caius led with the guide and his quarter of the men. Aulus followed, then Faber, commanding the third group. Marcus and his men brought up the rear. As they had promised, the refugees moved soundlessly. In single file they padded like hungry wolves to exact their revenge on the Saxon raiders.

Eventually they swung left handed off the track, through trees at first and then into a place of fields and open heathland. The column moved more slowly, taking advantage of any cover, closing up on itself, the tension rising like a tightening bowstring amongst them. They halted and the officers went forward. The farmstead lay just in front of them, a solid grey square of buildings in the moonlight. There was no sound from it, and no light.

Marcus whispered: 'You're sure they're still there?'

The guide said: 'They're there all right.'

Caius said: 'Their watcher reported in a mile or so back.'

'Ah. I see.'

Caius said: 'Off you go.' The guide vanished into the night. Ten minutes later he was back. 'The gates are open. There's no sign of a guard.'

They went back to the waiting men. Caius whispered his orders. 'Move up to the gate. No noise. Keep together. When I give the order, rush it. Aulus, you keep your men outside in reserve. Get any Saxons who escape. No noise.'

It was uncanny how quietly they moved. Aulus held his men back and the refugees went past him like shadows. He watched their faces. They were white and skull like in the moonlight. Forty yards from the gate Aulus saw Caius signal the men to close up and fan out round him. He saw the flash of Caius' sword as he raised it over his head and arced it down in the direction of the farm. He saw the line move forward, slowly for a pace or two and then the ragged forms of the refugees suddenly seemed to leap ahead and to shake off the restraining hands of the legionaries. A second later the fragile discipline broke. He saw the refugees rush forward through the open gateway. There was a shout from inside, taken up and answered in a howl of fury. The refugees of Aulus' reserve leapt past him, screaming. They vanished into the farm and as they disappeared he heard the yell of the attackers answered in wild bellowing from the defenders and the high pitched screams of wounded men cutting clear above the uproar.

And then it was all over. He saw the soldiers come doubling back through the gate, Caius and Marcus behind them. They halted and faced about, covering the entrance. He ran to join them.

'What's happening?'

Caius said: 'There's no need for us now.' He was not even out of breath. 'We'll just wait a while and see if any of the Saxons get away.'

'Is anyone hurt?'

'No, not of ours. It's gone just as I thought it would.'

'They only needed a lead,' Marcus said. 'There was enough hatred bottled up in those men to tackle a warband twice the size. We called the men off as soon as the refugees got at their throats.'

From inside the farm the yelling went on undiminished but its tone had changed. The answering Saxon shouts had faded. The noise carried an hysterical note of triumph, like a hound pack worrying a broken carcase. And then, more shockingly, came a single bellowed roar of fury as though the pack had turned its attention on a cornered quarry and the victim had screamed ferocious defiance at its tormentors. It came again, only this time it broke and rose to a scream.

'Come on,' said Caius. 'It's time we were off.'

With the morning they moved on. Towards midday they reached the crossroads where the military road cut across the track with its arrow straight paving lancing through the countryside. The soldiers looked about them curiously. The farm that the Saxons had used was not in sight. They crossed over, holding to their meandering track, confident with victory, determined now to deliver the wagons direct to Count Theodosius at Rutupiae.

With the afternoon their ragged escort of refugees reappeared. Their faces were relaxed. They smiled secretively to themselves. Only when the soldiers asked them about the attack and the fate of the Saxons did the blankness return.

For nearly two days Servius had writhed in frustration. Interminably the chieftain and his council had talked and argued. With savage humour the interpreter had explained to Servius that some of the men did not trust him and were for torturing him to test his story. Others were for going at once, leaving the livestock and the women. Several times he had been called to the chieftain's fire to be questioned about his warband and its annihilation by the Romans. Each time they had dismissed him and had gone on arguing loudly as he sat waiting with his giant escort and the interpreter.

On the first night he had been with them, two of the warriors had tried to crawl up on him, though whether to kill him or to question him he did not know. The giant had raised the alarm. In the morning the two men were brutally beaten up and he realised his guard was as much for his protection as to stop him escaping. As the second day had worn on he had judged that the argument had been settled. He was not to be tortured; at least not yet, not until his story had been put to the test. The warriors of the council had drawn closer together. Their voices had been quieter. They were planning how to move, whether as a raiding party or as a full warband with plunder and cattle. He watched them pick out several of the least emaciated cows and slaughter them.

When the meat was ready he was summoned again to the chieftain's fire and invited to sit and eat. They would leave in the morning, the youngest and ablest, with the chieftain to lead them and himself to guide. Smiling, the chieftain spoke to the interpreter. He translated: 'If you betray us your torture will be worse than you can dream possible. You will pray a thousand times for death.'

Servius looked at the chieftain. He was still smiling. Servius smiled back and shrugged his shoulders. He reached for a rib bone and bit into it. Again, he saw the flash of admiration in the man's eyes.

They headed south west to cross the Londinium road and leave Calleva unseen on their right. The chieftain led at a loping trot that ate up the miles and the warriors followed tirelessly. They ran all day. No one dropped out. When at last they stopped for the night Servius marvelled at their stamina and the discipline of their achievement. Nor did he fail to realise that the giant had never left his side.

They skirted round Calleva and reached the Noviomagus road next day. The wagons' iron-rimmed wheel marks were clear wherever mud overlaid the paving of the road. The trail was deeply etched at the crossroads where Caius had turned eastwards. Servius' heart leapt. With a shout of triumph he pointed to the marks and the prints of the escorting horses and soldiers. He and the chieftain looked at each other. The anticipation and cruelty that each read in the other's eyes spoke louder than words and broke the barriers between them. The chieftain called to his men and then they were crowding round him, slapping his back and pummelling his arms.

So, finally, with no regrets, Servius put aside his Roman life and went back to the people of his birth and childhood and when they set off again the giant no longer measured him pace for pace like an evil shadow.

They camped that night at a deserted pottery, effortlessly following the trail that Caius and his wagons had left. They were in boisterous spirits and Servius was the centre of attention. In the few hours since they had found Caius' tracks the prisoner had become the fêted hero. They stopped, puzzled, at the villa meeting place where Marcus had drilled the refugees. But the wheel marks led on and they followed while a flock of carrion crows pointed them off the track to the scene of the refugees' massacre.

Servius moved among the Saxon corpses. Even his hardened soul recoiled from the ghastly mutilations that he saw but he was puzzled. There was no evidence of any Roman dead and the vileness of the butchery could hardly be the work of disciplined troops.

'Cunning bastard,' he concluded admiringly. 'You let some bunch of butchers do your work for you. The locals who stayed behind, I'll be bound. Well, they've settled their scores here, right enough.'

The chieftain gripped his arm. 'Roman soldiers?'

'Yes.'

The chieftain nodded. Callously he kicked the nearest corpse and spat. He held up two fingers and pointed to the sky.

'Yes,' said Servius. 'Perhaps two days.' He looked around at the warriors. There was no compassion in their faces, but there was anger. He smiled to himself. 'You couldn't have done a stupider thing, Caius Martius. If these barbarians had any doubts they're forgotten now. They'll chase you to perdition. Tomorrow or the next day we'll tear you apart like wolves tear a lamb.'

Chapter XXI

Excitement, a subdued feeling of achievement, was mounting. Aulus could feel it as an almost physical thing. It showed in the soldiers' faces and in their step, in the set of their shoulders and the proud carriage of their helmeted heads. It rang in their voices and in their laughter. It was solid and tangible as they sat at the evening fires. They were almost there.

There was a different feel to the countryside. Almost, they were in range of Roman controlled territory. Instinctively they knew that there were no Saxons here. Their little flock of refugees had dwindled and bidden them farewell.

Tomorrow, they would be safe. They had reached their final crossroads where the military road south from Durobrivae cut across their ancient track. Durobrivae was no more than five miles away – Durobrivae, on the road from Londinium to Rutupiae, garrisoned , sanctuary, a final morning's march.

In high spirits and the rich warmth of comradeship Aulus wrapped his cloak and blanket round him, and settled down to sleep. He was tired, but at first he lay awake, excited and tense with the euphoria of their success. He went over the events of the past weeks in his mind and thought of the men with whom he had shared this adventure. There would always be a bond between them and a sort of love. Soon they would pass out of his life as he went back to Etruria and Flavia and they would join some new unit in the drive against the barbarians. But it would always be there, something he had never known before, an experience that was deeper and fuller than anything in his life.

He thought about Flavia and the farm and wondered again whether life could ever be the same. Between him and Flavia, yes, their love would perhaps be stronger for the winter's depredations and the suffering of the farm. But life itself? In his heart he knew that he had become a different man in a different world. But he could face it with a confidence and knowledge that he would never have known had Caius' wagon not broken its axle at the farm gate. He had learned so much about men and comradeship, about self-reliance and initiative and leadership. If it should be that Count Theodosius and his reinforcements failed to hold the country he would know how to defend himself and fight back. He settled his head more comfortably and fell asleep.

He was wakened by a rough and urgent shake at his shoulder. It was twilight, the start of the new day. Marcus was bending over him.

'For Mithras' sake wake up, Aulus. We're in mortal danger. There's a warband on our trail. They're only a few miles behind us. Get up, man! Get up!'

'There can't be,' Aulus groaned. He sat up, flinging the blanket aside, reaching for his helmet. 'How in Jupiter's name d'you know?'

'A refugee's just come into camp. He's been running all night. Come on. Quick. Here.' He handed Aulus his sword sling. 'Come on.'

Together they ran to Caius. The Chief Centurion was standing calmly beside the wagons, quietly supervising the harnessing of the teams. He looked detached and relaxed, a solid bulwark of confidence and strength. He nodded as they came up.

'Ride on to Durobrivae, Aulus. Take Lucian with you. Raise the town and get back here fast with as many men as you can get.'

'But what about you?'

'Don't argue.' Caius looked at him. 'It's the second time you've had to do this, eh? You'll succeed this time.' He gripped Aulus' arm for a moment and smiled. 'You'll do, lad. Remember all I've taught you. Now, get going.'

'Caius...'

'Go.'

'Marcus...'

'See you later, Aulus. Been a pleasure to know you.'

'Go!'

Spurred by the sudden fierceness in Caius' voice Aulus ran to the horse lines, shouting for Lucian. The troopers dashed to help them saddle up. They vaulted on and kicked their horses into a gallop. Behind them their companions shouted encouragement.

'Go to it, Sir.'

'Ride like hell, Sir.'

'Go on Lucian, lad, get them buggers back here double quick.'

And, ringing in Aulus' ears, Caius' words: 'You'll succeed this time.'

The sun had risen on a beautiful March morning, full of colour and the promise of spring when they reached the walls of Durobrivae.

'Thank the gods,' Aulus shouted to Lucian. On the ramparts of the gate were the familiar armour clad figures of Roman guards.

'Help! We need help! Saxons!' The horses slithered to a standstill.

'There's a cavalry ala camped on the Rutupiae road.' The guards shouted down, pointing to the east. 'About half a mile. Over there.'

Minutes later, they saw the camp, rows of neat horse picket lines, ranks of orderly tents, a big headquarters tent dominating the scene, and around the camp, the freshly turned earth of the familiar ditch and stake palisade of a military encampment.

Shouted exchanges with the sentries took them past the camp gates. Aulus flung himself off his horse at the entrance to the headquarters.

'What d'you want, soldier?' The dark skinned sentries crossed their spears in front of him, barring his path. 'You can't go in here.' Their Latin was heavily accented.

'Let me through! Saxons are attacking my unit!' Aulus' voice rose furiously as he demanded entrance. He grabbed the spear shafts to force them apart. The men shouted back, wrestling the weapons from his grasp, cursing him in their native tongue.

Behind him, Aulus heard Lucian draw his sword.

The tent flap was thrown violently aside. An officer stood in the opening. He roared a command. The sentries snapped back to attention, scowling murderously.

'For Mithras' sake, let me see your commanding officer. My unit's under attack from the Saxons. Every second's vital.'

The officer looked him up and down. His gaze took in the dripping horses. He jerked his head. 'Come on in.'

The ala Prefect was seated on a dais. He was looking towards the disturbance, frowning. His face was intelligent, fine featured in its frame of curly black hair. 'What's the trouble, Decurion?' He spoke with the cultured voice of a Roman patrician.

He grasped immediately the urgency of Aulus' plea. Before Aulus had finished speaking the Decurion had run from the tent. Trumpets were already calling the cavalrymen to horse as the commander took Aulus to a map that lay spread out on a nearby table. He stooped over it and pointed to the crossroads where Caius had camped last night.

'That's the place, right enough. Your Chief Centurion will have to fight a hard battle if we are to get there in time.'

Already three troops were mustering. Shouts and trumpet calls rose imperiously as the troopers rushed to saddle and form up.

The Prefect went with Aulus to the tent doorway. 'This is our first action in Britannia,' he smiled. 'We're from southern Gaul – ninth Gallic Auxiliary Ala. The men will welcome the diversion. They're not too taken with your miserable climate here and it doesn't look as though the Count will order a general advance for some time yet. A little action will do my homesick boys a power of good.'

They stood together for a minute, watching. The dark, foreign faces were eager: the sun flashed on helmets and spearheads. An orderly ran to them, leading two horses. He handed them to Lucian and took the two animals that he was holding. They mounted. Aulus saluted. 'Thank you, Sir,' he said.

The Prefect saluted back. He smiled. 'Don't thank me. You've done us a service.'

Aulus and Lucian took post beside the leading Decurion as he raised his arm and gave the signal for the column to move. File after file, over a hundred men, they spurred their horses and passed through the camp gates at a canter, as splendid and hopeful a sight to Aulus as anything he had ever witnessed before in his life. They passed Durobrivae's walls and settled to an easy hand canter down the grass verge of the southern road. Aulus begged the Decurion to go faster. The man shook his head.

'Can't be done, comrade. There's three troops behind us. If we ride any faster there'll only be half a troop with us by the time we reach your column. The horses will be half-blown and the men half-winded. What use would that be to your comrades, eh? Christos, what's that?'

As he had been speaking a column of black smoke had risen and was climbing in rolling billows into the blue sky somewhere ahead of them along the road. Through lips suddenly gone dry Aulus whispered: 'We're too late.'

The Decurion turned in his saddle. He raised his arm, sweeping it urgently forward. He settled back down into his saddle, kicking his horse. They bounded forward into a gallop. The Decurion shouted to Aulus: 'That is not your column, comrade. Only buildings burn like that. I think the Saxons are having themselves a little fun that we had not planned for. We shall see.'

He turned again in his saddle and swore in his own tongue. Aulus tore his eyes from the mesmerizing smoke and looked back as well. The orderly lines of troopers were stretching out, blurring shape, disintegrating into a long, disorganised throng of individual horsemen.

'Christos damn it,' the Decurion swore again. He scowled at his men and back at the tantalisingly distant smoke.

'See what I mean?' he shouted at Aulus. 'It can't be done.' He held up his arm and reined his horse back to the easy hand canter, riding half turned in the saddle, one hand on the pommel, the other on the cantel. At last he swivelled back with a grunt of satisfaction and Aulus saw that behind him the orderly ranks had reformed and they were again riding as a body. For all his desperate urgency he felt a surge of admiration at the restraint and discipline of this Gallic officer and his men.

The smoke rose high into the sky, billowing up in dark, evil clouds that mocked the sunlight. They passed through a screen of woodland and at last saw its cause. Off to their right, standing a way back from the road, was a farmstead, somewhat similar to Aulus' own. The smoke was pouring from its thatched roofs. Wicked dark red flame whirled below, devouring the timber structure, greedily racing the length of the buildings. And around the farmstead, leaping and prancing, they saw the marauders. Like the demons of a nightmare they were engrossed in their deadly work. Behind Aulus there was a roar from the troopers.

The Decurion's face broke into a wide grin. 'We'll get these sons of dogs.' He shouted: 'Galloper!' The trooper riding behind them drew level.

'The first two troops to follow me and engage those Saxons. The third troop to carry on with these two,' jerking a thumb at Aulus and Lucian, 'to meet up with his column. You have it?'

The trooper drew out and turned back down the ranks. The Decurion leaned across to Aulus, still grinning: 'Good luck, comrade. Our ways part here.'

Aulus and Lucian pulled up to let the two troops pass. Hardly a man glanced at them. All eyes were on the burning farmstead, all with the pale, fierce killer's look of men who are close to action. The third troop cantered up. Fuming with impatience Aulus and Lucian fell in beside its Decurion. The man nodded silently, dark, hard eyes in a dark, hard face.

They increased their pace and from behind them came the first shouts of battle as the troopers closed with the Saxons.

With every stride fear twisted Aulus into a tighter knot. By now they should have met Caius – they would certainly have met him had the wagons still been moving.

And then he saw them.

Caius and his men had been overtaken before they had covered three hundred yards. The Saxons must have been on their heels when Aulus had gone. He must have gone clear by minutes only.

The last of Caius' century lay as they had fallen, intermingled with the Saxon dead, grouped round the three wagons which still stood in the centre of the carriageway where their drivers had been struck down. The teams were gone, cut from their harness and taken as booty. The wagon tongues lay idly on the road. The canvas superstructures had been torn off and hung bundled over the sides. The equipment and stores of their cargo had been looted. Contents which the Saxons had not prized lay scattered about the roadway, pathetic in the ugliness of this massacre.

But the wagon beds were untouched. Even in the horror of this scene a violent rush of relief started and was instantly overwhelmed and forgotten. 'Oh, my gods.' Aulus drew breath in a groan of agony. He flung himself from his horse and ran forward, tears running unchecked down his face.

Stripped and mutilated, the hand-picked veterans of the field army lay within the very grasp of their goal. Blinded with tears Aulus stood among them. He raised his head and looked up at the Decurion who still sat his horse beside the carnage.

'Too late!' he said.

The man nodded. His face was blank. 'Good comrades, were they, friend?'

Aulus nodded.

'That's life, friend.' His face softened slightly. He looked again around the scene. 'There's nothing I can do here just now. You coming back with us?'

Aulus shook his head.

'Fair enough. We'll be back directly.' He wheeled his horse, raising his voice: 'Right, you lot. Let's go back and see if there's any action left for us this morning.'

There was an approving cheer from the troopers. Eager faced they wheeled after the Decurion and clattered away to join the fighting at the farmstead. Aulus and Lucian were alone. Silently they looked at each other. Lucian's face was ashen, his lips a thin bloodless slit. Incongruously Aulus saw that there were lines around his eyes and mouth. Unnoticed, the farm boy who had left Etruria had grown into a man. He said quietly; 'I think, Sir, I'll not be coming back to farm with thee.'

Aulus nodded. He indicated their dead comrades with a small gesture of his open hand. Lucian said: 'Aye, Sir.'

Aulus nodded again. He turned away and moved among them, looking for the familiar faces, praying that some might still be alive, knowing that it was impossible.

Four Saxons lay around Marcus. Perhaps he had been the last to die. Perhaps his skill at arms and strength and speed had held the Saxons off while around him his comrades lay dead. At any rate, his body had not been mutilated, nor stripped of its armour. His lips were drawn back as though he had died smiling, as he had lived.

It was not so with Caius. It seemed as though he had been singled out, and Aulus turned retching from the awful violations to his body. As he did so he heard again Caius' last words: 'You'll do, lad.' It was as though Caius was standing beside him. He felt again the Chief Centurion's grip on his arm and saw him smile: 'Remember all I've taught you.' Caius had foreseen his death. He had deliberately sent Aulus away, knowing that help could never come in time. Aulus drew himself erect and saluted the body at his feet. 'Thank you, Chief Centurion,' he said aloud. 'Thank you for everything.'

He moved on down to the third wagon. There were few dead here. It had obviously been overtaken first and probably abandoned as the driver was killed and the legionaries regrouped on the leading wagon. He leant against its side. The sun was warm on his body. Overhead, in the blue sky, the crows were gathering. Up by the first wagon Lucian had dismounted and was holding the horses, standing close to their heads. He seemed to be talking to them, his back towards Aulus. The world seemed quiet in the bright morning, gratefully soaking up the sunlight.

He said aloud: 'At least they didn't die entirely for nothing. The treasure is still there. They got it through. Other hands will deliver it, that's all.' He pictured the Gauls hitching new teams and climbing onto the boxes to drive the wagons on, escorted by their foreign, unfamiliar comrades. He turned to look into the bed of the wagon. He stiffened. He frowned. Three of the floorboards had been prised up and flung aside. Underneath, packed in their hidden bed in the false floor he saw for the first time the flat iron bound boxes of the wealth of the mobile army.

And there were two missing. There was a neat, rectangular void where they had been lifted clear. There was a faint outline of each box on the floor where the continual motion of the moving wagon had bedded them in. He stood and stared blankly.

His mind started to clear. His grief and shock were forgotten, replaced by a mounting anger. He climbed into the wagon and replaced the floorboards. Whoever had taken the boxes could not have gone far. Small and flat as they were they would be awkward and very heavy, more than enough for a man to carry. Whoever it was, it was not the Saxon warband. They had killed and mutilated and taken what they thought the column carried and gone on their way. Had they found the boxes the wagons would undoubtedly have been smashed to pieces.

Standing in the wagon Aulus frowned in concentration. How and why had the warband materialised so quickly? Had someone put it on to Caius' trail? Was it possible? Because if so, it could only point to one man. And yes, that one man could well be a Saxon by birth. Was it possible? Was such treachery possible? If so, where was he now? Automatically Aulus searched the grass verge with his eyes. It was unmarked. He looked back down the road. The crossroads, last night's camp site, was still in sight. There was a small farmstead beyond and what looked like a deserted pottery. His eyes flicked back to the crossroads. Close beside it, casually noted last night, was a wayside temple, a small, square building surrounded by a covered portico. Its red tiled roof was warm and homely in the sunlight.

He looked away, then suddenly back. In the shadow of the portico someone had moved. He jumped down from the wagon and walked back to Lucian.

'Hobble the horses, Lucian. Find a spade and start digging Caius' grave. If you finish, start one for Marcus.'

Lucian looked at him, blankly at first, then with growing concern. 'Are you all right, Sir? Thee look sort of odd.'

'I'm all right, Lucian. I've got something I've got to do.'

'I'll come with thee, Sir.'

'No, Lucian. This is my affair. Hold this, will you.' He unclasped his cloak and handed it to Lucian who took it reluctantly, frowning, searching Aulus' face with worried eyes. 'Be thee sure, master? I'd like to be with thee.'

'I know, Lucian. Thank you. Dig the graves.'

Aulus turned and walked back past his dead companions and the wagons for which they had died, towards the wayside temple. Behind him Lucian did not move. He stood watching, frowning.

Aulus walked fast, his head high and his shoulders straight. When he had gone two hundred yards he turned round. 'Get on with it,' he shouted. Lucian shook his head and, as Aulus watched, moved unwillingly to the saddlebags and got out the hobbles.

Aulus drew his sword.

The temple was windowless. The portico seemed empty. He walked slowly round it.

Looking from light into dark, it took him a moment to distinguish the form that stood in the temple's open doorway. Then it moved, stepping nonchalantly from the dark interior. They stared at each other.

'Well, well, well. Look who's here. If it isn't the little ploughboy himself.'

Aulus was silent. Rage was almost choking him. He was consciously feeling and testing every muscle in his body.

Servius laughed, an easy, relaxed chuckle. 'Well, now, ploughboy, have you come back for another beating? You mightn't be so lucky this time. I mightn't be so kind to you.' He was watching Aulus' eyes. They shouted death at him. And the ploughboy's face was different. When they had confronted each other in the courtyard at Etruria it had been open and easy going. Now it was a soldier's face – the lines hardened and sharply in focus, the mouth tight and purposeful. Servius laughed again.

'I've no quarrel with you, mister, nor you with me. I took your horse – well, I'm sorry for that. These things happen in war but there's no cause for us to fight about it. You just walk away from here and forget you ever saw me and you'll live to dangle your grandchildren on your knee.' He stepped easily to the edge of the portico. This time there was an edge to his voice. 'Now run along, ploughboy, before I lose my temper with you.'

Still Aulus said nothing. He had not heard what Servius had said. His whole being was concentrated on the Centurion. He saw the tension in Servius' body behind the casual step: he saw that the hidden right hand carried a sword: he saw the flash in Servius' eyes and he sprang aside as Servius leapt at him.

As he moved his sword arm arced up. It scythed down with all the concentrated strength of his body as Servius passed him.

The blow caught Servius horizontally in the small of his back with a crack like a breaking iceflow. The force of it shot his body forward and hurled him face down to the ground.

Before Servius had fallen Aulus was on him. He flung himself down on Servius' back, knees driving into the outstretched arms, pinning them to the ground. He seized Servius' hair and pulled his head up, jerking it round to expose his throat for the final blow. Servius' face was ash grey; blood was running from his mouth. His staring eyes were unfocused. Aulus checked his arm. He knelt there, sword poised, staring at Servius' face, wondering if he was already dead. The white hot anger seemed to drain from him and he shook uncontrollably. He let go of Servius' hair and the head fell leaden to the ground.

Slowly Aulus stood up. With his boot he lifted Servius' shoulder and half rolled the body over. Servius was staring up at him, his eyes blank with shock, blood and dirt smeared round his mouth. Servius tried to laugh but the sound came as a choking cough.

'You've grown up, ploughboy. It's yours now, then - except my boxes - you'll not have them.' Aulus could barely distinguish the words and as he bent to listen Servius' body relaxed and he went limp.

Aulus sighed. Mechanically he wiped his sword and sheathed it, staring down at Servius. Already the fierce blue eyes were glazing over. He put his boot on Servius' shoulder and rolled the body back into the dirt.

Aulus turned away. He walked slowly back towards Lucian.

THE END

Roman Place Names in Britain
With their Modern Counterparts.

Britannia	Britain
Corinium	Cirencester
Glevum	Gloucester
Deva	Chester
Eboracum	York
Durocornovium	Wanborough
Verulanium	St Albans
Calleva Atrebatum	Silchester
Pontes	Staines
Londinium	London
Durobrivae	Rochester
Rutupiae	Richborough
Regulbium	Reculver
Durovernum	Canterbury
Lindinis	Ilchester
Venta	Winchester
Dubris	Dover
Lemanis	Lympne
Anderida	Pevensey
Noviomagus	Chichester
Portus Adurni	Portchester
Venta Belgarum	Winchester.

Etruria is Etruria, Aulus Aurelius' farm, - it's house, it's buildings and it's boundaries have long since vanished.

14608695R00183

Printed in Great Britain
by Amazon